BABYHIP

BABYHIP

Patricia Welles

E. P. Dutton & Co., Inc.
New York   1967

Published simultaneously in Canada by Clarke, Irwin & Company Limited,
Toronto and Vancouver.

Library of Congress Catalog Card Number: 67–20537

FIRST EDITION

To Barbara

BABYHIP

1

SARAH HAD BEEN rummaging in the downstairs hall closet for nearly ten minutes when it occurred to her that her mother had hidden the hat.

"God damn it, where is it?" she muttered angrily and tossed everything she had found on the floor of the closet into the middle of the living room.

"God damn it," she said, looking at her father who was hanging about in the middle of the doorway. "Damn it, I'll lose my fucking mind. Where is that fucking hat?" She knew her mother had deliberately put it where she couldn't find it. For three days it had been missing. Some rotten nerve.

"What kind of dirty talk is this, already?" her father said dismayed, his eyebrows rising like Japanese moons. "You know you're not to wear the hat to school." His hands trembled. He was wearing his plaid bathrobe, the one Sarah loved to wear until she discovered funny brown stains all down the front of it. The spots were still there, even after she secretly sent the robe to the French cleaners.

"I know she hates my hat, but I dig it and it's none of her fucking business. Where is it?" Sarah's voice was threatening. "If you don't tell me I'm not going to Mr. Brownwise's class." She put her hands on her hips as though she were addressing a group of children who were just caught smearing mud on white walls. The idea that the pose she assumed would intimidate her father brought a smirk to her lips. She stood smirking at her father, wondering why men had to lose their nerve so young. It was like hair falling out. Were bald men cowards?

"Your mother says it's disgusting. And the blue on your eyes.

What's this, already?" He seemed to be studying her face. It was true that Sarah had penciled in thin blue lines across her eyelids. It was the new French makeup she had charged at The J. L. Hudson Co. Five-fifty a bottle was the price tag but Mr. Green wouldn't get the bill for a month. What's the difference, she told herself, he'll think Mother bought it.

Suddenly, Mr. Green stood very close to her, his eyeglasses bobbing up and down in anger. Grabbing her arm and pressing his stubby fingers into her flesh, he blustered, "Wipe the mouth." He made a motion as though he might very well shove his square and hairy fingers smack down her throat. She gritted her teeth.

The nerve of the man. What did he think he was doing? She leaned back, averting her head. There must be some decent way to handle the situation, some way to find the hat, and get the hell out of the house, and onto the bus and into the Art Museum, where she had planned to spend the day.

"Okay, Dad," she said soothingly, wondering what those brown stains could be. It couldn't be pooh-pooh, could it? Was this possible? After all most people and particularly elderly men did shit in their pants. This is a well-known fact. But no one shits on the front of bathrobes, do they?

"Why are you staring at me?" Mr. Green said defensively.

"Dad, okay, I'll fix my mouth," Sarah said, reaching into her greenbookbag and extracting a rococo hand mirror. Briefly inspecting her mouth, she decided it was gorgeous, a fantastic bright butterfly, and immediately pushed the mirror back into the greenbookbag.

"Well?" he said, observing she had done nothing. She knew she had to decide quickly which tack to take. It wasn't just possible to lie, saying you were doing something that you had no intention of doing, and then stand around not enforcing the lie. Parents were idiots but they weren't feebleminded.

"Tell me where the hat is and then I'll wipe the mouth." Mr. Green loved deals. He wasn't a businessman selling toilets wholesale for nothing.

He smiled. She did get herself up in strange outfits.

"There." He pointed to the top of the closet. Sarah scrambled in and dug out her hat which, squashed under a large gray empty hatbox, was flattened like a pancake. She threw her light tan cashmere coat over one shoulder and grabbed her greenbookbag as though immediate flight were imminent.

"Not the coat," her father pleaded. It was the coat Mrs. Green despised, mostly because she had wanted it for herself, and Aunt Ruth, who had married and divorced two Christians, had given it to Sarah. Aunt Ruth dyed her hair red and went to Greece in the summers. A thoroughly unorthodox woman.

"Please," he whined, glancing down to check to see his bathrobe had not fallen open to reveal the colorless paunch beneath. It wasn't that Sarah wasn't lovely in these clothes, it was more that Bertha would scream and nag when she peered into the closet and saw the coat was gone. His eyes grew steamy. It was his funny way, Sarah knew, and in a moment, he would begin to cry. Tenderly, she patted his shoulder.

"Dad, I have to wear this coat today. It's Tuesday."

"All right," he said, defeated. He shrugged his shoulders. The hat was plum colored. He didn't really understand why Bertha objected to it.

"So maybe she won't find out," he said solemnly. "Anyway, maybe it's a pretty hat. I think I like this hat. So why don't she like it, already?" The last words rose rapidly to a shout. His cheeks began to flush and his eyes to pop out like marbles.

"Dad, you're a winner," Sarah said quickly, kissing his rough cheek and catching a faint whiff of body odor, age and sleep mixed carelessly together.

"The clothes I don't mind," he said, trying to sound reasonable. "It's the words, Sarah, the language, all the dirty talk. I can't understand where you got such talk. We tried to raise you so good and give you everything and you talk like a truck driver."

Sarah pushed her American History book behind some dusty galoshes. There was no point in trekking it around with her all day, especially since she had no intention of attending the class where kooky Mr. Brownwise awaited her with his hot eager eyes and his semizipped fly.

"Dad," she said, sticking a tin of cigars into the greenbookbag, "you're always bugging me, driving me bananas. Why don't you just stop bugging me and leave me alone."

He looked hurt. "It's *mishugenah*," he said.

"You're all turned around, sugar," she said, wondering why he

]11[

always insisted on using obnoxious Jewish words. He must say *mishugenah* nine million times a day, and her mother nine trillion. It drove her crazy as though these creatures had totally failed to assimilate and were protecting themselves in some insane way by using these words. It was not to be tolerated. It was almost as peculiar as not knowing how to conjugate the verb To Do. Sarah became very annoyed when she heard them say he don't and she don't, for he doesn't and she doesn't. One afternoon she had even typed out the proper way to conjugate the verb To Do and tacked it to the bulletin board in the kitchen. They hadn't even noticed.

"What?" her father said dazedly, "all turned around?" She could hear him repeating it like a crazed moron to himself, over and over, as she walked down the porch steps and into the street. Poor Dad was so incredibly out of it. How had he ever found the right words to woo and capture her mother, the dear, darling 175-pound pain in the neck?

2

SARAH STOOD waiting for the bus, a twinge of guilt making its way from her kneecap to her groin. Guilt, heat and sexual excitement always affected her in the same way. Her pubic hair would, inevitably, begin to twitch and itch and sometimes even burn. She stuck her hand into the pocket of her cashmere coat and surreptitiously scratched herself, digging her nails hard against her suede jumper. The scratching barely made a dent in the groin area, but the activity caused her to forget what had made her feel guilty.

Well, crap what's the difference anyway, so they're angry, so it's another angry day at 10117 Cherrylawn. It would be a day just like all the other days as far as she could see. They were always on her ass, always beseeching her to do this or that boring, hopeless stupid thing, like visit her grandmother, or go to classes, or not listen to Ornette Coleman. She sighed and fished around in her green-bookbag, for her shades. One lens was cracked and the other broken. They were large and round and covered most of her face, perfect to shut out the silly square world.

The street was deserted except for a few cars speeding by at the usual Detroit pace of madness and folly. Much cooler, much wilder, tougher and terrible to drive slowly, preferably in a very old car. But what did these creeps know?

Sarah watched a baby blue Cadillac convertible lazying by. It came to a halt directly in front of her. Idiot One was in the front seat and in the back a gigantic, shaggy white dog bounced like a rubber doll. It was exactly the kind of car Hollywood moguls bought for their starlet chicks. Exactly.

She was aware of the picture she candidly presented to the Idiot, who leered out at her. She was standing in a stance similar to one she had seen in a television movie, with her hands deep into her pockets, and her plum-colored hat clinging like a wild animal to the side of her head. As soon as the baby blue appeared she turned her sun-glassed face in profile to give him the full impact of what a gorgeous, mysterious chick was really like. Despising idiots didn't preclude impressing them. It was amazing the enormous numbers of idiots afoot, particularly on Monday, Tuesday and Wednesday. Along about the middle of the week the idiots began to thin out and by Sunday, if you didn't include relatives and friends, they had all but disappeared. She never included school in the Idiot List because then the list would swell to ridiculous proportions, like the population of India, which, if she seriously thought about it, would cause the blood to rush to her head and a strange giddiness to overcome her.

The man, hollow-eyed, stared at her legs. His hair was dark, greased down with some ugly, geeky-looking ointment. Probably a gangster. His strange yellowish pallor screamed out at her like a violent wild bird. He must spend his days and nights playing poker with hoodlums. That much was obvious.

The dog was becoming hysterical, flipping and flopping around and tossing his head from side to side as if he were in a canoe about to sink. She could never quite decide whether cats and dogs were included in the Idiot List. They were probably in the category with friends and relatives. If you allowed them on the list, it would be like saving wagonloads of spaghetti, a fruitless activity.

"May I give you a lift, Miss?" the man said, revealing a mouth full of pink gums. He had a peculiar angular mouth with tiny little teeth all brown from nicotine. Sarah lifted her glasses, her large green eyes amazed even without the glasses his tiny little rodent teeth were brown. The dog thumped his tail into the man's ear.

"Shut up," he said, slapping the animal. "Shut up, you mutt." The dog panted nervously, saliva dripping down onto the man's suit.

"Well?" the man said, staring at her. "You want to get in or not?" He might be an ax murderer or a rapist. Sarah uttered a rude laugh. It was quite like the time she had to meet Moses, the maid's son, in the park near the house. She was seven and he was twelve and it was their custom, okayed by Mrs. Green, to make wild play in the park. Sarah had to pass an alley where neighborhood boys collected like old garbage. One of them beckoned to her. She went to see what he wanted and very sadly he took out his penis, saying, "See, see it, see, isn't it nice?" The question went unanswered and she fled to the park, where it took ten minutes to lure Moses out of a tree. He stubbornly refused to come down, and finally when he did, he laughed in her face and called her a liar. It was a true humiliation, not fair at all.

"You liar," he said, "you bad liar, you liar mouth. I'm going to tell your mama." The rat wouldn't believe her and had blushed scarlet, which was really a lie, because Moses was Negro and it was really closer to a dusky mauve.

"What's the matter?" the man said, "is something funny?" He swatted aimlessly at the dog who was thrashing crazily about in the back seat.

"Something funny?" he insisted. Sarah tried to smother her guffaws by pretending to nibble on the end of her glasses. He could kill her right on the spot. Who would know? He could just as easily throw her body into an empty lot or a used-car emporium.

"Nothing's funny," she said, smiling as best she could. "It's just that you and your dog, you and your dog," she groped for words, "look like an advertisement for toothpaste." The dog pounded his tail in agreement. The man, confusion in his eyes, hostilely regarded her.

"Oh, I mean in a men's magazine," she added in the hopes the explanation would cheer him up.

"Oh really?" he said and licked his bottom lip. It worked. He looked terribly interested. Must be flattered. She couldn't see his right hand, though, and this had been troubling her for about a minute. Where could it be? She had heard of these types. It was a special type of Idiot offshoot. These people were not actually murderers or violently destructive, not at all; they achieved their jollys in other ways.

"You want to go out?" he asked bluntly. The right hand hadn't yet appeared, but the bus was ambling down the street and would be in front of her in a matter of seconds. There wasn't much he could do in a matter of seconds; except maybe shoot her.

"I don't speak English," Sarah suddenly said in her best garbled voice. He couldn't possibly attack her in front of thirty people, thirty citizens of Detroit, Michigan, U.S.A., thirty Idiot residents

]15[

of IDIOTVILLE, could he? She felt a funny kind of rash-like sensation sliding along her leg toward her crotch.

The man flung her a filthy look, gunned the motor and jerked hastily away from the curb. The poor slob must feel very foolish, but that's what he gets for trying to pick up jailbait, hip chicks and all like that. Idiots should stick to Idiots. Sarah had a fine sense of the fitness of things, according to Moses, who mentioned this to her for the first time when she stood on the train platform waving good-bye the day he left for college. Mrs. Green strongly disapproved of such a meeting taking place, but was overruled by Carmine, Moses's mother. At the time Sarah hadn't known exactly what he meant by that particular remark, though she understood it was a kind of compliment. She understood a few years later, and this fitness for things had never left her.

She dug around in her purse for the exact change to hand the bus driver, who was waiting, door open, with a rotten cross expression on his face. The other passengers gaped with curiosity.

"I'm sorry," she said and clambered onto the bus gripping the money. It was tough titty when you had to depend on public transportation. The bus drivers acted as if they had thorns up their asses for many generations. But public servants couldn't be on the Idiot List, this was obvious. There were too many. The bus was crowded with freaks.

"For Christ's sake," a fat woman cried, "you dumb brat, why don't you watch your step." A large paper bag flew out of her hand and rolled down the aisle, strewing bananas under the seats. Sarah bent to retrieve them, blushing from the hurtful words. It wasn't that she was graceless, indeed not. Mrs. Green hadn't spent hard-earned money on ten years of ballet for nothing. Sarah was grace itself. It wasn't her fault that the slimy bus drivers made nasty movements with the bus just to bug the passengers. She handed the bananas back to the woman, whose feet were plastered inside sandals two sizes too small.

"Bananas to the bananas," Sarah said. The poor creature must have quadruple-size shoes. She's got the fattest feet I ever saw. She could be the featured attraction in a freak show, or a freak-out show. She studied the woman's blob of a face. The folds of flesh hung around her neck like an exotic necklace dug from the tomb of an ancient, obese monarch.

"Some snots ride the bus," the fat woman said and settled back in the seat like a turtle, her head shrinking grotesquely into her neck.

Sarah stumbled to a seat in the back of the bus and sat next to a gypsy type, whose son was playing desultorily with a chewed piece of bubble gum. She squeezed next to him and smiled into his great, sad, dark eyes. What were gypsies doing in Detroit? They must be from Canada. Had they slipped through Customs undetected? And where did they live? In some squalid rooming house in a garbagy slum?

The boy's lips were purple, giving him a kind of primordial monkey look. He was definitely part of the monkey kingdom.

"You dig my chapeau?" Sarah said, wondering if his father was the missing link or a king-size chimpanzee.

"You pretty," he said, yelling into her ear, "but the hat stink, it stink, stink, stink." Sarah began to laugh appreciatively at his ape reaction. His mother slapped her hand over his mouth and gave him a nasty clop in the ribs. Ignoring the reprimand, he continued to talk.

"Pretty lady," he said, biting down on his mother's quivering hand. She yanked it away, her bright rhinestone bracelets clanging together like the Fourth of July.

"Stinky hat, don't like," he said.

Sarah stared into his hungry eyes. She glanced up front to make certain the fat woman wasn't looking her way. Good. Surreptitiously she reached into her greenbookbag and removed a nice ripe though slightly grease-laden banana and began to peel it. The fat woman was involved in the tedious task of picking her nose with her little finger. She would be kept busy for at least as long as it took to engulf the banana.

"Want?" she offered the banana to the monkey child, who instantly reached out a dirty hand to grab a hunk.

"No, he wouldn't," the gypsy mother muttered. "He eats okay." So how gypsy could she be if she spoke such excellent English? Sarah had expected an accent, something strange, foreign, not understandable. What a bore! The old couze was just a fake gypsy, not the real thing at all. Why was she wearing rhinestone rings on every finger if she weren't a gypsy?

Sarah chewed the banana and dropped the peel on the floor,

praying that an Idiot would get his comeuppance; maybe even the bus driver in a vain attempt to clean the bus would fall on his brain. Just desserts. And could this woman be a whore? Where were a whore and her son going on such a day? And on public transportation. Peculiar. To the Art Museum? Most likely they were going down to Sam's Cut Rate Department Store for a little quiet Tuesday morning shoplifting.

She noticed a short, stout cat around sixteen was madly flagging down the bus, which zipped past as if he didn't exist. How silly, it was Morton Stein, the class fool, who, clearly, was going to be late. Morton Stein had passionately loved Sarah since the third grade, when to his extreme delight he discovered she would torture him free of charge. She would pinch, punch, scratch, bite and tickle. Along about the eighth grade she began to ignore him. After that the friendship waned until in the twelfth grade she didn't so much as acknowledge his existence.

Sarah shifted uncomfortably in the seat. Why were buses always so hot and stuffy? It was too stupid for words, and no one was about to make a move to do anything about it. She could complain to the driver, but it hardly seemed worth the effort. In ten minutes she would be at her destination. The museum was cool.

She looked out of the window at the early traffic, already reaching enormous proportions. What a detestable place Detroit was. It had no ambiance at all. The streets were ugly. There was street after street of houses, all with shingles in the front and small insipid yards. There was a horrible dreariness about the city that always depressed her. There were no plains, gradations, hills. It was all square. Fortunately, the trees were pretty and in the spring the lilacs sprung up in odd places. She had grown up on a street that no longer existed. It was a frightening experience to seek out the house she had lived in until she was seven and find it wasn't there. It had disappeared into the interstices of a superhighway. Where were the alleys of yesteryear, where the kids had played roof ball and created sadistic fantasies behind the garbage cans? There wasn't even an alley on Cherrylawn worth mentioning. Everything had changed in the city. It was beginning to resemble the inside of a cement factory.

Since the Green household had moved to Cherrylawn, the face of the city had changed from snow white to nearly pitch black.

] 18 [

The white folks had moved to the outskirts of town, or out of the city entirely. It seemed strange. Fortunately, her neighborhood was on the cusp of integration; soon it would change to darkness, which might add an element of interest. Not far from her house a Negro neighborhood was flourishing. It was there that Carmine and Moses lived with the memory of Moses' father who had long since disappeared.

Sarah pressed her face against the cool glass of the window. It felt good. The bus was stupefying. The idea of skipping Mr. Brownwise's class was a little compensation for the stupefaction of the ride. Poor Mr. Brownwise must have a severe constipation problem. Anyone who had his particular expression plastered onto his mug all the time must either have a lead pipe up his behind or be severely constipated. In this way Sarah could actually sympathize with him. She knew all too well the ins and outs of constipation, having been lectured on the subject ever since childhood. Mrs. Green believed sincerely in the power of high colonics, as did most of the older generation of Jewish creatures Sarah encountered. It occupied so much of their thinking that Sarah simply accepted it as an ethnic hang-up.

Poor Mr. Brownwise needed a good laxative to jolt the cramp off his face. Perhaps a kind of shock or jolt would help, an electric cattle prod or a buggy ride in upper Canada over rough terrain. She might even suggest to him that he spend the approaching summer in a dangerous section of the South in blackface. Surely, there must be something, some kind of device or life experience to loosen up Mr. Brownwise. It might change the entire color of his existence. Being overweight didn't help much either, because all his flesh, instead of turning into waste and leaving his system, simply hung around. Was this the reason Mr. Brownwise resembled two inverted pears? All the pears he had ever eaten in his whole life had remained in his system, till finally, in the end, he began to look like what he had eaten. If you are around a thing or a person long enough, you begin adopting its characteristics. Mr. and Mrs. Green were a prize example. They had become through association barely distinguishable from each other, both heavyset and flabby, both garbed in round nondescript glasses, both with graying flaccid hair and both with nearly identical sets of false teeth purchased from the same dentist, who had thrown himself out a window. At night they had to keep their teeth in separate places so there wouldn't be a mix-up. It was quite fitting there should be this situation that fit so very beautifully into Sarah's thesis regarding the fitness of things. It was her contention peculiar, odd, bizarre, off-beat and insane things fit together. It wasn't the ordinary things that were meant to be together but the strange ones. Life wasn't some kind of ordered whole at all; it was a weird and sinister combination of loose ends. And these loose, frayed and distorted ends were just crying and pleading to be put together.

And where were the beautiful, disjointed loose ends that would make her complete? The trouble with Detroit was that things, dull and mundane, and people only seemed to fit together. It was the middle-class, Establishment brainwash. It was a lie. They didn't fit, not in the least.

The question was, how to get out of the stifling, confining bag. In a way, her life was like the bus. She could make a fuss, but was it worth the trouble? She rubbed her fingers along the dirty windowpane. Was it worth the trouble? She would have to make a gigantic effort to get out of the city and change her life to something more bizarre, insane, off-beat, and therefore suitable. The idea was to get away from the nauseating restrictions of Mr. and Mrs. Green. To hell with college! They wanted her to attend Wayne University and no other place. This was so they could supervise, control and bug her life. She hadn't bothered to apply for the fall semester. But she would tell them her plan in due time. No point in arousing them for nothing. The master plan hadn't been worked out precisely enough. Carefully she would have to structure it. She would have to wait, find a job, save money and then—get the hell out.

She sighed. The bus seemed to be taking a ridiculously long time to get to the museum and the silly gypsy whore was pointedly ignoring her. Poor Mr. Brownwise with his semizipped fly. He really thinks he's sexy and what a horror! Why didn't the other dummies in class notice? They were a year or sometimes two years older than Sarah, but they weren't turned on to the world. What's the difference? Two more months and, free as a bird, she would fly anywhere and everywhere. No idiots, no absurd adults, no silly gypsy whores, no more dullass classes. Finished. And then she could work and save money and off, off, she would go. Finished. Finished. Finished with those asinine pep talks from the principal. What did he know? A person who wore short white socks so his skin showed couldn't know very much.

"You are lazy in the extreme," he pontificated, trying desperately to control his fury over the results of her college boards. To everyone's amazement she had done brilliantly. Underachiever, they shouted. It wasn't since the seventh grade, when she had skipped twice, accounting for her being only sixteen in the twelfth grade, that she had moved off her ass. It was true she refused to do homework, refused to study or do decent research. She even refused to go to class, where, she insisted, no one turned her on. None of those teacher creatures had a sense of humor. How could a humorless jerk turn her on? For one full day, one beautiful full day, she almost believed that Mr. Owens in Chemistry II was boss. He had a big, wide smile and said witty things, but holy mother, he had a tendency to repeat his jokes, which eventually landed him on the Idiot List for Academic Slobs. She irretrievably expunged him from her personal record.

Naturally, receiving the highest score on the college boards of anyone in the school enraged everyone. Ho hum. She could go to Radcliffe, they informed her.

She called Moses in Chicago and asked his advice. He wasn't much help.

"Come to the University of Chicago," he said, laughing, "but pretend you don't know people of color. It's like the Congo here."

She made her own decision. To hell with college. College was a who-needs-it syndrome. She could read on her own. She was sick of hearing from authorities, sick of it all. Not indicating any enthusiasm to the principal when informed of the strong chance of going to Radcliffe, she was dispatched immediately to the school psychologist, a young-faced woman with prematurely gray hair and dandruff that spread over her dark, bulky suit like a snowfall in the Himalayas.

Fortunately, she was terribly easy to con, tediously so. Sarah could tell right away that Miss Crenshaw found her disturbing, different.

She cleared her throat every few seconds in their first session together. "You can't have all Negro friends with parents such as yours," Miss Crenshaw said frankly, clearing her throat and secretly congratulating herself on the direct way she had selected to deal with this student.

"Why not?" Sarah asked, chainsmoking and blowing the smoke at Miss Crenshaw. Miss Crenshaw coughed and choked but went blindly on, stopping every now and then to clear her throat. She was not to be outdone, controlled or manipulated by this fresh-mouth juvenile delinquent. She had understood when she came casually strolling through the door that she would be a disturbing influence. Her clothes gave her away. A borderline case. A definite borderline case, dressed bizarrely and wearing some sort of peculiar white eye makeup which made her look like a sick raccoon.

"They will not tolerate your unorthodox behavior. You will be the one to suffer. They'll continue to put pressure on you. Is it worth it? Isn't it too rebellious for such a smart girl?" Miss Crenshaw didn't want to go too far, the kid had to keep a few defenses. She didn't want to break them down all at once. She glanced at Sarah's face. She seemed interested but did she have to keep twirling those enormous hoop earrings around her finger? It was too distracting.

"I mean," she said intelligently, "Mr. and Mrs. Green are very sheltered people." She would appeal to her rational sense. But wasn't it strange that the teachers' comments didn't jibe with the college boards. None of it made sense. Still, she must do her best to reach this kid and try to change her attitude, which was way out of kilter. She would get her on the right road, the road to college, to goals, to a future of adjustment, and success. She would make an underachiever into an achiever.

Sarah nodded her head and twisted her fake emerald so it looked like a wedding band.

"They're very sheltered people," Miss Crenshaw said again. Sarah seemed to be deep in thought. Had her words made an effect already?

Sarah looked at the clock behind Miss Crenshaw's head. Just a few more minutes and she could go to the drugstore and meet Jenny for lunch. Jenny was bringing a joint hidden in a ham sandwich.

"Mr. and Mrs. Green are good people," Miss Crenshaw said. For a moment, Sarah couldn't remember who Mr. and Mrs. Green were. It sounded familiar but then Miss Crenshaw's entire speech sounded familiar. She had heard it so many times before. Miss Crenshaw looked concerned, the worry lines spreading across her forehead like rabbit tracks in snow.

"Yeah, Mr. and Mrs. Green, I know them," Sarah exclaimed. "But I dig brown people, they're cool. They know how to ball."

Miss Crenshaw appeared puzzled. "Cool?" she said, trying to understand. It wasn't too good to allow Sarah to observe her lack of information on these slang expressions, but the truth was she could never understand argot. Nervously, she reached into the top drawer of her desk and pulled out an expensive silver cigarette case, a Christmas gift from her roommate.

"You smoke?" Sarah said.

"Yes, moderately, everything in moderation. The golden mean," Miss Crenshaw said, self-consciously sticking a cigarette into an ivory cigarette holder.

"What do you mean by cool?" She made it seem as if it were some special, peculiar usage Sarah had just invented. It occurred to Miss Crenshaw it was one of those bizarre words teenagers use to express hostility toward adults. It was obviously a word to exclude older people. Not that she didn't know they had their own language. She knew perfectly well, but she had never been able to comprehend the meaning of these words. In the last month she had heard at least five of her patients say groovy. It simply didn't mean a thing to her.

She was dimly aware that to them, to the hundreds of long-haired boys and girls who roamed the corridors like prehistoric beasts these words, these very strange words meant an entire universe.

"Well, you know like cool," Sarah said by way of explanation. Miss Crenshaw felt sure Sarah was staring at her as if she was some kind of ugly freak. "I mean intact," Sarah went on irritably.

"Oh yes," Miss Crenshaw said quickly, "I see what you mean."

How square could a human being be and still keep off the Idiot List for Academic Slobs, Sarah mused. The worst cubes were on top of the list. Was there room up there for Miss Crenshaw?

"Now," Miss Crenshaw said, forcing a smile, relieved the end of the hour was at hand. "Now," she said abruptly, clearing her throat, "this is all for today but I'll see you next week for another consultation at the same time. Tuesday, isn't it?" She looked at a piece of paper.

"Yeah, I think it's Tuesday," Sarah said.

"Right after American History. Okay? Now please remember, Sarah, this isn't a punishment or a reprimand. I'm trying to help you. You mustn't be ashamed." There was something demented about the way these kids watched her, something in the eyes, a kind of stubborn madness. And here this smarty kid was doing the same thing.

Sarah crossed her legs and yawned, her short dress rising up over her purple knit tights. Miss Crenshaw looked away. There were times, not too often, but times when she seriously regretted not taking more courses in Abnormal Psychology.

"I want to tell you one more thing," she said, wondering if Sarah took pills. "Remember complete liberty can only come with maturity." She slammed the desk drawer louder than she had wished. The noise reverberated through the room like a sonic boom.

"Well, I don't agree, sugar," Sarah said, imagining Miss Crenshaw prostrate in a darkened room, eye patches being applied to her fevered eyes. "Anyway, *ciao*," she said, opening the door. "*Ciao*, as Papa says."

"Papa? Your father? Your father speaks Italian?" Miss Crenshaw said, her voice cracking. She couldn't recall reading this curious fact in any of the records, and she had read them extremely carefully.

"Hemingway, Papa Hemingway, the great father of us all," Sarah said, softly closing the door.

She started toward the side exit. Jenny would be waiting at the drugstore, neat and tidy in her blue blazer, emblem of the parochial school she attended, and with the hidden treat pressed between the lettuce and ham sandwich her mother fixed for her each morning. Poor Miss Crenshaw, so dull, so bloody dull, so simple-minded. Miss Crenshaw would have to take her place on the Idiot List for Academic Slobs. There was just no getting away from it. Sarah bit a hangnail and looked around the bus.

The gypsy whore mother made a tiny hand signal at Sarah like some kooky hex. Sarah got up, moving rapidly to the exit. Tuesday

] 24 [

was a mother of a day for a hex. She could do without it quite nicely. And lo, there was the Detroit Museum of Art, white as ever, looming up. Sarah turned to the boy. "I'm going to see El Greco," she said, hoping her evident happy spirit would infuse him with a sense of culture, no matter how thin. He tried rising from his seat to follow her, but his mother nabbed him by the sleeve and pushed him back. He giggled, his monkey face pushing together gleefully. The poor darling idiot was really terribly small, his miserably pinched wrists and arms protruding obscenely from his body. Half-starved, no doubt. The old whore probably fed him zilch. He strained forward in a great effort to escape his mother's digging fingers. Poor obscene dirty darling, culture will never be a part of your forlorn life. Helplessly, he watched Sarah, his eyes an indictment. Take me away, they pleaded, take me away to your world, your plum-colored hat, your El Greco, your freedom.

The bus lurched to a stop and Sarah stepped down, looking over her shoulder for one last impression of the seated gypsy whore and her monkeychild, but the gypsy mother had risen majestically to her full height of five feet and was churning down the steps, dragging the boy behind. He kicked to be free, but she had him in a tight grip and succeeded in tugging him along the pavement. The poor thing, no knowledge of art, culture or even music would ever cross into his impoverished life. His evil witch mother would feed him ersatz chocolate till he wasted away. Sarah's heart went out to him. Forever ignorant, forever deprived. No Marshall McLuhan, no wine in Paris cafés, no Swedish movies, no digging of the scene, no nothing, just cheap rhinestones and insults.

Suddenly he sat down on the sidewalk and began kicking away at his mother's crotch.

Sarah clapped her hands at the unexpected show of courage. "Go baby, go," she said.

"Boo boo, bah, bah, blach blach, ich ich ich ich," he screamed in tantrum. "Boo boo, bah, blach, ich ich ich ich. Shit on you." His lips were a raving purple. Did he say shit? Yeah, he said the dirty word, all right. Sarah stared. He was saying it to her. He was looking right into her face and saying shit, the little ungrateful, underprivileged bastard. She stood riveted to the spot, her face a blank wall. The evil mother tried to drag him to his feet. But

]25[

steadfastly he lay on the ground. His arms flailed the air like a whirling dervish, his mouth moved like a giant fan.

"Shit," he said at Sarah. Ho hum. She better check them off her fantasy-life agenda and proceed to her destination. The day awaited her and hopefully with an absence of cretins and ungrateful little bastards from the slums. To hell with all of them! And to hell with Miss Crenshaw who would sit and smoke all by herself till her tongue dried up and fell off. She walked up the steps to the museum.

The limp-wrist at the postcard counter was in his usual tight jacket and tight trousers. He nodded sullenly and busied himself with a make-believe task he devised to avoid any conversation. No reason to get into a hassle so early in the day. By now he was on to the style and meaning of Sarah's conversations. After two years he had to acknowledge she was putting him on. At first it was difficult to accept. Her innocent green eyes and childish mouth had delayed the perception, but, finally, he had to admit, this sweet-looking girl had a ghastly serpent's tongue, not amusing in the least. Whenever he saw her, he began to sweat. Some days he had to rush home on his thirty-minute lunch hour and find fresh clothes. If she appeared in the afternoon, he was sunk, there would be no time to run home. But thank God, today it wasn't too bad, she didn't seem to want to talk. She was quietly leafing through the postcards, leaving a greasy mark on all those she touched. But it was all right, anything as long as she didn't assault him.

"This would turn on Jenny," Sarah said, winking. He ignored her and pretended to add up something. Sarah held up a Picasso. It would be a swell card to send Miss Crenshaw in lieu of her presence. Gifts were such lovely compensation. She would send Miss Crenshaw this perfectly groovy card. How could she be annoyed? It would show beyond a doubt that even though Sarah didn't appear for the scheduled appointment, she was thinking of Miss Crenshaw sitting there alone under her snowfall of dandruff.

"Maybe I'll buy these two," she said, "one for Jenny, the Virgin one and the other for Crenface." She would write a charming note for Miss Crenshaw and then Miss Crenshaw could lean it on her desk for the other flipped-out students to see. It had great pragmatic value.

"Are these cards more expensive?" she asked in an accusatory tone. He looked as though he were suffocating in his skintight clothes. It wasn't attractive.

"No," he said, turning away. He hoped it was time for his coffee break. Why did she always give him a hard time?

"Finally even art is commercial, in the market place," she said haughtily, handing him some money and wondering if she ought to inform him she was the museum president's daughter.

He gave her a hang-dog look, popped the cards into a small gray envelope and placed them on the counter. He couldn't bring himself to hand them to her. He might have to come into contact with her.

"Thanks, sugar," she said and flounced off in the direction of the El Greco she regarded as her own, passing the first floor guard and throwing him a quick smile.

"Morning, miss," he said. He knew her well from her weekly excursions to the museum. He had seen her grow from an ugly smart-alecky kid into a beautiful smart-alecky young lady. And not just once had he asked her to stop smoking those foul, stinking cigars. How her parents allowed such conduct was one of the mysteries of life.

Sarah sat down on a stone bench, took out the Picasso and in her best medieval scrawl wrote on the back of it.

Dear Miss Crenshaw:
    Sorry I couldn't make it to that gas of an appointment but I'm sick with a severe case of banana fever and gas. Last night I munched thirty-five bananas consecutively. I'll get in touch with you. No need to call me from class.
                                    Best ever,
                                    Sarah Green

She signed her name with an elaborate flourish and carefully tucked the postcard into the lining of the greenbookbag. Jenny would appreciate the card. She must remember to tell her exactly about it.

Sarah examined the Virgin, a gift for her friend. It was really beautiful but Jenny could put it down if she liked. Jenny wallowed in irreverence. Sometimes Sarah wondered why the nuns hadn't discovered this. She hid it well, even got good marks and was on her way to Sarah Lawrence.

"What's so good about going to college?" Sarah said. "Isn't it awfully middle-class?"

Jenny didn't know what to say, and looked at her with astonished eyes, her long blond hair slipping across her face and into her mouth.

It was Sarah who had turned Jenny on to Pot but then it was Jenny who really dug it.

"It's a religious experience," she said, inhaling deeply in the upstairs bathroom of the Green residence. Mrs. Green didn't like Jenny.

"You got to pick a Catholic," Mrs. Green whined. "Aren't there any Jewish girls to bring to your parents' home?"

"No," Sarah said, "there aren't." She hated the girls in her school. They all wore long bangs and identification bracelets, so boring. The girls in Jenny's school weren't much better, the saving grace being that they were more stupid and thus could be manipulated more easily. Jenny, of course, was an exception. Sarah couldn't possibly have a good friend who was a dummy.

Sarah sniffled and surveyed her wonderful El Greco. Her nose itched. Yeah, the suffering was there in El Greco, the despair, the confusion, the redemption. The suffering and confusion were reminiscent of the perpetual scowl on her mother's face. The despair was Mr. Green. Very interesting, she must tell Jenny. El Greco was a Jew? She hadn't heard or read anything to confirm this but wasn't it possible? After all, the great *goy* of them all was a Jew.

Though she didn't relish Jewish words at all, now and then one would creep into her speech. She tried thinking of something else, not wanting one of those silly ethnic words to creep into her brain and dominate her thoughts. Funny how you can't control your thoughts. She glanced at the El Greco again and tried to think of something else. She had to blow her nose, the urge becoming suddenly terribly strong. She sneezed, enjoying the sensation, then began to search through her greenbookbag for a tissue. There was nothing fit for the nose, no library card, no old book report, nothing, not even a scrap of paper. She looked down the room.

Was there no one on the scene to come to her aid? Where were all the swingers?

There weren't many people in the museum, too early. Across the room, five paintings down, she saw a young cat with straight blond hair, the kind of hair she detested, idly leaning against a painting. This in itself was rather nervy. She felt a sudden flash of interest wiggling around her kneecap. Oblivious, he leaned into the painting. His faded brown jacket looked as if he might have spent the night in the trunk of an abandoned car. She put her hand to her forehead, squinting her eyes for a better look and coughed to gain his attention. He wasn't a swinger exactly but he didn't look altogether uncool either. She would ask him for a tissue or a handkerchief. Yeah, a handkerchief was better and it would give her a task, something to do. She was bored, even the drama of St. Francis of Assisi wasn't enough to stir her imagination on such an innocuous Tuesday morning. It was a shame that Jenny never got the hang of cutting classes. They could have gone to Wayne University and cruised.

She sniffled and walked over to him. It was frustrating that he simply refused to look up and give his attention to her. What peculiar, nasty sexual thoughts must be coursing through his brain and nervous system for him to be so deeply concentrated? Frowning in exasperation, she stopped and took out her square tin of Danish cigars. It contained ten neat little cigars purchased at the drugstore near school. She lit one and proceeded to her target. In a way it seemed ridiculous to go to the trouble of cutting classes when nothing exciting seemed to be in the offing. Maybe Jenny was right about that. It was all so boring. The young man was absently running his hand through his hair. Was he hung up on it? She had met so many insufferable cats who were hung up on their own hair, much more vain than any of the chicks she knew. And he wasn't particularly tall, which was something of a disappointment, since Sarah detested small, thin, little or in any way deficient males. Fortunately, she noted, he had broad shoulders. He could defend her honor if necessary. He had nice, large hands and okay feet. All members seemed to be in order.

There was the possibility he was a college cat, Wayne being right across the street. She had met others in the museum. Once she had met a mad Armenian painter who told her she was a dupe of the Establishment. Her? A dupe of the Establishment? He wanted to take her to a group sex party but she smilingly refused.

The cat started moving away. She had to move fast before he drifted to the Rivera murals, where conversation was swallowed by the largeness of the room.

"Excuse me," she said huskily, her throat irritated by the cigar. She spoke very low. "Do you have a tissue?" Up close he wasn't too dreary, rather handsome. Tough enough with strange blue eyes. His hair needed a wash but wasn't nearly as disgusting as she had thought. Did he know how to do the piggy thing?

He jerked his head around in surprise. What was it, an elf, a woman, an apparition? She was pretty and small with long, thick shining black hair like a character in the Old Testament. Her green eyes were mischievous, amused. Where had she come from? His scrutiny came to rest on her bright red mouth. It didn't suit her otherwise delicate face.

"What?" he said, noticing a grease mark down the front of her light coat. Her hat was half-cocked. She was a funny combination of good taste and craziness.

"I need a tissue, I have to blow my nose," she said. "Drag out something for me, sugar, will you?"

Blow her nose? Blow her nose? What was she saying? Mechanically he handed her a copy of *Ramparts* magazine, which was stuffed into his back pocket. She shook her head. "No, no," she said, "a tissue or a handkerchief. I've got my own reading material." Oh, oh, he looked like the type of cat who might participate in peace-ins or teach-outs or whatever. A bit too organized for her. She didn't believe in such crap. People were who they were and nothing changed them, least of all humanitarian influences. The only possible scene to make was the freak-out scene. Anything else was square.

"Okay, don't get excited," he said as it sank into his brain what she requested. "I don't have these requests too often." He handed her a crumpled, soiled handkerchief. "Be my guest," he said.

"It's clean?" she said, making a wry face.

"Almost," he said.

She took the handkerchief and blew her nose into it. He was pale, such pale hair, but at least it went neatly to the collar, which was more than she could say about the jerks she knew. The guys in her class with long hair were so dopey and dull-witted that even the long hair didn't compensate. And a lot of them had pimples. She looked at his face. It was clear. On the fourth finger of his right hand, she noticed an interesting ring, which proved on closer inspection to be a skull and crossbones with sparkling red stones for eyes. Why the ring? It was a hood thing to do like wearing a chain with a St. Christopher around your neck. Or was it Camp?

"Now what?" she said, unfastening her coat to display the short, expensive blue suede jumper she had begged for until Mr. Green succumbed.

"Don't know," he said, looking over her trim body. What could she want, this child-woman? Conversation? She didn't look as if she wanted seduction, but it was difficult to know. He had been fooled before. The fact it was so near to examination time wasn't good. Girls got in the way, particularly beautiful ones.

"Do you want it back?" she said, holding out the handkerchief.

"Keep it," he said. What could he do with her? She was probably a virgin, which didn't necessarily put him off, but it did add an element of extra work, which could be better spent on his studies. He looked at her ankles. They were perfect. She was wearing silver net stockings and he could see through them to her skin. She was small, with small ankles and small wrists. He felt big standing beside her, big and strong and male.

Yet he felt something in him withdrawing. Something withdrawing and something surging forward. She could screw up his entire grade point average. He had counted on not meeting anyone until exams were finished. She was looking at him and smiling with the greenest eyes, her thick lashes outlining them.

"You look like Cleopatra," he said. "You should wear your hair on your forehead."

"In bangs, you mean," she said. Maybe he was a painter? He seemed to be a visual person. Anyway, a person with a good eye.

"Listen," he said suddenly as if he had decided something, "you want a beer? There's a bar across the street, nothing fancy, just a campus-type place. It's really a dump but we can sit and talk and stay all morning. No one bothers you." He seemed embarrassed but he didn't look away. There was something sincere about him, corny almost. But, somehow, the sincere squares were harder to dominate than the kooky ones. It might be tough to manipulate him, after all. She would have to give him a few tests.

"Oh no," she said, "Jewish people don't drink."

"You're Jewish?" he said.

"Yeah," she said, "Sabina Van Rothschild, the second. What's your name?" She took off her hat and crammed it into the greenbookbag. "My head's hot," she said.

"Honorable John O'Conner," he said. "But I thought men called themselves Junior, not women."

"Oh," she said and smothered a yawn. "Well, don't get all hung up on it. Just call me Sarah if you want. It's a nickname."

"Okay, Sarah," he said. She could definitely screw up his studying. "What's the last name?"

"Green," she said, smiling. "I don't dig it at all. I'm changing it as soon as I can."

John shoved his hands into his pockets and began to laugh.

"Shhh," she said, "they'll kick us out. I've already been kicked out twice this month for smoking. Shut up!"

"Sarah Green!" he laughed, "you're Jenny's friend." She suddenly came into focus for him. Sarah frowned. Anonymity had been shot to hell. How could she go around weaving fantasies for people if they were going to ruin it by knowing who she really was?

"Ah crap," she said, "Jenny has a big mouth."

"I've known Jenny since we were kids," John said. "She's nuts."

"She's not nuts," Sarah said, protecting her friend's image. "She's a boss chick, completely open to life. I love her. People should love each other more."

He nodded and took her arm to lead her away.

"I don't drink at ten in the morning," she said, pushing his arm. She hadn't expected him to be so aggressive. Where did he get off being so bleeding aggressive, insulting her best friend?

"Come on," he said, "we'll sit down and talk."

"Quiet," she said. "You're talking too loud, they'll throw us out." He couldn't really be too sincere, not if he were wearing a red sweater. Sincere people didn't wear red sweaters.

"But it doesn't matter," he said, "we're leaving anyway."

"Okay," she said, "I'll drink tea like my Russian ancestors."

] 32 [

"I'll tie one on like mine," John said, his cheeks flushed with excitement.

"Oh God, tie one on, tie one on," Sarah mocked, "it's such squaresville talk. Can't you say, get high?"

"Get high," John said, and smiled.

"Did you know," she said, "that a pint of alcohol is equal to ninety-two and a half rotten bananas? You could get banana fever or barf all night."

"You're against alcohol?" he said.

"No," she said, "but isn't it just a bit silly?"

"You have a virgin's mouth," he said, "but why do you wear whore's lipstick?"

"You must be an only child," she said. For a sincere person he certainly talked fresh. He held her arm down the steps. It might be okay. He seemed clever.

"Nope," he said, "twin. Twin brother. Jenny hates him. Would you rather have something to eat? Are you hungry?"

"No," she said, "I'm working on rotting my teeth. It's a groovy way to antagonize my parents. They flip." She glanced at his mouth. There was a rather large space between the two front uppers, which would definitely drive Mrs. Green straight out of her mind, since she had such a rigid teeth fixation. Not bad enough that he had an unkempt appearance and would be after her flesh, he had to have those teeth. And, of course, he already admitted he made piggies.

"You do make piggies, don't you?" she said, letting him guide her across the Woodward Avenue traffic.

"Piggies?" he said.

"Make the scene," she said, "fornicate, cohabit."

"I don't think Jenny speaks that way."

"We're quite different," Sarah said. "I'm a freer spirit." No doubt he was an uncircumcised dog, in the language of Mrs. Green, and naturally this would prove a problem. Mrs. Green had an incorrigible way of ferreting out all males, particularly Christian, who wished to make piggies with Sarah. She alienated them in one sitting so they never phoned her again for fear Mrs. Green would tear them limb from limb. Mrs. Green was obsessed with what she imagined was Sarah's sex life.

] 33 [

"Your behind, your behind!" she shrieked when Sarah emerged one Saturday morning wearing tight yellow corduroy bell bottom pants and an orange silk shirt with no brassiere underneath. The odd thing was she never ever said a thing about her fingernails, which were painted brilliant green.

Poor drab Mr. Green stood by, helpless, as they went at each other with insults. There didn't seem to be anything wrong with his daughter's behind as far as he could tell, but perhaps Bertha knew something about it he didn't know. It was true, of course, that Sarah wore crazy, *mishugenah* clothes. But then her friend Jenny, who came from a rich family, wore the same kind of clothes. Surely those rich people don't allow their children to dress badly.

"Watch out for the cars," John said, squeezing her arm through her coat.

"You know something about me," Sarah said, "but I don't know anything about you. It's not fair."

He pushed his arm across her shoulder. "I'm a rapist, philosopher, man-about-town, a pauper, a twin and an idealist. Does that explain who I am? Or did you mean it metaphysically?" He would have to be careful not to become involved. She was the sort who needed a lot of attention, and he didn't have the time. He had to study every minute. His abstinence had paid off. If he hadn't met Suzanne Belier, the French girl from Canada, he would have done even better. Nothing was going to interfere with his studies again. He had been granted a fellowship at Harvard by the skin of his teeth. The anxiety over Suzanne had nearly loused up everything.

"I'm freezing," Sarah said. "It's a motherfucking cold day."

John stared at her. "What?" he said.

"A motherfucking cold day," Sarah repeated.

"I don't appreciate swearing from women," he said. The lovely thing about the bitch Suzanne was her voice, the soft way she spoke and the gentle words. She was really feminine.

Sarah slapped her hands together for warmth. "Oh don't come on middle-class," she said. "I've had that bit up to here."

John held open the door for her and guided her into the dimness of the bar.

"Where do you live?" Sarah said.

] 34 [

"On Outer Drive," he said, "with my mother. My father's dead." He nodded at a waitress who had wandered over and was tugging at an artificial flower in her hair. "Whatdoyouwant?" she said. "Got your Id's?"

"You know me, Myrtle," John said. "I've been drinking here for three years. You don't need any Id's."

"Yeh? This broad looks about twelve," Myrtle said, standing firm.

"What makes you think I'm twelve?" Sarah snarled, digging into her greenbookbag and taking out a yellowed piece of paper.

She'd put her in her place, all right. Myrtle scanned it, shaking her head from side to side like a half-wit. "You kids," she sighed in a garlic breath, "you kids, I take so much. But, okay what'll you have?"

John helped Sarah into her seat. "Two beers," he ordered.

Myrtle vanished into the dim recesses of the bar.

"This says you're twenty-five," John said, examining the yellowed paper and glancing at Sarah. Her skin was soft and warm looking, faintly rosy as if she spent a lot of time outside. "It's impossible," he said. "You're a child, aren't you? You can't be more than fifteen."

Invariably he was attracted to small, dark girls with big eyes. It was a curse. Maybe it was because they looked Irish?

"Don't be an idiot," Sarah said. "I've had forged Id since fourteen. I'll be seventeen in the summer. The fourth of July."

"Still in high school, I suppose," John said, feeling sick. He knew she was young, but how did he manage with such regularity to pick up crazy high school girls? He would be much better off with Suzanne, though she didn't attract him. She was reliable and older.

"I graduate in June," Sarah said, pulling out the tin of cigars. "I'm young to be graduating in June but I skipped twice. They thought I was brilliant."

Fascinated, he watched her light the cigar.

"I wonder if Jenny's a virgin?" Sarah said. She looked at John's slate-blue eyes. Eyes were the first thing she noticed. The windows of his soul. He was probably too conventional for her tastes but maybe she could learn something from him, something new and enchanting, insane. Maybe this was the one to deflower her. It was

]35[

time. She had been sixteen for more than six months and still had her maidenhead. She was the only one in the twelfth grade who hadn't made the scene yet.

John tapped the table. "I don't know," he said impatiently. "My brother tried to date her, but she rejected him. She told him she didn't admire Catholics. I think that's pretty snotty. We did go to the same Sunday school."

Sarah bit down gently on her lower lip. There must be a way of turning this rather clever, handsome cat into more of a swinger. He was too tense. There probably was a way of getting him to relax. He looked sexy enough. Maybe this is where he swung? He swung with sex. She smiled at him. There was something seduce-able there, a kind of willingness, a desire that superseded his apparent middle-class point of view. It was better to be made by a Christian than one of her own kind. Wouldn't that make it sexier?

"People still go to Sunday school?" Sarah said. "Jesus Christ!" She wiggled out of her coat and threw it over a chair. What would Aunt Ruth think if she knew the coat was in a bar at ten in the morning?

"Yes," John said, looking around the room for Myrtle, "can you think of something better to do on Sunday morning?"

"Sure," Sarah said, impatiently, "sleep, screw or listen to music. Or figure out what to do with your life."

"Do you believe what you're saying?"

Sarah nodded. "I think I'd rather have a spiritual scene with music. It's not everyone who can have a strob-lit dream of love."

"Myrtle," John called into the back of the bar. "I don't know what you're talking about." He turned to Sarah. "Anyway, I've better things to do. I have endless studying to do. I'm going to Harvard summer session, then I have a fellowship." He pushed the hair away from his forehead.

"Anyone can go to college. Everyone, the dumbest, dummy, dumbbell, clown, idiot goes to college. The point is to find out what to do with your life."

"Well," John said, noticing his French professor had wandered in and was lurching aimlessly about in the back of the bar, "that's what school is for. Learning."

"Aah, fooey," Sarah said, "I'd rather smoke Pot for a real learning experience."

] 36 [

"Aha!" John said, sarcastically, "you're what's known as a hipster." There was something very dominating about her he wasn't sure he liked. She was opinionated. It was disconcerting to hear such absurd opinions coming from her. He had a sudden urge to reach over and touch her round, high breasts.

"I guess I'm hip," she said.

John took a cigar out of the tin and held it. "Anyone who says they're hip cannot be hip. I know." He lit the cigar and began to cough. It would be ridiculous to spend time with this girl except in bed. There she might function, but as a companion, a playmate, a friend, she was destructive. Her sense of herself was so strong, she was so narcissistic it would take one's every energy to bring her into focus.

Sarah yawned and stretched her tapered fingers like a cat stretching claws.

"Tired?" he said, coughing. What was a little girl doing smoking cigars? It was a masculine affectation at best.

"Just super bored," she said, lowering her thick lashes and sighing.

John leaned back in his chair. It was he who felt tired. He would need all the energy he could summon up to deal with this exotic creature. But how would he maintain his grade average? Maybe if he could straighten her out right away, right in the beginning, then later things could go more smoothly. If he allowed her to control him, all would be lost.

"Do you want to argue?" he said. "I went through this last month and last year. Why don't we try to enjoy each other. There isn't time for anything else." He touched her hand.

"I could show you how to enjoy yourself," he said.

Myrtle fluttered by and sloshed the beer onto the table and fluttered away in the direction of the French professor.

"Some kind of *klutz*," Sarah said. "I don't think I dig beer."

John picked up the mug of beer and gulped. The neurotic ones were always the interesting ones. Why? Sarah was insolent too, and nuts like her friend, Jenny. Two of a kind. But you weren't much of a man if you couldn't stand up to a challenge.

"Do you always complain?" he asked. He would intimidate her. Intimidate, dominate and seduce. He would make silly putty out of her and mold her into various shapes. She could retain the skin, the hair, the eyes, the body but the shape of her soul would be different.

"Not always, sugar," she said.

The French professor was standing at the bar, listening to Myrtle, whose jagged mouth moved in semi-literate circles. The professor looked drunkenly interested and finally reached over and patted her breasts, one by one.

"There's one of my teachers," John whispered, leaning toward Sarah and wondering when he would have the nerve to touch her. "His wife keeps trying to leave him. They have seven children. He tells us about it in class, the poor guy."

"It might be a good thing if she jumped," Sarah said. "If they want to hire a murderer, I'm available. I need bread. I've got to get out of this dead city. Money's the answer."

"Money?" John said. "What's that?" He knew exactly what he would do to her as soon as he found the place. He would take off her dress, and then her silver tights. He would take the pins out of her hair and let it fall loose. He would kiss her neck, her face, her green eyes. And that was merely the start. George would be jealous when he met her. The olive-skinned beauties didn't like George. They preferred John.

"I want to go to New York, that's where it's happening. All the groovy people are in New York. They're all bananas but there it works out." She felt dizzy. "The scene is New York." She should have eaten something for breakfast instead of zooming out of the house like a whirlwind. No breakfast and a beer wasn't too cool.

John finished the cigar and snuffed it out. Poor old George, never got the good-looking ones, was always stuck with the dogs. He took her hand again and pressed her fingers to his lips. "Ten kisses," he said, "from a rapist square to a wanted babyhip. A much-wanted babyhip."

"Babyhip?" she said, frowning. "I'm not such a babyhip." It sounded like a cross between a mythical beast and a teen-age crackpot. And, she certainly wasn't either. He better cool it. If he weren't too much of a cornball, she could manage to seduce him. She liked the idea of seducing him. Wasn't it time she gave up her maidenhood? She had been looking for just such a person as John. Not too wild, but sort of erotic. Reliable. Your first love should be reliable, then the rest could be bananas. Sarah had considered sleeping with others but had definitely decided to wait for the right reliable person. Moses had turned her down, the rat. He would have nothing to do with her.

"You know," she said, allowing her hand to remain in his, "I'm not such a babyhip or whatever you said. I'm thought to be an intellectual at school. My teachers think I'm a genius."

"And I'm a football," he said. The professor had taken a comb out of his pocket and was pulling it through Myrtle's electric hair.

"Hey," John said, "maybe that's his wife?"

Sarah shook her head. "No, girl friend. I have an instinct for these things."

John stood up. If Myrtle wasn't going to come to the table to take their order, he would have to interrupt her love-play.

"You do want another?"

"Yeah," she said, "does your twin make piggies?"

"I never heard that expression before." How could such a child-beauty be so muddled? He would have to straighten her out. What she needed to settle her were a lot of kisses in the right place. He looked at her ankles. Would George be at home? Was anyone at home? Tilly? George might be in the pits or zipping around the city in his car.

"When I left this morning my mother was sick," John said, remembering his mother's bleary, bloated face as she stared into her cereal. "Excuse me. I think I'll phone and see how she is."

3

SARAH SLAMMED the front door, deposited her coat on the banister and flung her hat across the room. Where could those maniacs be? The house seemed empty.

She ran into the kitchen and looked at the wall clock. It was later than she thought. They would be irritated she was late. But what difference did it make? It was late, yeah, too late. There was nothing they could do about it. She would never be a virgin again.

"Anyone home?" she yelled, "hey, dummies, where are you?" There was no reply. She looked down the hall joining the kitchen to the living room. It was mysteriously quiet except for a faint stirring from the closet. Slowly the closet door opened and Clytemnestra, the cat, lazily emerged. Sarah reached down and stroked her.

"You sexless creature," she murmured. It had been cozy in John's arms, lying against his chest with her head under his chin. He was more intense than she planned, which gave her a temporary uneasy feeling, as though she were falling down a well.

She picked up the cat and kissed the top of her head. She was so soft and cuddly. It would be nice to let Clytemnestra go out to the backyard and prowl in the flowers. She could roam freely playing with twigs and dirt and decayed leaves left over from the previous fall. It would be generous to let her go out.

Sarah smiled, thinking of how John had looked standing in his underwear. He turned off the bedroom light and let the hall light shine into the room, and then he kissed her warmly on the shoulder. It tickled.

"Don't laugh," he said, "please."

She giggled.

It wasn't the way she imagined it. When it was over she searched the sheets for blood. There wasn't any.

"Maybe we didn't actually do it," she said, rubbing his thigh.

"We did it, we did it," John said, sleepily.

"But there wasn't any blood."

"You're not a bleeder," he said. "Some aren't."

"You've known many?"

"Yes," John said, "many, many."

"Are you an English major?" she said.

He sat bolt upright in bed. "What?"

"Are you an English major. You know. At Wayne."

"Yes," he said. "What an odd thing to say." He lay down again. It was hard to figure her out. She was foxy.

"Did you like it?" he said, twisting his body so he faced her.

"Yes," Sarah said. "Can we do it again?"

"In a while."

They lay there quietly, not speaking, with their eyes shut.

"You know what I did when I went downstairs to use the phone?" Sarah said. "I called Jenny."

"What?" John said, sitting up. "You did what?" He got out of bed, shut the door and turned on the light. Over his dresser was a large picture of Elizabeth Taylor.

"Ugh," Sarah said, "turn out the light."

He stood over her, looking down at her perfectly formed body. Why was she so maddening?

"I called her at school to ask her if I should make piggies."

"Was that necessary?" John said, closing the venetian blinds. They were arranged so the neighbors could have a good view if they wanted.

Sarah pulled the sheet over her head. "She wasn't much help. She said I took her out of Mathematics class. It's her favorite. She's hung on Mathematics. I'm meeting her tomorrow at the drugstore. She's bringing me some Pot."

John pulled the sheet back so he could look at her. "Sarah," he said, feeling a ridiculous urge to hold her, "Sarah, I think Jenny's a lousy influence. Remember, I know her."

"She has a good brain," Sarah said. "John, you're wonderful, I dig you."

Sarah opened the back door, letting Clytemnestra jump out of

]41[

her arms and disappear into the dark intrigue of the backyard. The poor, idiot altered pussy would never know pleasure, the pleasure of floating down a stream in the middle of a lush, green jungle. She pulled some bits of hair off her suede jumper. Mrs. Green would rail if she saw the cat hair. She railed constantly about the cat hair. She was thoroughly disgusted with Clytemnestra and all attempts to get rid of her failed miserably. It wasn't two weeks before she suggested giving Clytemnestra away for the nine millionth time.

"I'll report you to the humane society, you bitch!" Sarah screamed. She banged her fist on the banister and grabbed the cat, locking her in the downstairs bathroom.

"I'm keeping her in the john forever, if necessary," she cried. Mrs. Green had been terrified of Clytemnestra since she first appeared, a tiny ball of fur in the front yard. Someone had, intentionally, put the animal there, and for an entire sleepless night she whined and whimpered in the new grass. It was a conspiracy, but who would do such a miserable thing? It was a plot a cruel sadist had whipped up to tease and torment her. Everyone knew how she detested and feared animals. It could be no one but Sarah in league with Moses. It was something they would concoct. And would it ever end?

She had tried various methods of getting rid of the animal. She left her on neighboring streets in the dead of night, abandoned her in the supermarket, shoved her into strange alleys. Somehow each time she wandered back. In desperation Mrs. Green had phoned the vet to inquire about the longevity of cats. It couldn't last forever. To her dismay she was told some animals, some cats live to be fifteen or sixteen, older even, if cared for properly. She placed an advertisement in the local paper. No one answered. She tried to bribe Mrs. Ferentz's little boy, Leon, to take the cat. He turned up his nose. For weeks she went around with a sour expression on her face as if to say, look at me, see how I suffer.

Assiduously she avoided the animal, who seemed forever underfoot. She placed a small gate across the entrance to the living room so Clytemnestra couldn't rip, tear and destroy the nice living room furniture and deposit fur balls wherever she went. To her great distress, Clytemnestra ate right through and for one nightmarish week nasty pieces of undigested chicken wire were to be found in all parts of the house. It was no wonder Mrs. Green had an underactive thyroid with that animal sapping her energy.

"I love you," she whispered into the backyard as the phone rang.

"Hello," she said, "Sarah Green's Pad." She pulled the run in her stocking wide open so her knee was exposed.

Mrs. Green's rasp floated over the wire. "What? What?" she said. "What? Sarah? Sarah? It's you, maybe?"

"Yeah," Sarah said, "*c'est moi*, baby."

"We'll be right home. Please put the beans in the oven and the chops in the broiler. We're shopping."

"Okay," Sarah said.

"We'll be right home. Where were you, why are you home so late, did they keep you at school, what did you do, why don't you call me when you're going to be late, I've told you a thousand times?" Mrs. Green said in one fat breath. Sarah held the phone away from her ear. The voice didn't fit into her otherwise perfect day. It came at her like poison arrows.

"Yeah, well like nine billion times, two trillion and sixty-nine is more like it."

"Don't start. Don't get fresh," her mother said. "We'll be right home. Get the dinner started." Click. She was gone. Sarah placed the receiver back on the phone. She had forgotten to ask John about the skull-and-crossbones ring. He had removed it after they made piggies. What did it mean?

"Shit," she said out loud, peering into the refrigerator. Mrs. Green had an uncanny way of preparing inedible food, the kind you find at kosher dairy restaurants. Being a lousy cook was only part of it, she actually believed herself to be divine. She was forever lecturing on calories, intake, output, the upper G.I. tract, the colon, puddings, spices, gefilte fish, and the secrets of avoiding constipation. Thinking she was an expert and having one hundred seventy-five pounds of flaccid flesh to prove it, invariably she starved her family. In a continuous state of hunger, it was Sarah's habit to journey to the kitchen after dinner was finished and fix herself an entire meal of her own exciting design. One night while Mrs. Green was watching the idiot tube, she discovered her father ingesting a herring sandwich on rye with mustard.

She caught him in the act and snapped on the light so suddenly tears came to his eyes. The old man was an amateur. Standing in his undershorts with obviously no place to hide the food put him in a nonprofessional status. Like a boob.

Sarah began to fix the same kind of sandwich. "What are you doing here?" she said loudly, trying to attract her mother's attention. She crammed the sandwich into her mouth. It would be amusing if Mrs. Green waltzed into the kitchen to find her husband, almost naked, sneaking food. Sarah polished off the sandwich in a second, making sure she dropped crumbs everywhere. The next day was Carmine's day off and Mrs. Green would be sweeping up.

"Having a *nosh*," Mr. Green said, guilty. "Don't tell your mother, we don't want to hurt the feelings."

Groaning, Sarah reached into the refrigerator and took out two lamb chops. They weren't very fresh. Was that all there was for dinner? "Ich," she said. The wax paper clung desperately in one soggy mess to the meat. She put it to her nose and smelled, then thrust it away behind a slimy jar of pickles that looked as if her Grandmother had bequeathed it a generation ago. No matter how hard Sarah tried to think of aesthetic delights or her intellectual concepts, each time she saw that jar of pickles she was reminded of a grotesque little pig fetus in Biology Lab. It was cruel of the school authorities to do such senseless, disgusting things. Squares. But it was their feeling for the fitness of things.

The clock said there was ample time to create her own culinary feat, a swinging little dinner. A boss meal. This would cool them out. They would come in and gape with pleasure. They would all sit down and eat just like civilized people. Carefully, she selected a dozen eggs, a rasher of bacon, and three English muffins. Dinner was such a bore. Sarah would prepare a superb, out-of-sight breakfast. No Establishment dinner for her. She had bigger fish to fry.

She began to mix and stir, scramble and beat. In a few moments the exotic smell brought Clytemnestra salivating into the room.

When everything was ready, the bacon warming and the eggs covered, awaiting Mr. and Mrs. Green's entrance, she set the dining room table with the Chanukah candles and the good silver. Then she selected a Lovin' Spoonful record. And just in time. She heard Mr. and Mrs. Green's new Chevrolet sidling into the driveway. She ran to the kitchen window and peered out. Yeah, there they were. Mom and Dad exactly like two plump phoenix birds. Mrs. Green was holding her old gray shopping bag and hysterically working her mouth. Mr. Green's arms flailed the air. They must be having the daily argument. And what a waste; with such grandiose energy he could easily have washed four or five of her cashmere sweaters.

Sarah rushed up the stairs to her bedroom, which was covered wall to wall with posters of her favorite music groups and movie stars she detested. Quickly, she stripped off her clothes and pulled on her Karate robe, a gift from Jenny.

"I thought you went shopping," she said to Mrs. Green. Could Mrs. Green intuit where she had been? "I thought you went shopping? The bag looks empty."

"We did," Mrs. Green said curtly. "What's the funny smell?"

"Oh, yeah," Sarah said, "I made dinner, that's all." She pulled at the sleeve of her robe.

"Uh huh," Mrs. Green said, eyeing the robe. "Did you find the chops?"

It had always been Sarah's contention Mrs. Green would have made a boss lawyer. What with her constant nagging and *noodging*, her paranoiac reactions and her feeling that everyone under the age of thirty was a criminal. It would have worked out super. Mr. Green sighed nervously and went into the kitchen. Sarah could hear him opening the refrigerator. The poor goose must be starved.

He searched in the refrigerator looking for a quick bite of something. There wasn't much there, only a jar of pickles. He didn't feel like eating a pickle. Not having eaten a thing since noon, he could have devoured almost anything, but not a pickle. For lunch he ordered an enormous corned beef sandwich to celebrate selling fifty-five orders of wholesale toilets to the J. L. Hudson Company. He had even ordered a piece of cherry pie. He felt he deserved something special, a reward for all the patience he maintained in the face of the housewares buyer's clear anti-Semitic tone. Mr. Green was equilibrium itself.

"Get out of there," Mrs. Green said and slammed the refrigerator door closed. "You won't eat dinner." Mrs. Green strictly forbade eating before meals.

"I couldn't find the lamb chops," Sarah said, pulling a French cigarette from the pocket of the Karate robe.

"You're not smoking that filthy thing in here. I'll *plotz*," Mrs. Green said.

"You're lucky it's not drugs," Sarah said and turned the fire on under the eggs. "I didn't dig making the dinner scene so I made breakfast, folks."

Mrs. Green glared at Sarah. "I'm *plotzing*."

"And I lit candles. Breakfast is a much more ridiculous meal than dinner."

"Candles. It's maybe a holiday?" Mr. Green said, smiling like a child. Would there be presents and songs and affection? Someone should give him a gift for all he had to put up with. The miserable *schnook* who hated Jews. It was so apparent. You could tell by the look on his face.

"Breakfast?" Mrs. Green said.

"Like I made breakfast a go go. You heard it right the first time. It'll be ready in a minute. Just cool it till then, and I don't want any off-the-wall conversation. Make it to the living room or something."

Mrs. Green backed out of the room, hitting her large cumbersome arm on the kitchen door. "What's this funny music I hear? Take it off. I won't have this. First you disobey, then you play this *schmutzik* stuff. Please, I can't stand it. What are you doing to us?" She thrust her hands together as though she might fall to her knees and begin to pray.

"Is this what we get for giving you everything? You're spoiled rotten. Why the kid was born with a silver spoon in her mouth. Is this what we get? Sass? No gratitude." Her voice was rising to a crescendo pitch, a habit she acquired from Mr. Green early in their marriage. Mr. Green always squealed when he spoke, particularly if he wished to underscore a point. He could almost reach as high as Renata Tebaldi.

"It's that *shicksa*," Mrs. Green said. "You used to be a good girl till you met the *shicksa*."

"Are you speaking of Jenny?" Sarah snapped. "She happens to be a very smart person and will probably have all A's this year and go to Sarah Lawrence and be famous." She opened the stove and looked inside. The bacon was baking beautifully. It would be a tasty little dinner unless she decided to throw it at them. "Let's cool it," she said. "No suicide tonight. I'll change the record." She walked to the kitchen door. "You can't dig a soul sound, anyway, what's the difference."

"So now we don't have a soul," her father said, absently sitting on top of Sarah's hat. He picked up the newspaper in an attempt to hide. Such discussions made his head pound. He would take refuge in the sports section.

"How about Nina and Frederick?" Sarah said.

"I've had enough," Mrs. Green screamed, seizing the album Sarah was about to play, "enough of that music."

"But they're the newest in thing," Sarah protested.

"To your room, go to your room," Mrs. Green breathed deeply. Mr. Green groaned and rustled the newspaper to drown out the sound. He glanced over the paper at Mrs. Green to check her welts. They hadn't appeared yet.

"Shhh," he said, "shhh, the rash, the skin, dear." Mrs. Green loomed over Sarah, a sick expression glued to her face. He wondered had she gained weight? Her dress seemed to be too tight across her bosom, holding her breasts like two fallen monuments. It was peculiar, must be due to menopause at an early age. He tried to remember what she looked like when he married her. She was little more than Sarah's age. Was she slim? She must have been a little thinner or he wouldn't have married her.

"What's the matter, dear?" he said. If only they'd go away and leave him to his paper. Why did they have to follow him into the living room night after night and prevent the one inexpensive relaxation of the day?

"I won't listen to this talk," Mrs. Green said, her face reddening. Her mouth looked puffier than usual, the skin slack near the chin. "Get to your room!" Sarah reached for a match and lit another French cigarette, the strong aroma filling the room and mixing with the smell of bacon and eggs. "Look," she said, "I'm sixteen and I'm not going to my room. Not now or ever." She regarded her mother as though she were confronting the enemy army. "Those days are gone forever. I'll do what I damned well please. Besides I'm getting married soon and we'll need a new relationship. One that's more equitable. It's a rite of passage in case you didn't dig."

Mr. Green threw down the paper and scanned his wife's face for an explanation for what his daughter had just said. She appeared astonished. What was going on? If she were given to fainting, she would have fainted, but it was important to be conscious at all times, no matter what. How else could you control the people around you, how would you know what transpired if you were unconscious? Married? MARRIED? A strange sensation passed through her body. Did Sarah say married?

"What married," she screamed, "to who?" There was something burning in the kitchen. They would have to eat out. Mrs. Green didn't like going to restaurants with Mr. Green. He didn't know how to order. It always embarrassed her. "Now," she said in a tight voice, suddenly very hungry, "who will marry such a *mishugenah* girl who never combs her hair? I ask you."

"Ha ha. John O'Conner, that's who."

Mr. Green got up. "It's Jewish?" he said.

"It isn't," Sarah shrieked and ran to the foot of the stairs. "It's Irish. Irish. Father from Ireland. Barely assimilated. I'll be marrying down. I love him, do you hear?" She stamped her foot on the bottom stair. They could never understand, never, never, never, the beautiful soul afternoon, perhaps the most interesting, out-of-sight afternoon of her whole life.

"Don't you get hysterics," Mrs. Green warned, "or I'll throw cold water on you. I'll have none of this sassing."

"Cold water," Sarah said furiously. "You square creeps. Hate, hate, hate, hate is all you know!"

Mr. Green advanced toward her, his voice shaking and beginning to ascend the scale. "How do you know this . . . uh . . . goy?" he said, peering at her breasts. "Where were you today?" His hands quivered in frustration. Tears came to his eyes. "Please," he said, "please tell your father." Sarah gaped at him. He had blown his wig, was totally out of his box. Bananas.

"I'm your father," he said.

"Yeah," she said. Poor Dad has flipped his wig.

"We'll take you for an examination," he said confusedly. "I'll go right with you. Did he touch one hair of your head? Where?

Where is he? This monster . . . this beast?" He threw his fists out at the air. So that's where she was all afternoon while they worried. Bertha had understood. "I'll break his wild Indian neck," he said, his voice like a whooping crane. "I'll get his father to the police station. He'll see. He'll see." Mr. Green began to sob. Mrs. Green sobbed, too, the tears cascading down her face and forming a small pool down on the front of her dress.

"How could you be so bad after all we've done?" she wailed. "Bernie, how did we fail? Oh Bernie, Bernie."

"Bertha," Mr. Green yelped, "Bertha." Sarah watched them. They had a trained-seal air, full of sound and fury, flapping around to no purpose. Flap, flap, flap.

"Listen," Sarah said. "You've seriously bugged me since I was twelve. I remember the exact moment when it began. It's a wonder I'm not in the looney bin." It had been a normally banal day in the middle of June. Mr. and Mrs. Green, Sarah, Carmine and Moses had driven to Lake Michigan for a picnic. Until three in the morning, Mrs. Green made hard-boiled eggs. There was fried chicken, southern style, tomatoes, potato salad, even beer for Carmine. Carmine made certain there was enough food. Moses had brought along a big striped umbrella for his mother. As they drove, Mrs. Green kept turning around to check on Sarah and Moses. They were too quiet. As soon as they arrived at the beach, they rushed into the water. Moses was going to teach Sarah to swim. At that point he was full-grown, six feet tall and muscular as any man.

For an hour they splashed and played in the water, until Sarah became tired. Moses agreed to life-saving, and it wasn't until years later Sarah realized from shore it must have looked as if they were fucking in the water. And try to explain that they weren't to Mrs. Green, who imagined her nubile daughter up to all kinds of evil doings. They were immediately bundled into the car, still wet from the swim, and driven swiftly back to the city. Sarah stared icily at her parents. Mr. Green shoved the glasses back on his nose. Somehow when he became annoyed his glasses tended to fall off his face. "Well," he said, "if he isn't Jewish, what is he?"

"As far as I know," Sarah said coldly, "Irish are Catholics, unless they live in the Protestant part of Ireland, which is as rare as a

]49[

black Jew. But let's eat, I'm hungry." At the mention of food Mrs. Green stirred from her funk. She wiped her tears away. Food would give her strength to argue.

"Put some nutmeg in the apple sauce," Sarah said, "it gives a groovy kind of high. Just ridiculous."

4

"THE DAY I STOPPED saying man to women I knew I had arrived," John said, stepping out of the shower and reaching for a towel. They had spent an hour.

"I'm hip," Sarah said. "It doesn't suit you." She wrapped herself in a large Turkish towel. "I feel divine like a saint." She leaned forward and kissed his chest.

"Kid stuff," he said. "Those words aren't interesting."

"That depends on the scene. Like on John R. it's okay or in the jazz community or some place that makes it."

John pulled his pants on and did a quick knee bend. "That's indigenous. It's different. If a Negro calls another Negro, nigger, it's all right. It's different. Anyway, those so-called hip words are out. They were used by musicians twenty years ago. Now it's pop culture."

"Ho hum," Sarah said. "I've heard that observation from about sixty-nine trillion people. If I hear it again I'll scream *merde* at the mayor's office." She looked at John's face reflected in the mirror. He brushed his hair one stroke at a time. So organized. So sweet. It was amazing they had met only a week before. Hadn't she known him always? It was like playing house with the man of your dreams. Could she ever feel differently about him? She touched his back.

"I love you," she said. He stopped brushing his hair.

"Do you?"

"Yeah," she said, "I do." It was exactly a week and so far, though it was Tuesday, and usually a good day for the Idiot List, she had only counted two.

"When do I meet Tilly?" she said. Perhaps they better split before Tilly came home. It could be awkward.

"Tomorrow," John said, "for tea. After school. Okay?" He smiled. She had fascinating calf muscles, very developed, like a dancer's. "Did you study ballet?" he said.

"No. I may not go to school tomorrow. I don't feel in the mood. Should I come here anyway?"

"Yes," he said, "about six. Tilly should be pulled together by then. She likes to have a few drinks after work. Then her boyfriend arrives and either they eat at home or go out."

"Your mother has a lover?" Sarah said, opening her eyes wide. She never knew anyone whose mother had a lover. It was exciting.

"Sure," John said, "what do you expect? She's young."

"Will you love me when I'm old like thirty?" Sarah said, putting her arms around his waist. "Will we always make love, always? Do old people really fuck?"

"Probably," John said. "I never really thought about it. You have the funniest way of saying things other people don't say."

"That's what Jenny says," Sarah said.

"I'd like to bite your leg," John said, "but I wish you wouldn't say fuck so often. It's disconcerting. Don't say it in front of Tilly."

"I might," she said. "Don't give me orders."

"And please go to school tomorrow," he continued. "Don't you want to go to a good college?"

"I loathe school," Sarah said. "It stinks. All those middle-class morons. They're imbeciles. I'm going to New York instead." She elbowed him away from the sink and began applying lipstick with a brush.

"Not too thick," he said.

Sarah turned around. "You sound like my parents," she said. "*Quelle* bore!"

"I'm not, can't you tell the difference?" John said, grabbing her. "I've got to bite your leg. It's an urge."

She pushed him away. "Later, sugar." She pulled a white turtleneck sweater over her head and slipped into a black leather skirt.

She tied a scarf in the back of her hair like a bow. "French," she said. "I'm ready now."

"We've got to straighten the bedroom," John said.

"You do it, I'm busy," she said.

"Busy? Busy doing what, madam?"

"Busy thinking, man," she said. "You do it."

John looked at her. "Are you kidding?"

"No," she answered. They confronted each other for a moment. "Oh come on, don't be bugged," Sarah said, teasing.

"Maybe you need a spanking," John said.

"That's all I ever got," she said. "Is that the doorbell?" The doorbell was ringing in a long groan like a dying canary.

"Must be George, it's too early for Mom."

"Oh George, the twin monster?" she said, patting a wrinkle out of her skirt. "How can there be two of you? It's dreadful."

John ran out of the bathroom and peered over the banister.

"We're different," he said and ran down the stairs. Sarah knew all twins made the same statement. She heard it before. However, John was accurate. They were very different. George was tall with dark-brown hair that curled mysteriously. His face was square. He had big hands and feet. They barely even looked like relatives. She scrutinized his appearance, looking from one to the other, making mental comparisons.

"Please don't do that," George said. "We don't admire that. Think of us as brothers, that's all that's necessary." He seemed crabby, a quality Sarah didn't particularly like in men. And, what's more, when they were introduced he had squeezed her hand till it hurt. He could be Idiot Three. An idiot handshake made you automatically an idiot as well as a creep. Like all the poor creeps in the annual party at her father's chapter of the Masons. Hearty handshakers, one and all, to the last man. Mr. Green belonged for twenty years and was used to the handshakes. He proudly proclaimed to anyone who would listen he was a Mason. He, a Jew, was a Mason. It was better than being number-one salesman in all of Michigan in the selling of wholesale toilets. It didn't matter one of the Jewish faith couldn't reach the holy zenith of the order, oh no, it was enough to simply belong. When he spoke of the Masons, she imagined a fat, swarthy man afloat on a magic carpet. He would offer a water pipe of the finest hashish to all those who made it to the top. If only Mr. Green weren't Jewish, he could swing around the world on the magic carpet, getting completely zonked out.

"I was at the pits," George explained. He was wearing a blue

]53[

crash helmet and a jump suit stained with grease. He was taken aback when John opened the door and he first glimpsed the exotic creature lurking in the upstairs bathroom. And then when she examined him minutely, he felt downright outraged.

"Should I undress?" he asked.

"Both sarcastic," she said, looking from one to the other.

"John isn't," George said.

"Let's go," John said and handed Sarah her coat.

"Ooooh, it scratches," she said, making a face.

"Let's go anyway," John said, trying to hurry her out the door. He looked back at George. "Maybe we'll double," he said, "with Jenny Oliver. Okay? This weekend maybe." George looked doubtful. "The kook?" he said.

"Do you appreciate this coat?" Sarah said as she climbed into George's car. It scratched but it was the only one that matched the black leather skirt. She bought it secondhand from a mad advertisement in the Detroit *Times*. It cost only two dollars and was the find of the century. The front was stitched with various colored beads. Undoubtedly it had belonged to a fancy millionaire. Henry Ford, maybe.

"Swell," John said, "just jim dandy."

5

"HI, SARAH," JENNY said, dropping down beside her at the counter. The drugstore was crammed with tousle-haired students eating lunch, smoking, talking and playing the jukebox.

"Hi," Sarah said, "what's happening?"

"Not much," Jenny said, casually slipping a joint into Sarah's hand.

"Should we smoke in here?" Sarah said.

Jenny shook her head. "No. Save for some other time. I just bought it. It's an early birthday gift to you."

"Thanks," Sarah said and put it into her greenbookbag.

"It's good stuff," Jenny said. "Oh, I saw the woman from Sarah Lawrence today. I think it's all set. Scholarship and all."

"A scholarship?" Sarah said incredulously. "But you have money."

Jenny smiled. "But I'm getting a scholarship." She pushed her blond, ironed hair out of her eyes.

"Did she say anything about the hair?"

"No," Jenny said, "not a word. Nothing."

"She's a cool couze," Sarah said and bit into a hamburger.

"I don't think I'll eat today," Jenny said, "out of penance for all our rotten foreign policy commitments."

"Okay," Sarah said, "but that's silly. You can't save the starving Armenians."

"Why not?" Jenny said. She was wearing her school uniform, a gray skirt and blue blazer with gold buttons and looked like any ordinary private school girl.

"They ain't worth saving, that's why," Sarah said and popped a stray piece of tomato into her mouth.

"I don't agree," Jenny said, "not at all." They were silent for a moment.

"I dig that sound," Sarah said.

"Who is it?" Jenny said, turning around and looking in the direction of the jukebox. A horde of boys were hanging around, moving their heads in time to the music.

"A new scene. I don't know the name. They swing."

"I suppose," Jenny said. "Did it work out with John O'Conner?"

"Oh did it," Sarah said. "I think I'll have another hamburger. Later I've got to rush over and meet his mother for tea."

"The brother George is not terribly intelligent," Jenny said. "Is John smarter?"

"Sure," Sarah said, "not brilliant but smart. He's going to Harvard for his Ph.D."

"Oh, that's interesting," Jenny said, her gaze wandering off. There was a girl at the end of the counter who looked as if she had just taken an overdose of LSD.

"Look at that maniacal girl," she whispered. Sarah looked down the counter. "That's just Emily Morton, the class hooker," Sarah said and pantomined another hamburger to the guy behind the counter.

"Hooker?" Jenny said. "What's hooker?"

"Whore," Sarah said, pleased she knew something Jenny didn't know. Jenny was clever, but she wasn't really hip. "Whore, prostitute, round-heels, strumpet, piggies-maker," she said. "You know. You read."

Jenny stared at Emily Morton. "Poor thing," she said.

"Yeah, that's what I always say," Sarah said and crammed the hamburger into her mouth.

6

SARAH STOOD FOR an instant on the porch, then drew a hand mirror from the greenbookbag. She would have time for one last penetrating look at herself before meeting Mrs. O'Conner. Mrs. O'Conner was conservative. Sarah inspected her reflection. The lipstick wasn't too dark. The hair was neatly pinned back with Spanish combs she found in Jenny's attic and no hoop earrings. Compromise and concession. Concession and compromise. John had convinced her it was important with people's parents. Why make waves? It was amazing what love could do. She had no desire, whatsoever, to say fuck to Mrs. O'Conner.

She pressed the buzzer and waited. Nothing happened. She pressed it again. She knew perfectly well it was the right day and the right hour. Where was she? She pushed the buzzer again. She banged the brass knocker. It was rude of Mrs. O'Conner.

"Mrs. O'Connor," she yelled. "Mrs. O'Connor, I'm here." Still, there was no response. "John," she screamed, "John, hey you mothers, you dirty bourgeoise mothers, where are you?" Was this an O'Conner habit? Is this the stuffing they're made of? Perhaps John had deliberately concocted this lousy scheme. He really hated her. He was simply preying on defenseless females, deflowering them and casting them aside. She always had the suspicion Detroit boys were that way. It was different in New York, more civilized. There were men in New York who respected women.

Furiously, she walked around to the side entrance. It was open. Should she go in? She looked into the backyard. No one seemed to be out there but, of course, what would anyone but a nut be doing in the backyard on such a gray day. She looked up at the sky. A bad omen. Some depravity was loose in the world. The skies didn't lie.

She pushed open the door and walked in. The backstairs were dark but ahead she could see there was a light. It must be the kitchen. She went in. Yeah, the kitchen and with a splendid silver tray covered with goodies. There were deviled eggs, carrots, olives, tiny little sandwiches done up like for a party. In the center was an odd mixture that didn't taste familiar. But it was good. It seemed to be a combination of egg plant, onions and mushrooms. She heaped some on a cracker and stuffed it into her mouth.

"Ummm," she murmured appreciatively, studying the tray. Egg sandwiches were supergroovy. She swallowed two down. Funny that no one was on the scene to greet her. She listened, poised like a vulture over the tray. Where was everyone? Had they all committed suicide? The kitchen looked as if Mrs. O'Conner had split the scene before she finished cleaning up.

Sarah yanked off her hooded burnoose and slung it over a chair. She chose a delicate Swiss cheese sandwich and quickly devoured it. At least Mrs. O'Conner could cook. She might be an alcoholic geek but she had taste, after all.

After selecting five or six sandwiches she decided to look around to see if there were any golems, idiots, or monsters around.

"Hey, baby," she said marching into the living room. A woman clad in her slip lay peacefully snoring, her mouth open, her arms crossed.

"Hey, what's this? Bob Dylan's grandmother?" Sarah said. It wasn't very nice of Mrs. O'Conner to have crumped out. It wasn't every day she had the opportunity to meet a celebrity such as Sarah.

"Hey, you!" Sarah said loudly. Mrs. O'Conner moved restlessly for a few seconds, then jerked open her eyes, gaped at Sarah and gave a piercing scream.

"Aaaaaaaaa," she screamed, throwing her hands over her face to protect herself from an assault. "Who is it?"

Sarah stood speechless. Didn't the dunce know who she was?

"Hamlet's ghost," she said, finally.

"Oh goodness," Mrs. O'Conner said. "I'm sorry, you must be Sarah Green." She tried to rouse herself from the couch.

"I was invited to tea," Sarah said, doing a curtsey.

"Really?" Mrs. O'Conner said, struggling with one of the pillows on the couch. "Oh yes," she said, the dawn of recollection crossing her brow. "Sandwiches and tea. I've made them. I must have fallen asleep." She tried to smile. "I must have fallen asleep," she said weakly. "I'm so tired after work. I had a glass of brandy for my stomach."

"Uh-huh," Sarah said. It was taking Mrs. O'Conner an awfully long time to get herself loose from the couch, which had wrapped itself about her like an octopus.

Sarah glanced around, looking for an ashtray. The olive pit lying in her mouth had to be thrown somewhere.

"Call me Tilly," Mrs. O'Conner said, putting out a clammy hand. Her breath reeked of drink.

"Where's John?" Sarah said. When Tilly stood she was smaller than Sarah. A troglydyte? Her hair was a mess but her eyes were slate blue like her son's. She lurched toward the kitchen. "He'll be along soon," she said. "Just sit down. I'll make tea."

Sarah threw the olive pit under one of the couch cushions and picked up a copy of *In Cold Blood*, which was lying on the coffee table.

"You dig this book, *In Cold Blood*?" she called.

"Wonderful," Tilly answered. "Excellent. He can write. And so morbid! Just wonderful. All the neighbors read it. It was on the best-seller list for weeks."

"I thought it stank," Sarah said, lighting up a cigar. "There's no such thing as a nonfiction novel. It's a bloody lie. He's not so clever." How could Mrs. O'Conner be such an idiot? Oh, oh, Idiot List? Any kid in the eighth grade knows there's no such thing. A novel is a novel. Finish. It's not even good reportage." She had managed to get her hands on *The New York Times* to read the reviews. They were all crazy. It didn't fit her opinion of New York at all. This discrepancy was part of the fitness of things. It was okay.

"Reportage?" Mrs. O'Conner said. "Is that French?"

"Yes," Sarah said. Tilly came back into the room, holding the tray of half-eaten sandwiches. "John was nibbling," she said apologetically, "but I could make more if you're hungry." She set the tray down on the coffee table. "What I really liked about the book was the Cutter family, was that the name? Yes, well the Cutters. Such a peculiar family. I hear it's going to be a movie."

"Well," Sarah said, "It's all passé by now. There are thirty books since that one that are better. I thought people had forgotten about it. It was two years ago wasn't it? Barbra Striesand in the movie?"

"I don't know," Mrs. O'Conner said. "Oh, I forgot I'm wearing my slip. I'll have to put on my robe." She began edging toward the hallway.

"Oh no," Sarah said, "just wear my burnoose. It's in the kitchen. Go ahead. I don't mind. I think Screaming Lord Sutch and Mia Farrow are going to be in the movie," she added.

"I don't know," Mrs. O'Conner said from the kitchen. Why did John invariably pick raven-haired girls who spoke aggressively? He had babbled about this girl as if she were the only girl in the world. And what was this strange cloak she was wearing? She slipped into it. It was as heavy as a rug. It must weigh five or six pounds.

"John will be here with his brother soon," she said. It was difficult to understand this generation. Their ways were so different. It was like trying to bridge a chasm. They were two steps ahead at all times. It was frustrating. She looked at her watch. Michael would pick her up in an hour. They could escape to a bar. She sipped her tea and tried to think of conversation.

Fortunately, John and George came bursting into the house.

"That's Sarah's coat," John said, kissing his mother. He grabbed an egg sandwich. "I'm starved," he said, "and, hey, today is boxing day. Come on Sarah, let's go to the basement. We'll show you how we box."

George took off his crash helmet and handed it to his mother. "I've got a date, let's make it quick."

"Now boys," Mrs. O'Conner said, gripping the crash helmet, "please keep your voices down. I'm tired of complaints from the neighbors. It's not very nice."

"Nice, shmice, what is it?" Sarah said.

"You'll see," John said leading her to the basement steps. The basement was damp, smelling of wet wool and decaying wood. Cobwebs caught her face.

] 60 [

"God bless me," she said, sneezing violently.

They had roped off a part of the basement to resemble a boxing ring. On the walls were various types of weapons, swords, rifles, hatchets, chains.

"Like it's a nice pad for Marquis de Sade," she said.

"You're not supposed to know about that," George said, pulling off his shirt and flinging it to the floor. He pulled on the boxing gloves and punched the air, a sullen, nasty grimace sticking itself to his face.

"Eleanor Rigby," he said, "is a bore. So is Jenny Oliver and so is Sarah Green."

"Hey, cut it," John said, striking him lightly. They sparred for a moment, then began punching each other with force. They moved rapidly, graceful as dancers. Sarah found a semiclean step and sat down. Ho hum. It seemed a silly occupation when she and John could be in bed somewhere making piggies. John connected a right to the jaw, George a crushing left to the shoulder. It certainly didn't equal making piggies.

"I'll tear your heart out," John said, swinging hard. He missed, his hand crashing into the hot-water heater. He moaned in pain, danced around the ring for a moment then continued fighting, his breath coming in short gasps.

"Break your ass," George said and punched John on the side of the head. Sarah watched them with interest. She had never heard John swear.

"Scum," John mumbled. His mouth was beginning to bleed, the blood trickling down the front of his shirt.

"Ratfucker, prick," George said. It was turning into a freak-out. What fun! How amusing! Still, it didn't beat the bed scene. John could use his body in a better way, aside from venting his hostility on his twin. Of course, they wouldn't really hurt each other. For all the apparent hostility, she felt they dug each other.

"Eat shit!" John said, clouting George on the nose.

"Bugger off, jerk," George said. His eye was beginning to ache fiercely.

It looked as if they were getting serious, a truly objectionable thing to be doing. Seriousness about nothing was so unbearable, so dullass, so pointless. She arose.

"Stop it," she said. "What are you doing?" She really wanted to stop this senseless fight so she could speak to John alone. The important question was not whether George should wipe out John or whether John should wipe out George, the important question was whether she should buy a diaphragm. She knew about them but had never actually seen one. And who would she go to for a fitting? She couldn't go to the family doctor, because he would most certainly fink on her. So who? Would Jenny know? Maybe she wouldn't know. It was probably too sophisticated. Sarah was sure in New York all the high school girls had diaphragms. They had clinics there for such matters.

George and John heaved from side to side, smashing into each other. John's ear was bleeding. Pavane for Two Dead Creeps or Dirge for Two Stupid Trolls.

Sarah screamed, "Hey you, Mrs. O'Conner, they're killing me. Help!" What the hell was Mrs. O'Conner's first name? She couldn't remember it. Matilda? Tanya? Wilma? She had said to call her by her first name and now she couldn't remember it.

"Mrs. O'Conner," she shrieked, "save me, they're attacking me. Rape. Rape. Matilda!" The name was familiar but wasn't quite right. She grabbed a sword off the wall. "Stop," she said, threatening them by lifting it over their heads. They ignored her and continued beating on each other.

"Tanya," she screamed. "Tanya, come quick!" She ran up the stairs. Down below she could hear the violent noises, crash, crack, bang, smash, smack, slap, break. It was a bad scene, not interesting at all, and it must come to a rapid end. She could pour cold water on them. Mrs. Green lived by that method. It was tried and true.

She poured water into a glass and started down the steps.

"What's wrong?" John said breathlessly, rushing at her up the steps, "where did you go?"

"Is he dead?" Sarah said, taking a sip. Might as well use it. The fitness of things.

"Dead? Who?" John said and tried to hug her. She backed away, not wanting to spill water on her orange silk blouse. It would stain.

"Come on," he said, wondering what time his mother would return with her boyfriend. "Don't be upset. It's just exercise. We always behave this way." He kissed her cheek.

"I've got to talk to you about something," Sarah said. George bounded up the steps. "Got to go," he said crossly. "Got a date."

"Who's stopping you?" Sarah said. There was something nasty about George, rather idiotic. But he was too smart to fit the Idiot List. She would have to invent a whole new list just for him like The Nasty Fuckers List. It was a pity John hadn't just gone ahead and crushed his skull. George stopped at the top of the stairs and bent over the banister. "I'd ask Jenny Oliver out but she always refuses. She thinks if you don't smoke Pot you're irreligious. Pot's her religion, you know." He addressed the speech to Sarah, who simply stared blankly at him. She wasn't about to make a statement, or betray her friend. Is that what he wanted?

"Yep," John echoed. "Pot's her religion." It was always the same, just as it was in gym class when the boys lined up against one side of the room, and the girls stayed on the other.

"You don't have to side with him just cause he's a guy," Sarah said. John knew the tone of voice. It was an anti-romance, anti-sex, anti-love voice. There might not be any chance for an encounter. He frowned at his brother. George had screwed up.

"I'm seeing Consuela Zachi tonight," George said profoundly.

John grinned. "She's like some ordinary girl-next-door type, you sap," he said. George fled upstairs.

"She's pale with red hair and freckles all over. Big bust," John said and spilled a tiny drop of water on Sarah's blouse.

"What do you think of my breasts?" Sarah said. He looked at her thoughtfully, removing his boxing gloves.

"Ripe pears," he said, putting his arms around her. "Could you stay for dinner? Tilly won't be back till later, I hope."

"Maybe," she said. "Anyway, breasts aren't everything. It's the whole that counts."

"I GRADUATE IN less than a month," Sarah said and pulled the sheet over her head. "It seems funny. Lawrence Tech is such a fink name. But it won't say that on the certificate so that's cool."

"Yes," John said and peered at his watch. Tilly wouldn't be home for some time. Obviously had gone to a restaurant or the movies with Michael. Was probably blotto at this very moment. He looked at Sarah's navel under the sheet. It was perfect.

"Your belly button leads to Heaven," he said, touching her.

"No more, enough is enough."

"A diamond would fit there, all right," he said.

"Diamonds are middle-class," she said.

"But you're middle-class, Sarah," he said, holding her buttocks and sliding on top of her. He put his penis quietly between her legs for warmth.

"I feel used," she moaned.

"I thought you liked it," he said.

"I do," she said, "but not every minute."

"The idea is to submit. You've read those books."

"I know," she said. "I read Freud at fourteen. I know."

"Better get a diaphragm or take those pills."

"I'm too young for that." she giggled.

"I think you better," he said. "I'm tired of our system. It takes the energy away." He jumped out of bed and switched on the light. "Did you hear something? A car?"

"God no, turn off the fucking light," she said, shielding her eyes.

John looked at his well-proportioned body in the mirror.

"A good specimen," he said, "twenty-two or so, intelligent and in love. All set for the Army sending me to Southeast Asia to be blown to smithereens."

"You're in love with yourself," Sarah said, climbing out of bed. "I don't think I like sex anymore."

"Should we try again?" he said, holding her.

"No."

He watched her with his slate-blue eyes.

"You're neurotic," he said.

"Yeah," she said, "it's a way of life like being rich or something."

They stood in front of the mirror, regarding their bodies and listening to the phone ring.

"I'll answer it," John said. "It might be important. I hope it's not Tilly."

"What a drag," Sarah said and got back into bed.

John ran to the hall and picked up the phone. Could he keep an erection if it were his mother? And for how long? A rasping voice pushed its way into his ear.

"Who is this?" John asked. It was the kind of voice that bore into you like chalk against a blackboard.

"Who is this?" the voice answered.

"Look, you called here. So you identify yourself."

"Is this that John O'Conner?" the voice said.

"Yes, who is this?" John answered. His erection had dwindled. What fool could be calling at such a time? Sarah was smiling seductively from across the bed.

"This is Mrs. Green, where's my Sarah?" John gaped into the receiver then motioned frantically for Sarah to get out of bed. "Get dressed," he whispered.

"Mrs. Green?" he said to the receiver. "Mrs. Green? Sarah's mother?"

"Mrs. Green, yes," she said.

Sarah leaped out of bed and hastily began to gather her clothes together. She stuffed her stockings into the greenbookbag and grabbed her hairbrush.

"Oh," John said stupidly, "Mrs. Green." Sarah was pinning her hair back so it would look exactly as it had when Mrs. Green saw her last. She slapped on some lipstick and stepped into her shoes.

"I'm calling the police," Mrs. Green rasped and hung up.

"She's calling the police," John said.

"Oh no, she's always putting me on saying that. I don't believe her. Just don't blow your cool, baby."

"I'm sorry," John said.

"Yeah, I'm sorry I have parents." She went to the bedroom window and looked out. "I think that's George backing into the driveway. You could drive me home."

"Okay," he said. He stood next to her at the window and leaned his shoulders into hers.

"We could live together," she said. "The hell with parents."

"Are you serious?" John said. George was very sloppily backing over the new rosebush.

"Yeah," she said, "in New York they all do."

"But how?" he said, "where? I'm going to Cambridge soon. You know the summer session begins in six weeks."

"No guts. You're a cop-out," she said, turning to face him. He was handsome with his thin Christian hair and his slate blue eyes, but did she want to live with him? Wasn't that some kind of wild commitment?

"I could live with you in Cambridge," she said. "Who would stop us?"

"Mrs. Green."

"I think Mrs. Green will flip when I get home. It's late, isn't it? We're too young to be married. Anyway, who in their right mind wants to be married? We could live together. I have a plan."

John groaned. "I don't know," he said uncertainly.

"I'll finish school at Lawrence Tech. Night school like I explained before. They don't care at Highland Park. I looked into it yesterday. I think they're pleased to get rid of me. And then I could maybe work in the day and save some bread."

"But how does that allow you to live in Cambridge? Your parents could prevent it."

"No," Sarah said persuasively, "we'll get engaged. They'll think we intend to be married. And then I'll say I'm going to work in Cambridge six months before we get married. How can they say no? It's so decent. So reasonable. Middle-class and respectable."

"Let's go," John said, "before she calls the National Guard." He took her arm and began to lead her downstairs.

"What's that noise?"

"I didn't hear anything," he said. "What noise?"

"I heard a funny sound," Sarah said. "It sounds like a noise a drunken pervert makes immediately before death or like someone making piggies, possibly."

They stood in the dark at the side entrance to the house. John squinted his eyes. It wasn't George. He must have parked the car and gone for a walk.

"I'd quit day school, go to night school, work and save up some money for the plane flight and I could be in Cambridge in the middle of the summer."

John could faintly see her, but the outline of her face was visible. He touched her cheek. She had it all figured out. Was it a trap?

"But we don't have to be married," she said. "I don't want it, not yet. I'm too young."

A loud moan came from the side of the house.

"Did you hear it?" Sarah said. "I knew I wasn't going bananas. I have a good ear." The moan grew louder. It sounded very human.

"My God!" John said, disgusted. "It's Mom." He was looking down at a form writhing in the driveway. He bent over.

"My God, maybe George ran over her." He ran his hands over her body. She seemed to be all right, no blood. She opened her eyes.

"Who's there?" she said thickly.

"Take it easy," John said, relieved she was plastered instead of run over. "Let's get you to your feet." He tried to help her up but she resisted and lay there squirming.

"Do you like my wig?" she said, giggling. She patted her hair. "St. Patrick's Day, and such dear, dear boys . . . twins."

"Where's Michael?" John said, lifting her. Michael, the reliable alcoholic, had fled evidently, or had never arrived.

"Didn't he bring you home?"

"Fell asleep under the weather," Tilly said, trying to focus her eyes. There was someone besides John standing in front of her. Who was it? She peered into the darkness.

"A pretty girl," she said, "so dark. An Egyptian princess." Her voice trailed off into space. She wavered between them.

"They think they're eating caviar," she murmured, "and it's only porridge."

"I'll call you tomorrow," John said and hoisted his mother over his shoulder. "I'll put her to bed."

"Yeah, like later," Sarah said. It was a shocking sight to see a grown woman, though she be small as a child, making an utter ass of herself. "Was there any insanity in your family?" she said into John's ear.

Tilly began to sing, her voice as tinkly as a doorbell. She waved to Sarah as John lugged her through the side door. Sarah walked to the street.

It was so late Sarah knew Mrs. Green would be nervously looking for her, hanging out the window like a kook. It was a dark night with few stars. They seemed incredibly far away, like her childhood. Had it ever actually happened? And here she was walking down the street, already a woman, already grown up. She would go to Cambridge. It was, perhaps, merely a step on the way to the real scene. She might even be in love with John. Of course there would be a scene from a Russian play to be gotten through with her parents. This could not be avoided. But, in the end, she knew she would win. She would defeat them. But it had to be planned wisely for a minimum of chaos. Chaos of that kind was such a bore. And if they didn't give in as she had planned, if they didn't agree, or if they complained and *kvetched* too long she would simply have to transfer them from The Idiot List for Close Relatives to the Nasty Fuckers List for all and sundry.

8

SARAH SAT at her desk in Mr. Brownwise's class, playing with an eraser and trying to ignore the cretin sounds issuing from Mr. Brownwise's throat. The class had to end soon. It seemed to be going on for an eternity. Mr. Brownwise was wearing his cheap summer jacket a month early. It was obscene. It was such a pity Jenny never caught sight of him. They had waited one whole afternoon in a cold drizzle so Jenny could actually see Mr. Brownwise was a real person. Somehow, he hadn't materialized. He must have slipped out another exit.

It was difficult to believe he wasn't a type of kinky sex maniac, what with his half-open fly and his lurid staring. He must go home and tattoo himself with pictures of naked children or something like that.

Recurrent fantasies of Mr. Brownwise had plagued and fascinated Sarah since her first semester at Highland Park High School. The disgusting idea of Mr. Brownwise laying one of his aging paws on the nubile body of a female student made Sarah gasp with delight. Mr. Brownwise's mouth turned rapidly like a flashing light in front of the inattentive class, the words pouring out in profusion, making little or no sense. The Board of Education must have wigged out when they hired him. Blah. Blah. Blah. High, very high on the Idiot List for Academic Slobs, very high.

Sarah yawned and pulled her skirt over her knees so Paul Kravitz, thin, gaunt, troubled youth sitting next to her could have his jollies. As she was concentrating on Paul Kravitz's startled smile the door opened and an efficient girl walked in. She whispered something, looking at Sarah the entire time, in Mr. Brownwise's large, ugly ear. Mr. Brownwise's mouth dropped open, resembling the slot in a piggy bank. If she put a quarter in, would change drop out?

"Did you hear me, Sarah?" Mr. Brownwise was declaiming. He snapped his fingers, at the same time trying to sneak up his zipper. "Sarah," his voice shot forth, "did you hear me?" He knew she was pretending not to hear. She did it often. It aggravated him. If she were less attractive and dumber he would fail her. At the rate she was going she might even maintain B plus. Who could resist those knees that hung out like emblems of a great empire.

"What?" Sarah said dreamily.

"You are wanted," he said. "I mean you are wanted by the principal. I mean you're wanted in Miss Crenshaw's office right away. It's important." He stared at her breasts. She had pulled her green jersey down tight. Mr. Brownwise snapped his fingers again. "Right now, miss," he said, blushing and picking at his zipper.

Sarah slowly emerged from her chair and followed the girl out of the room. She knew all eyes were upon her, boring into her rear end. She reached into her greenbookbag and in front of the class took out a stick of chewing gum and popped it into her mouth.

She walked to Miss Crenshaw's office, checking off the whores, the freaks, the fools, and the idiots as she went along. She spied Janet Frame, her archenemy, just as she arrived at Miss Crenshaw's door, which was open.

"Hi, Jan," she said, "how's the daisy chain gang-bang scene?" The girl ignored her and ran into the ladies' room, slamming the door.

"Want some gum?" Sarah said, offering a stick to the efficient one.

"It's not allowed," she said coldly.

"Well, aren't you the holy couze."

Sarah decided to go into Miss Crenshaw's office and get it over with. To her surprise Miss Crenshaw was seated at her desk, her back to the door, busily applying eye makeup. She didn't hear Sarah's entrance and continued patting her eyelids with a white liquid as though she had an out-of-sight date waiting for her in the school yard. Sarah laughed.

"Oh!" Miss Crenshaw said, looking up. "I didn't see you. Please sit down." Her voice was shaky. She tossed the eye shadow into the desk drawer and swiveled around so she was facing Sarah. The kid was wearing lavender net stockings like a burlesque dancer and a tight blouse of some kind of clinging, silky material. Where did she think she was? Her skirt was way over her knees, in fact almost to her underwear. The lavender stockings disappeared under the short skirt. It was a costume, not school attire.

"I wear white eye shadow," Sarah said helpfully, "especially when I make the scene at spade hangouts."

Miss Crenshaw coughed, stalling for time. "Oh?" she said. She had to figure out the best approach, the most intelligent, the one with the least pitfalls. Her training, the B.A., the year of graduate work were at stake. Had she all that training for nothing? She must proceed with caution. Education must mean something. Her teacher, Mr. Crumb, was wrong, of course. He had advised her not to go into counseling.

"Uh huh," she said. Sarah raised her left eyebrow and shifted from one foot to the other.

"Do sit down," Miss Crenshaw said. "Is that right?"

"Is what right?" Sarah said. Okay so she would sit down. She'd humor her, the poor biddy, virgin, ugly, goose.

"You said something about spade?" Miss Crenshaw said carefully, racking her brain for the meaning. Spade? Like a shovel? Something to dig with? It associated nothing. Was it the name of a teen-age hangout? Sarah had said something about a hangout.

"Spade means Negro," Sarah explained, "but don't use it to a Negro. I think it's rude. I'm not sure, though. There are spade jazz clubs all around the city. Detroit." She emphasized Detroit so Miss Crenshaw could orient herself. She did look terribly puzzled. There was a silence while Miss Crenshaw coughed and then blew her nose into a white handkerchief.

"Like jazz," Sarah continued, "it's the only true American art form. In fact, there are those who believe that's all America has given the world. The jazz scene, though it's disappearing, is still extant. It's not a freak-out scene anymore, it's disappointing, but it's still cool. The rock scene is more interesting." She examined Miss Crenshaw's fingernails. Amazing she never tuned in on them before. They were stubby, bitten down to the quick like cigar butts. Very unattractive, repulsive even. If the fingernails, visible as they were, seemed to be disgusting, imagine the toenails hidden under Miss Crenshaw's plain stockings. Too bad she could never investigate the toenails. It would be an experience! She could envision poor Miss Crenshaw at home soaking her flabby body in the tub, her beaten down toenails peeping out of the water like drowned rats. Miss Crenshaw ought to lose a few pounds. The flab didn't go well with the gray hair.

"Actually," Sarah said, trying to grab Miss Crenshaw's attention, which seemed to be flagging, "the Japanese play very good jazz. You can barely tell it from the real thing."

Miss Crenshaw noticed the tree across the street from the school yard. She must have the window in her office washed so she could have a better view. There were a couple of TV dinners she'd had the foresight to take out of the freezer for dinner. Her roommate did so dislike TV dinners but Miss Crenshaw hadn't as yet done the week's shopping. She did the cooking as well as the shopping and the roommate did all the cleaning up. It had been an extremely equitable arrangement for five years. Recently, the roommate had begun to criticize Miss Crenshaw for practically everything.

"I've been digging music since I was a child. And I dig classical, too, you know. Not just folk, jazz and rock. I don't like to get hung on things. Freedom and variety are very important." She noticed Miss Crenshaw's gaze seemed to be fixed on something outside. Was it flip-out time?

"Of course," Sarah said, "in New York, there's more variety. And that's why ultimately I'll have to make that scene. I hear Los Angeles is interesting too. I knew a girl, Marsha Stephenson, Terry Stephenson's sister, who visited there. She said it was a gas. Very far out."

"Yes," Miss Crenshaw said, "yes." She searched her mind for something to say in response. Counseling was a two-way street. She coughed again and spat into the handkerchief. Her roommate hadn't mopped the kitchen floor in a month. Was she angry at her?

She tried to smile. Sarah was scrutinizing her. She mustn't let the kid manipulate her. The roles must be seriously sorted out so there would be no confusion.

"I received your postcard," she said.

"Postcard? I never sent you a postcard. I haven't been anywhere. Been right here in Detroit." She emphasized Detroit so Miss

Crenshaw, who did seem remarkably out to lunch, could get a grip on herself.

"Yes, you did," Miss Crenshaw said nervously. "It said you ate thirty-five bananas." She paused. "Are you feeling better?" Her roommate had identified the card as an El Greco and thrown it out.

"Oh yeah," Sarah said, "thirty-five. Yeah, much better thanks." It seemed like years ago. That was the day she met John in the museum. It was also the day she lost or rather gave up her maidenhood. Where did all the hymens go? It was a folk song in its way. Where did all the hymens go, da da, dee dee, dee dee.

Miss Crenshaw looked at her watch. She could always fix hamburgers, she supposed. Even pick up a nice cold bottle of wine on the way home. Or a steak. A steak would be good.

"Very nice," she said. It could be a celebration. But for what? The roommate's anger had to come to an end sometime.

"Oh, I'm dropping out of school this week and finishing at Lawrence Tech. It's all arranged," Sarah said, "and I'd like to thank you for all the help you've given me."

"Yes, help," Miss Crenshaw said. School would be over in a month. They could celebrate the closing of school. It was something to celebrate, wasn't it? They could go to a movie. Jack Lemmon was playing.

"I've made all the arrangements. It was tough getting through to that idiot principal, Mr. Leeway, but I finally made it. I lied somewhat but he seemed to dig it," Sarah said.

A steak? Carrots? Carrots might be nice. Or even a roast. But was there time to make a roast? If they were going to a movie she would have to hurry. The wine could be saved for another night. There was no point in drinking wine and then going to a movie. She tried to focus on what the kid was saying. What was it? Something about changing schools. Sarah crossed her legs so her skirt slid up to the top of her net stockings. "I'm getting engaged." She smiled. "I'll invite you to the engagement party. It should be fun. There'll be some older people, too."

"Fine," Miss Crenshaw said. Engaged? She was engaged. Miss Crenshaw jerked her head around. But she was only a child. A tot. A little girl. She was barely out of the cradle. Miss Crenshaw had never been engaged. It didn't make sense. Why she hadn't had a date since 1964. She had begun to think she might be a lesbian. It started one day when she trudged home from school, exhausted from the crazed kids who sat raving in her office all day. A familiar-looking brat, probably one of her patients, with a great mane of hair flapping in his face, had screamed Dike, Dike at her. Not knowing what this meant she had asked the Italian grocer, Mr. Viviano, a silly, ignorant man with two boys in college. He giggled and pointed and acted like a fool. Gladly she would have smashed his face with her purse. Her roommate had laughed, too, which was the cruelest cut of all.

"I did want to thank you for all your help," Sarah said. "The engagement party will be at the Detroit Leland as soon as I tell my parents about it. I'm working up to it. They don't know John yet. It's none of their business but they have to pay." She would have to consult Jenny as to the number of people to invite. She didn't want too many. And, actually, there were few people at school she liked. She could forget about them. Maybe she could invite Janet Frame as a joke. She could come wearing a whore's dress, whatever that was.

"None of their business?" Miss Crenshaw said, gazing at Sarah's enormous hoop earrings, which swung back and forth. There was something primitive about them, almost African. They were scarlet and hung to her shoulders like elephant ears.

"Yeah," Sarah said, "so ungroovy. They're so ungroovy but we have to do it this way. We're not getting married, just living together. We'll be living together at Harvard. He's going to Harvard, getting a Ph.D. in English Literature. He's smart."

Miss Crenshaw started to choke, the blood rushing to her pale cheeks.

"We'll be engaged, so it's not like living entirely in sin. I'm not Catholic so I don't have a concept of sin, anyway."

There was a sale on tomatoes and eggplant at Mr. Viviano's. If she rushed there after school, she'd have time to scoop up the remains. Actually they could eat out. There was a small Chinese restaurant on the corner. The waiter was rude but it was cheap. The roommate always seemed happy in there.

"Want a glass of water?" Sarah said, getting up. Miss Crenshaw was gasping as if she were about to have a seizure.

"I don't think it's wise for a young girl to marry," she said. "You

] 74 [

could go to Radcliffe, too," she added lamely. "You did well on the college boards. You have a high I.Q. You mustn't let these men get ahead of you."

"Radcliffe, schmadcliffe, who wants to go to college?" Sarah said, airily noticing Miss Crenshaw was slopping around in her desk drawer trying to find something. Miss Crenshaw finally fished out a cigarette and lit the wrong end. She sputtered and gave a racking cough.

"You want one of mine?" Sarah said, offering her a filtered Gauloise. "They're the end!"

"No, thanks," Miss Crenshaw said, exhausted. It was another one of those tiring days filled with hysterical mouthings of juvenile delinquents. Maybe flattering the kid was the best policy. Her ego might need bolstering.

"You see," she said, "you're very smart. College material. Good college material."

"Hey, what is Radcliffe, anyway?" Sarah said. What could the time be? The hour must be nearing its end. She craned her neck to see the time on Miss Crenshaw's watch and began edging toward the door.

"A good school in Massachusetts," Miss Crenshaw said. Miss Crenshaw had gone to the University of Michigan. It was good enough for her but the principal had given her specific instructions to mention Radcliffe to Sarah. After all it was prestige for the school if one of their own was admitted to Radcliffe.

"Oh yeah," Sarah said, "the chicks who hang in at Harvard. Promiscuous, I hear."

"I don't know," Miss Crenshaw said. "I don't know."

"I'd rather *do something* than go to college," Sarah said, "but I don't know what it is yet. I guess I'll find out."

Miss Crenshaw gave her a cold stare.

"Gee willikers," Sarah said, "I better get my youknowwhat back to class. I don't want to ruin my chances of getting into Lawrence Tech."

Miss Crenshaw sat, the dandruff floating to her shoulders, and watched Sarah's earring swinging back and forth, back and forth. There was something hypnotic about the motion.

"Yes," Miss Crenshaw thought, nodding her head. Cauliflower probably, or maybe macaroni. Her roommate adored macaroni.

9

MR. AND MRS. GREEN sat with arms folded, attempting to comprehend what Sarah was saying without having congestive heart failure.

"It's near seven, he'll be here soon," Sarah said. She was lying on the floor with her feet up on the couch. It was all so boring. So perfectly predictable. That was the trouble with parents, they were all so predictable. Explanations, and counter explanations. It was like a child's game. You had to go through certain steps, certain rules, knowing all along the ending. And would she always be on trial? She supposed so. If only Kafka could have visited 10117 Cherrylawn. She looked at her parents, sitting side by side like Tweedledee and Tweedledum. Mrs. Green's lip twitched, Mr. Green's face was set in mud, as if no nerve endings were present. Mrs. Green touched his arm with her fat hand. "So, okay already," she said, "so she'll have a wedding. So we should tear out our hair. No. Life's too short." Mrs. Green did seem to be taking it well for a person of such attitudes and insane expectations.

"Engaged," Sarah corrected, "engaged at the Detroit Leland in two weeks. We can invite Rabbi Morris. But we don't want to get married for a year." Rabbi Morris was a definite concession. Didn't they realize what a good sport she was being?

"You have to marry a *goy*," Mr. Green said sadly, his voice muffled. "You got to go out of your way to marry a *goy*. It's just as easy to marry a Jew."

"I don't know any Jews," Sarah said. "They're not around." He should arrive any minute. She would have to convince them entirely before he got there, otherwise he might be exposed to an absurd situation.

"At least he's dark," Mrs. Green said.

"Oh no," Sarah said, "blond. Aren't there blond Jews? It seems to me the Israeli Jews are all blond."

"Not true," Mrs. Green said. She wagged her finger at Sarah. "Very dark, black even."

"Hmmm," Sarah said and stretched her legs. She was wearing a wildly colored, flowered dress that looked like a painting of the future. She had drawn blue and black abstracts on her legs with colored pencils. She ran a pointed silver nail along the edge of one of the drawings.

"I looked for Jewish boys," she said, "but they don't seem to dig my style. They run when they see me coming."

"No wonder," Mrs. Green said.

"Why should they run? Such a beautiful girl," Mr. Green said. Sarah had her legs arranged in such a position he could see up her dress, or down, whichever the case. He recognized the bottom of Mrs. Green's slip, the one he gave her for her last birthday. It cost twelve ninety-five at Himelhochs and she reported it missing a week after. The bottom was beautifully embroidered.

"How about Dr. Kantrowitzsky's son?" Mrs. Green said.

"He's at school," Sarah said, "away at school. He hated me, anyway."

"Marvin Kantrowitzsky was crazy about you," Mrs. Green said. "His mother told me." She sighed. "So much money. He got a good practice. They belong to Franklyn Hills, you know."

"Country clubs are disgusting," Sarah said, "and anyway, he's a moron with a fat behind. I like slim hips myself."

"Such funny talk," Mrs. Green said.

"Well, don't bug me."

"Don't start," Mrs. Green said, "please."

"Well, don't bug me," Sarah said.

"I'm warning you," Mrs. Green said.

"A fat ass and kike eyes," Sarah said.

"Another word, and I'll slap your face," Mrs. Green said, deeply offended, her face flushed in a preview of the angry red welts that were momentarily to appear.

Mr. Green got up quickly. "Yes," he said, echoing his wife, "she'll slap your face."

Sarah stood up. Somehow one of the drawings around her ankle had flaked off and was lying in a heap on the carpet.

"That's what you do to dogs," she yelled, "to dogs. You slap their faces."

"You started," Mrs. Green said grimly. She noticed out of the corner of her now swelling eye that Clytemnestra was secretly tearing at the drapes.

"I can't stand it," she said.

"Well, leave me alone then."

"No sass," Mr. Green said, "none of it. We'll have none of that *klippeh* wild Indian sass," Mr. Green said. If only they would go away so he could quietly read the paper. *The News* had started a new contest he was thinking about entering. You could win up to fifteen hundred dollars or a trip to Mexico. He could go to Mexico alone.

"Marvin Kantrowitzsky is at Ann Arbor and comes home every weekend. He don't have a girl yet," Mrs. Green said.

"No wonder they burned you in the ovens," Sarah said. There was a moment immediately after the words spun out of her mouth when large welts emerged on Mrs. Green's face like dancers coming out for a curtain call. Mr. Green grabbed her arm.

He screamed into her face, "Up to your room, you monster, you've gone too far. How could you say such a terrible thing after all the suffering, the pain. She don't know. She don't know." He tried to push her out of the room and toward the stairs but she stood her ground. Being exactly the same height but much stronger gave her an advantage. She shoved him back, ripping the arm of her dress.

"Jesus, you're ruining my dress," she cried and *klopped* him on the chest, sending him reeling across the room and into a chair. The impact knocked over the chair, which fell on him as he flopped in a heap to the floor.

"She killed me," he screamed. "She killed me. My own child. My own Sarah." His glasses whirled about somewhere in front of him on the floor. He could hear the crack of the lens as they hit the floor. He had worn those glasses for two years. There was a certain attachment as well as a financial investment. How shameful! He would take the money for the glasses out of her allowance. She would be made to pay for them.

The room was spinning. He reached out for the glasses. Maybe he could salvage enough to see.

"*Oy, guttinu,*" Mrs. Green said, rushing across the room and yanking him to his feet, "*Oy vey is mir,* what is it? A massacre? She killed him!"

"My glasses," he screamed, "my glasses, Bertha. We'll put you in a convent. You'll see." Dazed he struggled toward where he thought Sarah was standing, his cloudy eyes straining to find her. "To your room," he said desperately. He had to have a gorgeous daughter, a spoiled brat? It wasn't enough. Yet she had to be stronger, too? Such a humiliation. Such humiliation. He felt the anger welling up inside. And so why couldn't Jews have places to send bad girls? Why was it only the Catholics had convents? Surely, it wasn't fair. Surely, someone in power had made a terrible mistake. Mechanically, he put his hand to his face to straighten the glasses that weren't there.

"Here," Sarah said, handing something to him. She was standing next to him. He put out his hand and grasped at the air. "Here," she said and put the broken glasses in his hand.

"I'm sorry, the door was unlocked. I rang, but no one answered, so I just came in." The three of them turned to see John O'Conner looking quite puzzled, standing in the doorway, a dozen long-stem roses in his arms.

Sarah stepped forward. "Come in," she said. "It's freak-out time." He came gingerly into the room.

"Well," he said with a false smile, "this must be Mr. and Mrs. Green." Something was askew, something was definitely askew. Mr. Green gaped in his direction like a mentally retarded child. Sarah snickered. What was the matter? Suddenly Mr. Green jerked loose of Mrs. Green, who had been hanging onto his arm, and lunged at him like a bull charging across a pen.

"Out!" he shrieked. "Out, you *goy,* you defiler of flesh, out of my house!" He whacked wildly in John's direction, his fingers suddenly coming in contact with the bouquet of flowers. Quickly, he grabbed them and slung them with all the strength he could muster over the couch, across the room and into Mrs. Green's fat belly, where they made a thwack sound like a hand slapping a face.

"Oh, oh," Sarah said, "let's split the scene. It's Sodom and Gomorrah in Tel Aviv. The meeks have become the freaks!"

She took John's hand and pulled him out the door. "Bye," she shouted. They ran to the street and leapt into the back seat of George's waiting car. "Hurry up, let's split," she said to George who gave her a dirty look and started the car.

"This is Connie Zachi," he said crossly. Connie, laded down with thick red hair, turned around and smiled feebly.

George swerved around the corner. "We're going to a party," he said.

"A party," Connie said. She wore her face as if it were the family jewels. It was liberally sprinkled with freckles like tiny topaz stones.

"A What's Happenin'?" Sarah said, making conversation. She felt shaky after such an unpleasant hassle and took John's hand.

"He's wearing your ring," she whispered.

"Be quiet," John said, "don't say anything."

"What's Happenin'?" Connie said, looking embarrassed. "I hope it's not one of those far-out things. They make me uncomfortable." Sarah leaned forward. It was a square. Why hadn't she noticed right away. Connie was a square.

"Do you use Tampax?" she said quietly.

"Huh?" Connie said.

"Be quiet," John said.

"Tampax?" Sarah repeated. "Are you deaf?"

"Why . . . uh . . . why," Connie stuttered, "why yes I do."

"Can't you keep quiet," John said and pinched her arm.

"We're not going to any party," George said and began to make a U turn.

"But I want to go to a What's Happenin'," Sarah pouted, "and otherwise I'm putting this scene down."

"Country music," George snarled.

"Country music?" John said.

"Country music," George said. "We're going to hear some country music."

"I hate country music," Sarah said. How dare he wear the skull-

and-crossbones ring? Wasn't it John's property? What did it mean? And then he had the utter fucking nerve to drag her to hear sounds she wouldn't enjoy at all.

"I hate country music. Twang, twang, twang," she said. "Though Moses, come to think of it, used to dig it."

"Moses?" Connie said, turning around again, her face hanging out like a flag. "Moses? The one who crossed the Red Sea?"

"Yeah, babe, the same one," Sarah said. She dug her foot into John's leg.

"Oh these women!" George said, pushing his crash helmet over to Connie. She better learn to have contact with it immediately if she wished to go out with him again.

"Nasty Fuckers," Sarah said, "way on top of the list."

"Please," John said, poking her. "George hates swearing from girls."

"What's wrong with Nasty Fuckers?" Sarah said. "It's a category like Immanuel Kant's or Martin Buber's."

"Martin Buber didn't have categories," George said.

"Ho ho, an intellectual," Sarah said, "ho ho." She touched George's corduroy jacket. "Why are you wearing that ring?"

"None of your business," George said, passing the speed limit. They were sailing down Outer Drive like a comet through space. Connie clutched at the helmet.

"Let's not talk about the ring," she said tearfully. "Please." There was a tiny crack in her voice. Her eyes began to brim up with tears, giving her topaz-studded face a somewhat redundant look. Gently, John placed his hand over Sarah's mouth. If she couldn't shut it herself, he would have to shut it for her. Gently, she clamped down on his hand, her teeth biting into his flesh. Connie wept silently, her tears glistening like tiny moons in the reflected light of passing cars.

10

"BUT A PERSON has to be something, even if a person is a chick," Sarah said to Jenny. They were walking near Jenny's house after lunch. Jenny lived on a private road about a mile from Sarah's, in a mansion, where she kept three tame field mice, a lizard, three hamsters and a rabbit.

"Or," Sarah said, "a chick is a person is a person is a person."

"I see what you mean," Jenny said. "Shall we light up here or wait till we get home?" She stopped in the middle of the sidewalk and reached into the pocket of her black trench coat.

"No, let's wait, it's better," Sarah said, marveling at her restraint.

"I'd like to meet this Moses you keep yapping about," Jenny said. Her hair was falling forward out of her beret and stringing itself around her mouth.

Sarah rubbed her boot along the gutter. "I think I stepped in *merde*," she said.

"Quite possible," Jenny said. "This man, Moses, sounds so bright. Does he smoke Pot?"

"I don't think so," Sarah said. "He's hip but not so daring. Sort of well organized. But groovy with the African haircut."

They came in sight of Jenny's house, a huge red brick affair surrounded by trees.

"*Nous voici*," she said. "I like the African look, don't you?"

"Yeah," Sarah said. "Is your mother home?"

Jenny gave a quick frown. "I hope not. She's at a meeting, a luncheon or something. A Charity Ball for Female Impersonators or something. All my mother's friends impersonate females."

] 82 [

"Yeah, I know what you mean," Sarah said. "Those society broads are too much."

"Selfish, essentially selfish," Jenny said. "Let's go to my room and turn on. No one's home but the maid and she's making dinner."

They proceeded up the grand staircase to the third floor where Jenny had her studio, or what she called her studio, a gigantic room with large windows overlooking a garden. She locked the door from the inside and motioned Sarah to plop down on the kingsize bed.

"Why do you have a white maid?" Sarah said, removing a green suede coat and dropping it to the floor.

"Why not?" Jenny said. "I think she's a relative and Father won't say anything. She looks like him."

"Maybe an illegitimate daughter?"

"No, she's too old. More like a mistress."

"As I was saying," Sarah said, "a person has to be something."

"I don't know," Jenny said, lighting up. "Here, have some," she said, offering it to Sarah.

"I think I want to be a singer," Sarah said and dragged hard on the joint. "Good," she said, "as good as the other day."

"The Olivers have only the best," Jenny said, laughing and tossing her hair out of her mouth.

"I like music so much," Sarah said, opening her green eyes wide. "So why can't I be a singer?"

"Well, for openers, can you sing?" Jenny said. She looked at her friend dressed from head to toe in green. Green boots, green dress, green scarf, green earrings, green stockings. Green. Green. Green. "Green's a good color," she said.

"Yeah," Sarah said. "No, I can't sing."

Jenny sat down on the thick Persian rug and crossed her legs into a double lotus position.

"I can't wait to go to Sarah Lawrence," she said.

"College is for the birds," Sarah said, taking another drag. "It'll be down to the roach soon."

"That's nice," Jenny said. "No, it's all right for me. I want a Ph.D."

"Why?"

"For power," Jenny said. "I need power."

"I could study singing," Sarah said. "The idea has been coming to me for a long time."

"I need a Ph.D.," Jenny said. "I want to teach at a university. I want to influence young minds. I want power."

Sarah stretched out on the bed and closed her eyes.

"I could study singing in New York," she said, opening her eyes and looking at the ceiling, which was decorated with cherubim. "I dig the ceiling," she said.

"Don't smoke the whole thing!" Jenny said, getting up and taking the end of the cigarette away from her.

"I could sing," Sarah said, giggling.

"I'll go to a great university for my Ph.D.," Jenny said, giggling, too. "Oxford or Cambridge. American universities are all poor. A poor education."

"I wouldn't know," Sarah said, turning over on her stomach. "I know I could sing," she said, snickering into the pillow.

"You could be a great opera star," Jenny said, laughing, "and I'll be the first female President."

"Opera?" Sarah sat up in the bed. "Opera? Have you gone bananas?" She began to shriek with laughter. "I'm talking about rock. I want to be a rock 'n' roll singer." She rolled around the bed helpless with laughter.

Jenny's shoulders shook, loud guffaws pouring out of her mouth like a brass band.

"You witch," Sarah laughed, "you witch, you swallowed the roach!"

11

SARAH PRESSED her early morning sleepy face against the windowsill and peered out at the sun.

"Nice," she said and crept back to bed, pulling the covers over her head. It wasn't actually time to be up. It was about seven, instinct told her. The engagement brunch was to happen at noon. There was plenty of time. Everything had gone according to plan. Predictability, predictability. Ho hum. The Great Engagement was going to take place. The Russian play with Mr. and Mrs. Green had turned out to be a one-acter. In some way she felt sorry for them. How they did cling to the past. At dinner, when they met John, they searched his face for one remnant of Judaism. And to their disappointment, there wasn't any, not a trace. They could barely eat, a rare occurrence. Mrs. Green had flown into one final rage directly after dinner over the prune yogurt. Mr. Green looked unhappy but said nothing.

Sarah didn't consider the first meeting as an actual meeting. She instructed them not to mention it at all. Mrs. Green made one fleeting reference to it and that was just to shakily thank John for the flowers. Then they had phoned Tilly to make sure she wasn't a criminal and to arrange a time for them to get together. What could they do? They had to meet the mother of the boy to make sure she was respectable.

Privately, Mr. Green said, "Better she should be engaged than run off and be married. It'll run its course. It won't last. You'll see, she'll end up married to a Jew. Maybe Jerry Blum or someone like that."

"Jerry Blum?" Mrs. Green said incredulously. "You mean the

lousy bum who don't have manners? Who used to pull our Sarah's panties down behind the garage?"

Sarah could sleep for at least three more hours. It wouldn't take long to dress, since her clothes were hanging in the bathroom waiting for her to step into them. It was cozy under the blanket and she could feel a soft, furry thing near her feet. Did Rabbi Morris accept the invitation? She hoped so. He was such a camp. He rarely passed up an invitation where food and drink and pretty women were involved. She would keep an eye out for him.

To bad Moses couldn't be there. He always added a note of elegance. And he would be the only dark face except for Carmine, his mother, and her ten-year-old schizy nephew she said she had to bring. Three dark faces. And Tilly would flirt with her boy friend right in front of everyone. And Mrs. Green would whisper stupid explanations to her Hadassah ladies about John's Christianity.

She felt a wet, rough thing on her leg. Clytemnestra was amusing herself. Sarah pushed her away. She hadn't invited any of her friends except Jenny, mostly because she didn't have any friends. She had arranged for George to pick up Jenny. He seemed to want to go out with her and here was the perfect opportunity.

"Sarah," a voice rasped. "Sarah." Sarah moved deep inside the blanket. The voice came closer. It was coming from under the blanket. Had Clytemnestra suddenly found a voice? Sarah felt around with her hand. The creature had disappeared. She poked her head over the blanket to see whether Clytemnestra had become a dragon. A grotesque face appeared, hovering above her, its hair knotted up in something shiny and awful, its form wrapped in rags.

"All right already," it said, "get up, it's time. She's called three times and I'm going *mishugah*." It was only Mrs. Green in her old bathrobe, her hair in curlers.

Sarah looked at her sleepily. "It's you," she said.

"You expect maybe Jesus?" Mrs. Green said, jerking the blanket off. "Up," she said. "This Mrs. O'Conner has called three times. Is this what these people are like? Did you know the twin, the George or whatever, don't go to school. He drives and *schpatziers* around in a car or something funny. He's a real Indian."

"He's a racing-car driver," Sarah said. "He gets prizes and money for it. He saved enough money to go to New York."

] 86 [

"New York, so," Mrs. Green said.

"He'll probably marry a rich girl," Sarah said, trying to appeal to Mrs. Green's sympathy. No point in having a fight before a party.

"You got the educated one, be happy," Mrs. Green said disgustedly and opened the window. "The room smells. You need a bath, maybe."

"Go away, will you," Sarah said. "Don't bug."

"You got that beautiful dress we bought you," Mrs. Green said, standing with her arms on her large hips. "Be happy."

"I hate it," Sarah said, sneering.

"Come on," Mrs. Green urged, "up and at 'em. Up and at 'em. Out at the world. The *goyim*."

Sarah climbed out of bed.

"You're nervous," Mrs. Green said. "After the engagement you'll settle down. Maybe you'll show more interest in school. I don't understand," she said, her voice beginning to climb the scale, "how you would want to go to that funny school instead of finishing at Highland Park where you know everyone." She shook her head.

"It's my life," Sarah said, waking up. "Let me live it."

"I know it's your life," Mrs. Green said. Sarah looked at her suspiciously. Mrs. Green had never uttered such a statement, never. Had something mystical happened?

"It's your life?" Sarah said.

"No, no it's *your* life," Mrs. Green said. "Here, brush your hair, it's a mess." She gave Sarah a brush. "Quickly," she went on, "we can't keep the rabbi waiting." She stood behind her watching her brush her shiny, black hair, then began to move out of the room. There were many things she had to do and that *mishugenah* Tilly might have her on the phone for the fourth time. Slyly, Clytemnestra flew out of a dresser drawer and landed on Mrs. Green's head, her claws fastening onto Mrs. Green's curlers like clamps.

"*Oy*," she screamed, "*oy*, what's this?" She grabbed at her head and tore the animal off. "No time," she screamed, throwing him on Sarah's bed, "no time for monkey business!" She rushed from the room.

Sarah brushed her hair with great vigor, then applied her party makeup, which consisted of giant white rings around her eyes, false eyelashes and no lipstick. She was tired of a scarlet mouth.

She wore three rings on her right hand and none on her left, the engagement ring, a large garnet anointing the middle finger of her right hand. It was the fitness of things. Wasn't that also the utility finger?

Under the beige and silver dress purchased for the glad occasion, she wore slightly metallic silver threaded tights. And then there were the silver brocaded shoes with the tiny bows. She had bought them on the sly, knowing full well Mrs. Green would never consider spending fifty dollars for a pair of shoes. But what the hell!

She would have to present the next step in the plan very subtly so as not to incur the parental wrath. The next step was to communicate to them the idea of leaving for Cambridge. The plan would involve some lying. She didn't want them to know she would be living with John. She would have to arrange a phony Cambridge address but John could do that by writing a friend who was already there. She would simply tell them she was going there to work and save money, which would in itself be quite true. Really, living with someone was none of their business.

12

THERE WERE AT least sixty people at the hotel when Sarah arrived twenty minutes late.

"You look like a nurse," Mrs. Green said, eyeing her metallic stockings distrustfully. "How you do get yourself up. It's amazing!"

"Hey, the peons are all here," she said to her father, who had taken a haircut for the occasion and looked like a plucked chicken. He peered around the room through his sunglasses trying to see who was there. One by one the guests came up to Sarah to congratulate her. It was like the reception committee for Custer's Last Stand. But she allowed them to smile and praise her and look doubtful and then move away toward the champagne that was being passed by a bizarre waiter with pop eyes and a tight mouth.

Sarah waved at John, who was ensconced between two chattering magpies across the room. "Everyone has creep, freak, bore hairdos, did you notice?" she said to the pop-eyed waiter, who reluctantly offered her a glass of champagne. She drank it down in one gulp and reached for another.

"Don't worry, we'll eat soon, they won't know what hit them, it's so delicious," Mrs. Green said. She patted her hair self-consciously and tugged at her girdle, which was pressing into her flesh like a torture machine.

Sarah surveyed the room. A motley crew, as they say. And where were Jenny and George? He was to pick her up early so she could be one of the first to arrive. Ritina Glass, for years her mother's foe, stood in a corner talking to Mr. Green and slurping down a drink. After they had unexpectedly met at a funeral, she and Mrs. Green became best friends. It was revolting, Ritina argued with everyone she met. She seemed to be making fun of Mr. Green's glasses. After a few moments he walked off, looking for someone else to talk to.

"Hey, did Ritina dye her hair? It looks like worms," Sarah said, walking over to Mr. Green. He shrugged and said nothing.

The sixty people were making a terrific racket talking and carrying on with each other. Sarah put her hands to her ears to drown out the babble. "Don't do that," her father said.

"Hey, look at Tilly plastered," Sarah said.

The hubbub of aimless sound suddenly ceased as George O'Conner made a grand entrance dressed in his pit suit and crash helmet. Walking behind him and smiling slightly was Jenny, dressed in a severe black silk dress, her long blond hair hanging loose, a strand or two in her mouth.

"What's this?" Mrs. Green said. "What's this? He must be in the wrong place."

"It's George, my brother," John said, rushing over to introduce him to Mr. and Mrs. Green.

"This is okay already for a party that costs Mr. Green plenty?" Mrs. Green sputtered outraged.

Jenny kissed Sarah on the cheek and shook hands with Mr. Green. "You're looking well," she said to him. "Why is he wearing dark glasses?" she said to Sarah. "He's become a hipster?"

John presented George to Mr. and Mrs. Green, who stood with startled looks on their faces. The hubbub began again after a minute of gaping at George, whose pit suit was as usual covered in grease.

"Been down to the pits," he said and rubbed the skull-and-crossbones ring as if it were a talisman.

"Maybe you should go home and change," John said. George shook his head. "No," he said.

Jenny smiled and wandered off for a drink.

Mrs. Green began to go red. She grabbed George's arm. "It won't do," she said. "The rabbi would scream."

"Oh, Mother," Sarah said, "the rabbi isn't even here."

"We're Catholic," George said. "Who needs a rabbi?"

"Shut up," John said, unbuttoning the jacket to his dark gray suit. It was beginning to be terribly warm in the room, what with all the people packed in and the alcohol rushing through his body.

Mrs. Green turned to Sarah accusingly. "What have you done?

What have you done? After all we've done for you, so ungrateful, what's this?" She pointed to George. "What is it? We gave you your own bedroom and bath, camp when you were little, spending money, we even let you borrow the car." Mrs. Green looked around for a place to sit. The varicose vein in her left leg was beginning to throb from the anger she was expressing. But it didn't work that way when she was sitting. If she sat and *shried,* the vein was quiet. A couch on the other side of the room was occupied by Tilly O'Conner and a tall, dark handsome man, who seemed to have his hand on her breasts. Mrs. Green squinted her eyes.

"Who's that?" she said, pointing across the room.

"It's Michael, my mother's friend," John said.

"The rabbi, the rabbi would scream," Mrs. Green said. "We'll be asked to leave the temple. *Oy vey.*" She wrung her hands.

"Listen," John said, "I have a fine idea, George and I can change clothes. We're almost the same size." Sarah began to titter. Mrs. Green looked at him as if he were a lunatic smashing rotten eggs in his hair. Where was Mr. Green? He had disappeared. Why wasn't he standing next to her helping her with these wild Indians? Why did he always leave just when she needed him. She looked at the circle surrounding her.

"And," she said, frantically eyeing the guests who had moved further and further away and were standing in a tight cluster around the couch. "Who are those other dark men on the far side of the couch. They're thirsty," she said.

"Oh," Sarah said airily, "it's just Maco Maco and Bill Fitts, my friends, musicians from John R. One blows tenor and the other vibes."

Mrs. Green stared. "They're colored," she said. George walked off in search of Jenny. She wasn't getting away so easy.

"Spanish and African," Sarah said in exasperation. "Spanish and African. They told me so themselves. One of them sings and might give me a few lessons." Now there were four dark faces, Carmine, her nephew, and the two musicians. It gave Sarah a peaceful feeling. She would have liked to invite more dark faces but she didn't know any.

"Like a cantor?" Mrs. Green said, trying to make sense out of the situation. "Girls aren't cantors."

] 91 [

"Yeah," Sarah said, "uh-huh, that's right." She saw George had apprehended Jenny and was busy talking to her. She looked at Jenny's expression. It was one of dreamy tuned-outsville. Jenny had the ability to tune out whenever she felt like it. She was almost as tall as George in her heels, her eyes level with his. Sarah could tell she was pretending to listen, fluttering her eyes in a fake response, and occasionally nodding her head. What a phoney!

"Maybe you should talk to Tilly," Sarah said.

"Yes," Mrs. Green said, "later, after the food."

Tilly was laughing and freely gesticulating on the couch, her skirt edging up, revealing bony knees. She was probably on her tenth drink, having downed them liberally since her arrival.

"I never heard of drinking in the morning," Sarah said, to amuse herself. "Jews don't drink, do they?" she said, surveying the room. It was like an alcoholics' ward.

"They don't," Mrs. Green said emphatically. "Just the *goyem*." She pressed her lips together and made a nasty clicking sound. "There's Rabbi," she said and tried to smile in his direction. He had glided into the room twitching his mustache and looking for a good-looking woman.

As soon as Mr. Green caught sight of him, a button switched on in his brain. He instantly rushed to him and grabbed his lapels as if the rabbi were an escaped convict.

"Glad you came, Rabbi," he gasped. "My baby is going with a non-Jew, a *goy* even. He seems nice. A scholar or something." Mr. Green cherished a respect for scholarship.

"Yes, yes," the rabbi said and tore Mr. Green's hands from his lapels. "We do our best," he said, sternly trying to get loose of Mr. Green, who was wearing Hollywood sunglasses and appeared demented. The rabbi really had nothing against interfaith marriages. It seemed like much ado over nothing. The Jews assimilated the others, what did it matter? And wasn't Judaism rich enough to take in everyone? He was for direct proselytizing, unlike the rabbis he had known. Why not try to convert someone? Why not? He began to gracefully move away from Mr. Green and toward a particularly attractive blond woman who was seated on a couch with her skirts up to her *pupik*. She waved her hands dramatically. The rabbi loved expressive women. It was so Jewish. It fulfilled his need for directing, for playacting. He loved nothing more than taking an attractive woman, regardless of her religion, to the theater. Perhaps he had missed his calling. In a way, the theater was his true home. He patted Sarah's shoulder as he passed her, took a glass of champagne from the tray, and went directly to the couch.

"Hello." Sarah turned around.

"Holy Doobie Doo," she said. It was Miss Crenshaw, standing shyly in an ill-fitting summer suit.

"Why, Miss Crenshaw," she said, enthusiastically. She would put the forlorn Miss Crenshaw at ease. "I'm so glad you came. This is my mother, Mrs. Green." She tapped her mother's shoulder. "Mother," she said, pulling her around, "This is Miss Crenshaw." Poor Miss Crenshaw must be freezing.

"The school guidance lady, remember," Sarah said.

"Oh yes," Mrs. Green said uncomfortably, "would you like a drink?" So this was the doctor woman from school, who phoned and reported Sarah as a truant. Why should she give her a drink?

"She don't deserve it," Mrs. Green said.

"What?" Miss Crenshaw said.

"Nothing." Mrs. Green blushed. "Would you like a drink?"

"I don't drink," Miss Crenshaw said, slipping her hand into her worn purse and taking out the ivory cigarette holder.

"Excuse me," Mrs. Green said, "I must see to the rabbi." He was sitting close to Tilly O'Conner and appeared to be deep in conversation with her. The boyfriend, or whatever that handsome man was to her, was talking to Carmine, of all people, who was stuffing peanuts into her mouth at a fast clip.

"Where is the bridegroom?" Miss Crenshaw said, looking around the room. Who could she talk to? She glanced at Sarah. The kid still had the wild look in her eyes. Her roommate had said without a doubt she was schizophrenic. Miss Crenshaw's belief was she took drugs.

"Oh this is the engagement party, didn't I tell you?" Sarah said. "I wasn't putting you on, it's the truth. I don't lie." She smiled politely at Miss Crenshaw. Poor Miss Crenshaw. Had she no zest for life? No feeling for the fitness of things? Did nothing turn her on? How could she be so lifeless?

"I'll be going to Cambridge to live with him," Sarah said, "and we won't be married. We'll be having sex, too. I might even start

]93[

taking the pill." There must be some way of getting a reaction out of Miss Crenshaw, of putting some color into those dreary cheeks. "We like making piggies," she continued, "we really do. Did you read the book that came out about a year ago on female sexuality?" She could always slap Miss Crenshaw's face. This would put life into her.

Miss Crenshaw fidgeted with her purse. Had she heard correctly? Maybe the roommate was right. She hated to admit her diagnosis might be the right one. The roommate wasn't even a psychologist, it wasn't her field at all. She was an electrical engineer.

"That's a lovely dress," Miss Crenshaw said, feeling she must humor the kid. Schizophrenics can't help it, she knew that much. It could even be brain damage.

"A spring dress," Sarah said, rolling her eyes. She felt rather annoyed at Miss Crenshaw's limited reaction.

"I'm going to Europe this summer," Miss Crenshaw said, changing the subject. It was strange how awkward she felt with this sick kid. It should be the other way around.

"Really?" Sarah said. "Where?" Where was Jenny? Couldn't she rescue her from this creep?

"To Greece," Miss Crenshaw said. She looked around for an ashtray. Her cigarette was down to the filter and what was she to do with it?

"To Greece. My Aunt Ruth goes every summer and makes it with the fishermen. Greek fishermen. Gorgeous. Absolute rough trade."

"Rough trade?" She dropped the ash into the pocket of her jacket and glanced around to see if anyone had seen her doing it.

"Male whores, like that," Sarah said helpfully. "You're not the hippest, are you?"

Miss Crenshaw licked her lip. "No," she said.

"I'll get you an ashtray," Sarah said, "wait right here, I'll be back in a flash. Help yourself to a drink, don't be shy. Live it up as they used to say in the eighth grade." She smiled, her lipstickless mouth dimpling like an angel's.

]94[

13

TO DO WELL AT Lawrence Tech, Sarah discovered, was no great
feat. On the first day she understood she would despise it, yet it
was important to get through without a fuss. Highland Park would
grant her the diploma even though she was finishing at Lawrence
Tech. It was mighty white of them at that. Being one of the few
females in the school gave her a distinct advantage. She was the
star, unrivaled in all her classes. Mr. Montclair of English Literature bowed to her when she came into the room. And Mr. Duncan
Bones of Biology, who lisped, was totally fixated on her. He could
barely rip his glance away. He was an intriguing character for a
teacher. He looked a little young to be teaching, but when she
questioned him about age he gave her an equivocal answer. She
decided he was somewhere in the shadow of twenty-five. He was
tall and thin and occasionally limped, which gave him a strange
romantic air. On days when he looked particularly exhausted the
limp appeared. It was cute. The lisp was even cuter. The first time
she heard him lisping she had an urge to break up, falling into
great clouds of hysterical laughter.

Mr. Duncan Bones was an automatic, obvious and unadul-
terated A+ grade. She knew she didn't have to knock herself out.
The minimum would do. Usually she devoted the class time to
reading the want ads. Nothing seemed terribly exciting. The jobs
looked dullassed as hell. But she must find a job. School was over
on June 6th. She must have a job before or the point of switching
to a nightschool would be altogether lost. In one month she could
save enough for the plane fare to Cambridge. She had to pay her
own way, since John was without funds, dependent on what Tilly
or George threw his way.

Finally, she discovered something that seemed all right. She had decided she might as well work for a really insipid place and in that way try to make a camp scene out of it. In the end it might be more fun than working in a loftier environment. She picked The Michigan Insurance Company, phoned them and was given an appointment for four o'clock on May 29th. Insurance companies were the lowest, all the better. It was the beautiful fitness of things.

On May 29th she parked her parents' car in front of the school building next to a fire hydrant and dashed inside in search of Mr. Duncan Bones. Under one arm the newspaper was safely tucked, and under the other was a theme for Mr. Duncan Bones, one week late.

He was quite surprised to see her. As he caught sight of her, he was standing idly near the men's first-floor john.

"What are you doing here in the daytime?" he said, touching a slender, refined hand to a green ascot wrapped around his aristocratic neck.

The cool bit was to act humble. Humbleness got to them.

"I brought my paper," Sarah said humbly. But did he really give a crap it was late? He looked above such nonsense.

"Yes, good," he said, moving his head so his sandy-brown hair fell partially over one eye. He smiled.

"You've got your ascot backwards," Sarah said, looking at his mouth. It was a wide and handsome mouth, and he had lovely teeth, like a real upper upper type. "I could dig you if I wasn't engaged," she said seriously.

"Why don't you fix it," he said, fingering his ascot. Was it covering a hickey? She would have liked to yank it off and see whether there was a making-piggies mark there.

"Fix your ascot?" she said. It would be soft and silky like his deep brown eyes.

"No, child," he said, "the engagement."

"I should feel intimidated but I don't," Sarah said, watching the derriere of an older student scurrying down the hall.

"That cat ought to wear a truss on his behind," she said.

Mr. Duncan Bones burst into laughter and clapped Sarah on the back.

"Oh, but you are a charming child," he said.

"Thank you," she said. She could still feel the sting on her back. Was he bananas? That's how you treated men, not women, not ladies, gentle maidens such as she.

"And you've finished the paper?" Mr. Duncan Bones inquired.

"Oh yeah," she said, "and it's passable. I mean not bad. Not my usual brilliant work but I've been distracted lately."

"Distracted?" he said.

"Yeah . . . by you."

"Oh," he said, looking at his watch. "I have to be in class in three minutes. But it's a pleasure to chat with you. Can't we get together later? Cocktails? Coffee? Anything you want." He was sweet, a dear, and so well mannered.

"I can't later, I have to go study and then I'm meeting my fiancé. I mean I'm looking for employment."

"What an ambitious girl," Mr. Duncan Bones said and began to limp away. "Well, another time. You'll fix that, won't you?"

"Fix what?" Sarah said. Would she have a black and blue mark from where he assaulted her?

"The engagement, dear girl, the engagement," he said. "And then we'll make merry."

Make merry? Make merry? Didn't he mean make piggies?

14

SARAH THOUGHT ABOUT Mr. Duncan Bones all the way downtown and up until the moment when she reached the door of The Michigan Insurance Company. The name was printed in bold gilt letters quite unashamedly on a dirty glass door. He was definitely a sophisticate. He wasn't very Detroit, he was cooler, more like an Eastern character. He wasn't a hippie in any way but he had a quality that was better. In her experience he seemed to be from a Henry James novel or Edith Wharton. He had taste, that was evident, and he was cultured. He knew about the ballet, for instance, and how many high school teachers in the entire world dug ballet?

Jenny looked skeptical when Sarah gave the report on Mr. Duncan Bones.

"A fag," she said, "or a fraud. I never neard of The Boneses. He can't be too social. My family knows every other important family in this city and Mummy said she never heard of him."

But Sarah didn't give one fucking damn what Jenny said about him. After all, Jenny, though she was smart, could be wrong.

Mr. Duncan Bones had even seen Sarah surreptitiously drinking tea in the teachers' cafeteria and had looked the other way. He was a definite gentleman. There was nothing faggy about him whatsoever.

Sarah opened the dirty glass door to The Michigan Insurance Company and went in. A fat girl was squatting in the reception area. She looked up.

"Yeah?" she said hostilely, "whatdoyouwant?" She stood up, her fat legs creaking. Her eyes were dull. They took in Sarah slowly, getting hung up on her shoes.

"Miss Abercrombie," Sarah said, "that's what they told me on the phone." The girl's waist was pathetically thick, like a telephone pole.

"Be seated," she said, staring at Sarah's shoes. "I'll ring for Miss Abercrombie now. She's expecting you?"

"Uh-huh," Sarah said. She'd be damned if she'd sit down. The girl pressed a button. "There are magazines to read," she said, pointing to a stack of torn magazines shoved behind an ugly Japanese lamp.

"Uh-huh," Sarah said. She took her silk scarf from her head and tied it around her neck.

"You can sit down," the fat girl said.

"Thanks," Sarah said. Yeah, the place looked rotten enough for an insurance company. It was the wonderful raunchy fitness of things. Cheap prints hung crookedly on the walls, alone and forgotten, unnoticed by human eyes. An orange plastic couch decorated one wall, its stuffing falling out as though a wild beast had fornicated on it.

"How's business?" Sarah said, imagining the president of the company in a rest home nursing an enormous ulcer.

"There are magazines behind the lamp," the girl said mechanically, writing on a ripped piece of paper.

"Where's the *Daily Worker* or the Socialist Workers' rag?" Sarah asked.

"Behind the lamp," the girl said. She made a face like an old prune. Such a pity, the poor fat thing was only about nineteen and with her body already shot to smithereens.

"You're putting me on," Sarah said. "There's no *Daily Worker* unless this is a Communist front. Maybe it's a William DuBois Club in disguise. Or part of the Mafia. I heard the Mafia controlled all the insurance companies except in New York."

The girl glanced up from her work.

"Huh?" she said stupidly. "Daily? We have periodicals."

Sarah reached into the greenbookbag and took out a book. "I'll just read this if no one minds," she said, grinning. At least the chick knew what a periodical was. Might get her a five-dollar-a-year raise.

"This is a swinger's book," she said, "for those who like to blow their minds without taking LSD."

]99[

"Is it good?" the girl said, a flicker of life appearing in her cow eyes. "Is it good? I'm always looking for something good to read. I can never find it. Good books are hard to find. I kinda like those nurse books."

"There's a shitwagon full of sex in this book," Sarah said, "if that's what you mean by good." She sat down on the broken couch. "It really swings," she said, opening *Pride and Prejudice*.

A tall, angular woman wearing a huge pair of round glasses poked her head through the door.

"This way," she said like a doctor. "I'm Miss Abercrombie." She turned her back and dashed away. Sarah followed her down a long, dim corridor where most of the lights had burned out, and into a tiny cubicle office. Miss Abercrombie walked fast, her high heels click, click, clicking on the uncarpeted floor. There was something breathless and no-nonsense about her. *Quelle* bore!

"Sarah Green," she said, giving Sarah a quick inspection.

"Yes," Sarah said smartly, offering her hand.

Miss Abercrombie ignored the hand and yanked a yellow notebook out of her desk. "Let's see," she said, fixing the glasses on her beak nose. "I'll quickly review your qualifications, if any," she said. "We have many applicants, you know. For some reason all the girls want to work here. We have Major Medical, maybe that's why. They all want free psychiatric treatment."

"Is that right?" Sarah said, with interest. Miss Abercrombie's dress fitted her like a sack. She looked closely. It might actually be a sack.

"You gave this information on the phone, didn't you?" Miss Abercrombie asked.

"Yeah," Sarah said. How long would it take her to save the plane fare? How long? Was taking crap in an office worth it? On the other hand, if she didn't take crap she would be languishing in Detroit forever. This was the way out of the middle-class bag. She had to earn some money. If she put a little aside she might take a few singing lessons from Maco Maco. He had offered to teach her real cheap. And why not? Others had made it from Detroit. It was the backwash, but occasionally a person broke away and did what was important to them. She could make it too, but it would take bread.

She smiled at Miss Abercrombie, who was watching her with

caution, then Miss Abercrombie's bird eyes lit upon something on the piece of yellow paper. "No," she said *sotto voce*, "it's impossible." She jangled a well-worn enormous silver bracelet and said, "You've never worked before? It's not possible."

"Oh, but I want to work," Sarah said quickly. "I'm more than willing. I need a job. I'd love to work. I don't care about Major Medical. I'm very sound mentally." She tried to make her voice as sweet and appealing as possible. Miss Abercrombie was looking at her with fierceness, waves of incredulity emanating from her voice.

"It's not possible," she said, shaking her head in disbelief.

"For God's sake," Sarah said, "I'm only sixteen. What do you want? How can I have experience when I just crept out of the womb three seconds ago?" Miss Abercrombie's mouth came apart slightly, revealing chipmunk teeth. She wasn't all bird evidently.

"It seems to me I read about this company. You're supposed to be very liberal with the employees. I want to work here very badly. I read about it in *Consumer's Report*."

Miss Abercrombie scratched the side of her face.

"We try never to hire people without business experience," she said.

"Oh yeah," Sarah said, "I heard it was a fine company. Gives turkeys at Thanksgiving and a whopping bonus at Christmas, even to Jews."

"It's a rule," Miss Abercrombie said, a tiny smile flitting across her chipmunk mouth.

"A rule? No kidding," Sarah said, bored. She yawned. "I'm not used to going to school at night, I suppose. I'm really very tired."

Miss Abercrombie watched her. "School?" she said. "You're at school at night and working during the day?"

"Yeah," Sarah said, yawning again. "It'll be a drag, but I have to do it. I'm going to make something of myself."

"Yes," Miss Abercrombie said, "I went to Wayne at night for ten years and then I received a lousy B.A."

Sarah perked up.

"Oh," she said with interest, "I'm a hard worker, too."

"I'll jot that down," Miss Abercrombie said, writing something in shorthand on the yellow paper. "I'm certain you're a hard worker," she said, tapping her high heel on the linoleum. She took off her glasses and propped them on the desk.

Sarah yawned again. "Excuse me," she said. "I've been working so hard, I'm almost faint from exhaustion."

"Sit down," Miss Abercrombie said, "please sit down." She pointed to a greasy chair in the corner. "Do you think you could manage a job in the day and still get to classes at night? It won't be easy."

"Yeah, sure, nothing's easy," Sarah said, sitting down in the chair, "but I'm as strong as a horse. I may be small but I'm not weak."

Miss Abercrombie tapped her foot and scratched her head.

"I'd really love to work for this company," Sarah said.

Suddenly Miss Abercrombie jerked her head up. "Are you serious, Miss Green?" she said. "This company is absurd."

"Oh," Sarah said.

"That's correct," Miss Abercrombie said, hastily looking toward the door to see if anyone was lingering in the hallway. "Look, I can hire you for the public relations department. They're starting a new policy, trying to create a new image for the company. It's going bankrupt. But you can never mention to anyone here that you didn't work previously. Understand?"

"Yeah, yeah," Sarah said.

"Can you start at nine o'clock sharp tomorrow?"

"Yeah, I'd love it," Sarah said.

"All right," Miss Abercrombie said. "But try never, ever to say yeah. Say yes, y-e-s. And please," she went on, "try to keep the lip buttoned about loving this place. No one will believe you."

"Okay," Sarah said.

Miss Abercrombie walked to the door and stuck out her head. "Sam," she called down the corridor, "Sam, could you come here a moment?" Sarah heard the shuffling of feet coming along the corridor. An elderly man with the depressed face of an abandoned child stepped into the room. His hands shook like a drunkard's.

"This buzzard is your boss," Miss Abercrombie stage whispered. "Just keep calm with him. Keep the lip buttoned. He's been here twenty years and he's deaf."

There were two buttons missing from his jacket. His shoulders sloped downward. "Afternoon," he said, a bit of spittle slipping out of his mouth and disappearing under the collar of the jacket.

"This is your new assistant," Miss Abercrombie yelled. "Very smart girl, well qualified, plenty of experience. She starts tomorrow at nine sharp."

Sam stared at Sarah, then nodded approval. "Glad you got a girl," he said very quietly. "I'm swamped in this new department, swamped."

"We allow for no late arrivals," Miss Abercrombie said at the top of her lungs, "and we'll pay sixty-five dollars a week, that's the minimum wage. Sam, Mr. Cox, is your superior."

"Yeah, I see," Sarah said.

"What?" Sam said, "what?" He came close to Sarah to look her over. Evidently he liked what he saw as he smiled, a long slow smile like a moron.

"Fine, that's cool," Sarah said loudly.

"Don't shout," he said. "It's not necessary. I hear."

"No, he doesn't," Miss Abercrombie said. "He's stone deaf."

"Glad to meet you, Mr. Cox," Sarah said.

"I like the young ones," he said.

"Yes, yes," Miss Abercrombie said. "She'll do a good job. Now it's time for you to go back to work, Sam."

He stood gazing at Sarah for a moment, then turned and reluctantly shuffled out of the room.

"Thanks, Miss Abercrombie," Sarah said. "I'll see you tomorrow at nine."

"Sharp," Miss Abercrombie said, dismissing her with a short nod.

"Is there anything I should bring tomorrow?" Sarah asked.

"Just keep the lip buttoned, you'll do," Miss Abercrombie said, turning her back to Sarah and opening a dirty old file cabinet.

15

SARAH DOUBLE-PARKED Mr. Green's car and jumped out. There was still time to find Mr. Duncan Bones again before class began. She'd just make the one class and then go meet John. There was no point in attending all the classes when no one would know the difference.

She found Mr. Duncan Bones in exactly the same place, near the men's john on the first floor.

"Twice in the same day," she said.

"It's a secret society like the Masons," he said, "but it's an honor to see you twice in the same day." He was lisping, which sent a strange, twitching sensation from her groin down her leg to her kneecap.

"Do you always lisp?" Sarah said. "It's quite altogether super."

Mr. Duncan Bones looked at her with a queer expression on his handsome face. "No," he said, "I don't have a lisp, not really. I don't know why people seem to think I do. Would you like to have tea in the teachers' cafeteria?"

As they walked to the cafeteria, the students lingering in the hallway eyed them curiously. It wasn't every day they were treated to the sight of a beautiful girl accompanied by her teacher. Sarah felt happy. Not that prestige was important to her, but it did count for something.

They took the tea off the counter and found a small table behind a pillar.

"It's quieter here," he said.

"But it's not noisy," Sarah said. "The place is almost empty."

"It's emptier here," he said, helping her into her seat.

] 104 [

"Did you have a lisp as a child?" she said.

"No, no," he said. "I don't lisp now nor have I ever lisped." He smiled engagingly and began to sip the tea.

"I came a little early to school to study," she lied, dropping her engagement ring into the tea. "Tea is good for cleaning."

"I'd like to see you alone one evening, may we?"

"I don't know," she said.

He touched his ascot. It was soft. "I think we have something to say to each other. I wonder if you will let me say it?"

Sarah looked into her tea. Her engagement ring was at the bottom. How could she be so madly attracted to one man, and supposedly in love with another? It didn't make sense. She would like to throw herself into the long arms of Mr. Duncan Bones.

"How can you be my teacher and my . . . uh . . . friend at the same time?"

"A teacher is a teacher," he said. "I mean what I'm saying."

"Is that Zen?"

"Yes, a Zen saying."

"Maybe after I graduate we could see each other."

"No," he said.

"But can't you wait for a month?"

"No," he said, "why should we? These feelings are always mutual. We could have a drink together soon. Don't worry, it'll be casual."

Sarah got up and slipped her engagement ring back on her finger. "I've got to go and do some studying," she said. "But I'll consider it."

"You won't do any studying," he said, "you know that."

"How do you know?" she said.

"I know you," he said, "my dear girl, dear, dear girl." When he said such things, how could she resist? He was the sort of person who would send a girl flowers and perfume.

"I want to see you, be with you very soon, don't deny me," he said, his warm brown eyes searching her face.

"I'm meeting my fiancé after school," she said. "Another night, soon."

"Yes, soon," he said. She left him sitting at the table touching his ascot. How could she be so passionately attracted? How? Was she in love with him?

John was waiting for her after school, dressed in his brown leather jacket.

"Hi," he said and kissed her cheek. "Where's the car?"

"Oh, hi, it's there." The car was double-parked in front of the school.

"There's a ticket on it," John said. "Give me the keys, I'll drive."

"Oh, blazes! Ho hum," she said, "can you drive it?"

He made a face. "You know I can," he said. "What do you think, I'm a fool?"

"Oh you're irritable," Sarah said, getting into the car. "I thought George was the sulky number of the family."

She thought about Mr. Duncan Bones' lisp as John started the car.

"You're very silent."

"Thinking, don't bug me," she said.

"What's the matter?" he said. "It's your period?" She was in her bitch mood.

"Nothing's the matter with me, don't bug me."

"Are you upset?"

"For Christ sake, you're the one who's upset," she said.

"No, I'm not," he said.

"Well, I'm not either. Maybe you are, or maybe it's your Irish temperament. The Irish have visions, everyone knows that. Remember Yeats?"

"You want to go for a ride? Maybe that will calm you," he said.

"No," she said, "drive me home, I'm tired."

"All right."

"I don't think Jenny will ever go out with your brother again," she said.

"Why not?"

"He was such a slob and a bore. He tried to rape her."

"I doubt that."

"Give me a cigarette," she said.

"You smoke too much," he said, handing her a cigarette.

"Fuck off."

"You do that," he suggested. "Are you sure you want to go home? We could still go for a drive. We could drive to the river."

"And jump in."

He put his arm across her shoulder. "Sit next to me."

"No," she said.

"I'd like to make love to you."

"No," she said, "no piggies tonight. What's the matter? Sex words get you hot or something?"

John said nothing, simply drove and was silent. She reached out and turned on the radio.

"You're crude at times," he finally said. "I don't think you'd make it in Cambridge and would you please turn the station over?"

"Leave me alone," she said. "You're some kind of sex fiend. And anyway, I'm looking for raga rock." She turned the station to another.

"Turn it down, it's too loud," John said.

"You're mean and nasty," she said. "Why are you torturing me?"

"You're torturing me," he said. "You've got it mixed up."

"Don't blow your mind."

"Can't you find something classical? That stuff gives me a headache."

"A mind ache." How tall was Mr. Duncan Bones? He was lean, but he looked as if he would have nice swimmers' muscles rippling down his back.

"You're upset, aren't you, Sarah, what's wrong?"

"Drop dead," she said, dragging on her cigarette. "Mind your own bananas."

John reached over and turned off the radio. "I can't think straight with that junk. Now," he said, "stop acting like a spoiled brat and tell me what's the matter."

"Nothing's the matter," Sarah said, tears coming to her eyes. "Leave me alone, I hate you."

"Why?" John said. "You nut. It must be your period."

"You're too short," she said, racking her brain for something critical. "Too short."

"Short of what?" he said.

"Short of tall," she said, wiping the tears away.

"I'm not short for you," he said. "You're a swallow, a hummingbird, a dwarf. You're a tiny girl. You know. You look twelve."

"Take me home quickly," she said. "I'm going to have a breakdown."

John gave her a long look. "You need a drink," he said and swerved around a corner in the opposite direction. "We'll stop at my house and drink some of Tilly's good brandy. It's good for breakdowns. You need it."

"You're kind," Sarah said, "but I'm not getting my period for ten days and you've got the whole thing confused."

"I think you're confused," he said, accelerating.

"I'm going home or I will leap out of the car and break my legs this minute," she said, putting her hand on the door handle. John grabbed her shoulder and pulled her next to him.

"Okay, bitch, okay," he said, "you'll go home."

16

PULLING INTO THE Green driveway, Sarah noticed the house was ablaze with lights as if her parents were giving a ball.

"Mah jong party?"

"I'll take you to the door," John said, getting out of the car and going around to the other side. "I don't know why you're so moody, maybe I should go into abnormal psychology."

"Forget it," Sarah said. "I'm not bananas because of an unhappy childhood but because everything was so very perfect."

"I doubt it," John said, taking her hand.

Mrs. Green was sitting, eyes closed, with Clytemnestra curled up on her ample lap.

"Is she asleep?" Sarah said, dumbfounded to see Mrs. Green coming into actual physical contact with the cat. Mrs. Green was clad in one of her oldest house dresses, a flowered affair that was ripped down both sides. She looked a wholesome picture.

"I'm not asleep," Mrs. Green whispered, "where were you? I called all over. Jenny don't know. No one knew." Wearily she opened her eyes.

"It's you?" she said to John with undisguised disapproval.

"I was at school," Sarah said.

"I forgot," Mrs. Green said and sighed. "*Oy vey*, it's your father. He's sick."

"Oh, should I say good night to him or what?" Sarah said, already bored with the conversation. Her mother was always bugging her with one thing or another. If only she could go somewhere where she didn't have any relatives, no boyfriend and no one at all, she would manage much better. New York was the place. She didn't know one solitary human being or one solitary

] 109 [

animal in New York. She could take a jet and fly free as a bird to New York, where she would have immediate success as America's leading singer. She could even change her name to Sabina. It was a good name for a singer.

"Where were you?" Mrs. Green said.

"I told you, at school," Sarah said.

"Your father, your father," Mrs. Green moaned.

"Will you stop the scene, Mother," Sarah said.

"He's in the hospital," Mrs. Green said. "It's no scene."

"Hospital?" Sarah said. "Why? Are you bugging me or is this for real?"

"One foot in the grave," Mrs. Green moaned, "and you're *schpatziering* all over town with this one."

"What's the matter with Daddy?" Sarah asked anxiously. "Please tell me. Why won't you tell me?"

"Calm down, no tantrums," Mrs. Green said, throwing Clytemnestra off her lap, "or I'll have to use the cold water."

"So?" Sarah said, rolling her eyes at John.

"I just come from the hospital and I needed you there, but you weren't around. It's a special circumstance. Your father don't drop dead every day, you know."

"What happened, Mrs. Green?" John said, stepping forward.

"What happened?" Sarah screamed. "Tell me or I'll flip."

"Not that tone," Mrs. Green warned.

"Is he dead?" Sarah screamed, and held her mother tightly by her fat arm.

"What's this *mishugenah* question? Of course not! He had a bad time, but Dr. Kantrowitzsky says he'll be good. Marvin's father, you remember. A good man, he don't charge much, and your father's going to do his bathroom in exchange for low rates."

"Well, what the hell happened?" Sarah said.

"He broke his hip," Mrs. Green said, revealing the secret. "It's the hip. It snapped like that." She snapped her fingers to indicate the misfortune. "But the doctor don't charge much."

Sarah tugged at her mother's arm. "My father's crippled for life and you're talking about money."

"Your father said he'd do his bathroom."

"Money, money, I'm sick of it. All you talk about is bread."

"Will Mr. Green be okay?" John said. "That's the important fact."

"He'll be all right," she said, "but the doctor says he has to lie in bed for a long time and then with a crutch."

"In bed with a crutch," Sarah said.

"We can't afford a nurse, we're not millionaires," she said, looking accusingly at Sarah and lifting her arm to reveal the rips in the side of her dress.

"You go in the morning and make a visit, your father wants to see you."

"Yeah," Sarah said. Mrs. Green looked overstuffed, as if she were poured into her dress, a rich, fattening glass of Kosher coconut juice. "I'll go, I'm not such a bad daughter as you may think."

"No lip," Mrs. Green said.

"Keep calm," John said.

"Shut up," she said.

"I'll need you here this summer," Mrs. Green continued, her voice becoming hysterical. "We can't afford a nurse. Mr. Green don't have millions in case you thought you'd go *schpatziering* somewhere. You said something about Cambridge the other day, didn't you? Or was it New York?"

"Both," Sarah said. "You mean I'm supposed to hang around this palace of boredom?" Her plan was shot to hell. The utter fucking nerve! How could he do such a miserable thing? Did he have to fall on his behind just when she had her whole future arranged? In her mind she had saved the money for the plane and was already ensconced in a pad with John. The lie had been sorted out, the emotions set and here Mr. Green had come along and ruined everything. It had all seemed so reasonable. She was going to tell them she was willing to wait and not marry for one year, if in the interim they would allow her to work in Cambridge. Everyone would be happy. She could, openly, go to Cambridge. They'd wish she'd change her mind and not marry the *goy*. They would never visit her in Cambridge, consequently they would never know she was living with John. They never went anywhere except for the trip to Israel two years ago. And what a fantastic occasion! Fifteen years they argued about going and when Grandmother Green died and left her savings, it had been enough for a round trip to Israel. The millennium had struck.

"The poor soul was hit down, one, two, three," Mrs. Green said, snapping her fingers. "One second he was in the shower, the next he was sitting on the toilet, one, two, three, and then he was on the floor. He don't know what hit him, the poor soul. It was like lightning. He was spread all over the floor. And I had just scrubbed it. Imagine? He don't know what hit him."

"Did it hurt?" Sarah said, realizing she was asking a stupid question. Poor Daddy with his pale face on the hospital pillow? What could he be thinking about lying in the sick bed? He probably didn't have sexual fantasies anymore.

Sarah had little connection with sickness. In fact, she had been to a rest home only once when Jenny's mother had a nervous breakdown in the middle of playing Gin Rummy. Jenny and she had visited the rest home, where Mrs. Oliver seemed extremely happy.

"I heard the crash and came running. I called the police," Mrs. Green said excitedly, "or I thought I did but it was the fire department and they came, twenty men carrying ax handles."

"Oh crap," Sarah said.

"But Marvin's father came right away with the ambulance. Those no-goods from the fire department were mad. They don't know what sickness is."

"Yeah," Sarah said.

"He slipped getting up from the toilet and hit his hip, the right one and it broke, one, two, three, just like that," she said.

"Please," Sarah begged, "don't snap your fingers."

"Should I visit him in the hospital? Does he want visitors?" John said. "Some people want to be alone when they're sick."

Mrs. Green's face darkened. "No," she said firmly, "it's a Jewish hospital."

"Mother," Sarah said, "Christians can go to Jewish hospitals, and Jews to Christian ones, have you blown your cool completely? For God's sake, how can you be so dumb?"

Mrs. Green, bewildered, looked from John to Sarah and back again. "Oh," she said.

"Well, good night," John said. "I guess I'll go home, it's late, I

] 112 [

have an early class. If you like I'll take you tomorrow. What time?"

"After work," Sarah said. "I'll call you."

"Work?" Mrs. Green said. "Now she's working."

"Bye," John said, scooting out the front door.

"I want to talk serious with you," Mrs. Green said. "You want a cup of tea?" This was Mrs. Green's way of ingratiating herself. A cup of tea was all she could offer. She kept no liquor in the house, not even for company. The most a person could get was a cup of tea or a piece of hard candy, usually stale.

"Make it quick," Sarah said. "I have to be at work at nine sharp tomorrow. Like who works and goes to school, but your work-horse daughter has arranged to do so." But what a pity she didn't have Biology class for two days. She wouldn't see Mr. Duncan Bones for two whole days.

"So? You got a job?"

"Yeah," Sarah said, sitting on the edge of the couch. "Is his foot in a sling?"

"Yes," Mrs. Green said, "it's packed in concrete."

"Uh-huh."

"He must rest, be quiet, no aggravation for a few months. I don't want him to see the inside of his office," Mrs. Green said.

"Or the inside of a toilet," Sarah said.

"Okay, okay," Mrs. Green said, "you said you want the tea or not?"

"Okay, okay," Sarah said, following her into the kitchen.

"I got no one to help me," Mrs. Green said, beginning to whimper. "You'll have to help. We'll have to lift him. We can't let him down."

Sarah leaned against the stove and unpinned her hair, letting it fall loose over her shoulder. "It seems to me," she said, "that between you and Carmine you could lift a football team. I mean between the two of you, you must weigh four hundred pounds. Dad weighs one hundred and thirty-five, I think."

Mrs. Green pushed Sarah away from the stove. "Get your hair out of the water," she said. She never boiled water in a teapot but in a regular pot. It was quicker.

"The doctor is putting me on a diet," Mrs. Green said, "and

Carmine is going to visit Moses for the month of August. He's at summer school. Imagine? The *schwartza* gets a vacation."

"Moses is in his first year of graduate school, that's right," Sarah said, thinking of Carmine sitting in her son's apartment listening to music and drinking a Coke. Carmine was addicted to Coca-Cola. She wasn't as flabby as Mrs. Green though, and dug music, which was definitely something in her favor. Mrs. Green's arms were like tapioca pudding not yet congealed.

"Moses isn't staying long in Chicago, so it's Carmine's only chance to visit Chicago. That's the *bubamisah* she tells me, anyway. Imagine those *schwartzas*. Pretty soon they'll be living next door."

"They already are," Sarah said.

Mrs. Green's eyes widened, her nostrils flared. "Is that right?"

"I don't know," Sarah said. "I thought you liked Carmine. Where's Moses going, the Army?"

"New York," Mrs. Green said, curtly spilling the water into breakfast cups.

"I want the good cup," Sarah said. So Moses was going to New York and hadn't even written her one single word about it. How could he be so inconsiderate?

"Okay," Mrs. Green said and took a china cup decorated with flowers out of the cupboard.

"Don't you like Carmine?" Sarah persisted.

"What are you talking about? When I was a girl it was different, they lived on the other side of town. Now they don't know their place, talking about black power all the time. What do they want, to be President?"

"Why not?" Sarah said. "There's white power, why not black power? They're human like the rest of us finks. Why can't a brown person be crazy, too? White people want white power."

"Brown," Mrs. Green said, confused, "but they say they want black power."

"Let's drop it," Sarah said, "but answer me, don't you like Carmine? She's been here so long, I thought you dug her."

"I like her," Mrs. Green said, "but her husband is a bum."

"Uh-huh, well, I have to go to bed," Sarah said, putting the cup in the sink. "Keep your pecker up as they say. I'll call Daddy in the morning." Moses' father had bugged out when Moses was barely a year old and was never heard from again except to send an occasional postcard from various cities around the United States. There was no denying he was a bum, or at least a bum on some level. Who knows, he might have been quite intelligent. Moses was smart and he must have got it somewhere.

"I don't get it," Sarah said as a parting word. "You tell Carmine the most personal, intimate soul things and then you talk about her as if she's a nigger. I don't understand."

"She's just the *schwartza*," Mrs. Green said. "I don't call her a nigger, it isn't nice."

17

MR. COX WAS EXTREMELY helpful to Sarah on her first day at work. He kindly showed her the supplies kept in a converted bathroom, and even pulled up the shade in his cubicle so a few scraggly remnants of sun could filter through the filthy windowpane. Every now and then Miss Abercrombie popped into the room, her thin body stiff as a Ping-Pong paddle, her enormous round glasses bobbing on the end of her nose.

The day whizzed by and before she knew it, it was time to leave. At exactly five sharp she was seen flying past Miss Abercrombie's open door in order to get to the hospital in time to visit Mr. Green. The fat girl with the telephone waist didn't bother to look up as she whirled by. "A lazy pig," Sarah muttered, slamming the door.

The first person she saw standing in the hospital lobby was Mrs. Green, who looked as if she owned the place. Mrs. Green beckoned to her.

"Good, you're not *schpatziering* around. He'll be all right. The doctor said it'll take about three months. We'll have to lift him."

"Where is he?" Sarah said, "in the loony ward?"

"He's down there." Mrs. Green pointed a chubby finger toward the end of the corridor. "With another man. It's the bone ward. I don't know who that other man is. The bed don't smell so good."

"You mean he's not in *Who's Who* and doesn't spend his vacation at The Concord?" She started to walk to where Mrs. Green had pointed but she grabbed her arm. "Wait a minute," Mrs. Green said, "we got to talk." She motioned her toward a small drafty waiting room and sat her down on a cold bench. An old man wearing a derby sat quietly in the corner reading the newspaper. When he saw them, he quietly left, lowering his eyes.

"Remember," Mrs. Green said, "you're going to help me. A good daughter don't go back on her word like a wild Indian."

"I can never do a damn thing that I want to do," Sarah said, feeling sorry for herself. Why couldn't she have had a nutty sister or a fruitcake brother, big and strong, to stay and help? Why? The fitness of things was botched up. She wiggled around on the bench in a paroxysm of guilt. Poor daddy, all alone in a bleak hospital with nothing but an evil-smelling man to keep him company and a glaring absence of sexual fantasy.

"What're you doing?" Mrs. Green said sharply, noticing Sarah wiggling on the bench. Her eyebrows pulled together like oars in a rowboat. "What're you doing?"

"I've got an itch," Sarah said, "that's all. Can't I have an itch?" It was so utterly boring. Boring. Boring. Boring. Everything ruined. It was exactly like the summer she thought she could visit Reed College. She had whined, cajoled, theatened. And finally became violent. But it was no good, no damned good. They had refused to let her go. They had even gone so far in their madness to investigate Reed. They had phoned Rabbi Morris and forced him to find out what he could. And when he had given his report, they were thoroughly disgusted. The off-campus students took drugs, and all of them had sex entanglements. They were certainly not going to allow their daughter to be exposed to such a terrible atmosphere.

"It's unhealthy," Mr. Green had the gall to say at the breakfast table over his usual dry, tight fried eggs. She stared at him in hatred, and then seized a thickly buttered piece of toast and flung it right into his startled face. It spilled over his only good suit, a pinstripe affair, and left a pale ring like a halo even the French cleaners couldn't remove.

"Will you stop wiggling," Mrs. Green commanded, "someone will see."

Jenny Oliver couldn't believe her parents wouldn't let her go. Mrs. Oliver had said it was just fine, except for her psychiatric treatment she would have flown to Oregon with them.

"Will you stop that wiggling," Mrs. Green said.

"Oh, Mother, I've got the clap," Sarah said.

Mrs. Green gazed down the corridor. The nurses were so slim and clean-looking in their starched white uniforms. She had been on Dr. Kantrowitzsky's diet for three days. She regarded her plump belly. It would never be like those nurses, no, she was going to be realistic but she could lose a few pounds. It was possible. If only Sarah wouldn't say such nasty things, perhaps she would eat less. She had seen on television that fat people eat to console themselves.

"Why do you have to talk that way?" she said.

"What way?" Sarah said, wiggling.

"Such a face, such a face," Mrs. Green said. "You should see his face."

Sarah felt a sudden impulse to strangle her mother. She was so bloody dramatic, so ridiculously hysterical, couldn't she say anything, anything at all in a normal voice? It would be so easy to slip her fingers around her large neck and squeeze. No one need know.

"Such a face," Mrs. Green said. "He still don't know what hit him." She reached into her purse and took out a lace handkerchief and blew her nose into it.

"That's mine," Sarah said. "Daddy gave it to me."

Mrs. Green looked hurt. "Since when do I steal things from my own daughter. Your father gave it to me on my birthday."

"He didn't," Sarah said. "But I'll let it go."

It would be so easy to rip the handkerchief out of Mrs. Green's hand and stuff it into her mouth, so easy. Mrs. Green daubed at her eyes with the handkerchief as if she were crying. She could tie her arms together with her belt and drop her down the nearest laundry chute. That would give her something to cry about. She could whimper the entire way down. The headline in *The Detroit News* would read "Nasty Fucker Found Among Dirty Linen."

Sarah was aware for many years she had had such strange impulses, and did not worry about it. A lot of people want to kill their parents and vice versa. The impulse came at unexpected moments and particularly and invariably on Sunday, when she watched her parents going mechanically in and out of the bathroom, lugging the papers to and fro for the entire day. After breakfast they would listen to a stupefyingly dull religious program about Israel. The drone drove her bananas.

] 118 [

"I want to be able to count on you," Mrs. Green said. "You've been irresponsible, and now here's your chance to prove yourself."

Sarah looked at her shoe. It was gorgeous, the square gold buckle reflecting the dim light of the waiting room. What punishment was meted out to parent killers? It probably varied from state to state. Were the courts lenient? It could be a touchy subject. Most people had parents, after all, and from time to time most would like to cut their throats. Naturally, the punishment meted out to such offenders would have to be very strong in order to prevent everyone, just everyone from doing it. If a person was only dealt a minor punishment, most assuredly there would be few, if any, parents left in the world. The majority would be six feet under contemplating their navels.

"You don't like me, do you?" Sarah said, looking up from her shoe and directly into Mrs. Green's eyes.

"Sarah, you know we love you. Why do you ask such *mishugenah* things? *Oy.*"

"Prove it," Sarah said. The little old man was coming back with his paper, his derby hat tucked under his arm.

"Please," Mrs. Green said, "don't start, not today."

"Why do you always bug me about Moses," Sarah said. "If you want me to help this summer, I want quick answers to this question and all the others I may ask."

"Moses?" Mrs. Green asked, her voice strained, her bosom beginning to heave. "You ought to know something about your heritage, that's all," she said.

"Oh oh, freak-out time," Sarah said, remembering Connie Zachi of the freckles and red hair had made the same error. "I mean our Moses, Moses Jones, for Christ's sake."

"Why didn't you say so?" Mrs. Green said irritably. "He's in Chicago, you know that."

"You don't like him. Remember you were so rotten to him."

Mrs. Green looked uneasy, her bottom lip beginning to quiver. She daubed at her tearless eyes with the lace handkerchief and tried to ignore the little old man with the derby hat, who peered at her over the top of his paper.

Sarah scrutinized her mother, outrage in her eyes. How could a human being forget such treatment? Everything was designed to bring Negro people down, to make them feel as depressed and deprived as possible. Why didn't white people understand? Or maybe they did, and that was the real point. It wasn't as if Mrs. Green behaved unconsciously, or unawares. *Au contraire,* she knew perfectly well what she was doing when insults were directed at Moses or any other person of color. Out of the blue Mrs. Green would confront Moses, her face contorted, eyes bulged, temper flaring.

"What are you doing?" she would shout as they sat quietly playing chess on the back porch. Moses taught Sarah to play when she was thirteen.

"What are you doing?" she shouted in his face. He shrugged his shoulders in his phoney Steppin Fetchit pose and went home, leaving a perfectly groovy strategy unfinished.

"I used to give Carmine our old clothes, Daddy's old clothes," Mrs. Green said.

"Yeah, sure and they fit Moses' left toe," Sarah said. The little old man had discovered a spindly spider creeping around on the floor and was playing with it with one end of the paper.

"I've had enough." Mrs. Green stood up. "How much *mishegas* is there in this world? Come, let's go to Daddy."

Mr. Green smiled like a baby when they came into the room.

"I don't know what hit me," he said eagerly, thrilled at seeing his daughter's pretty face. She sat down on the bed and held his hand. "Poor Daddy," she said, "we'll take you home to Loxley Hall soon and take care of you."

"Thank God," Mrs. Green said, sighing with relief, interpreting Sarah's words as a commitment for the summer.

Sarah looked around the white antiseptic room. In the other bed a form moved beneath the sheets. It would be a human body underneath though the head wasn't visible.

"What's in there?" Sarah whispered.

"Shhh," Mr. Green said, "Mr. Ginzberg, Home Improvements, Livernois and Seven Mile Road, I think. His son's in special school."

"An idiot?" Sarah said.

"No, shhh," Mr. Green said, "blind."

Mr. Ginzberg rustled the sheets.

"He might hear you," Mr. Green said.

"But we're not saying anything," Sarah said.

"Shhh, be quiet," Mrs. Green said.

"How do you feel, Daddy?"

"Not bad," he said, "but I don't want to lay here too long. I got work to do. You can't lay around too long." He looked guiltily at Mrs. Green, who had instructed him he was not to go to his office for the entire summer.

"Don't think about that now, Bernie," Mrs. Green said.

A muffled sound came bursting out of Mr. Ginzberg's bed.

"Oy, what is it?" Mrs. Green said, alarmed. "What is it? Maybe we should get the lazy nurse who's never around when you want her. You could drop dead and what would anyone care. No one would know."

"Look," Sarah said, "don't lose your cool, can't you tell a fart when you hear one?"

"Shhh," Mr. and Mrs. Green said together, "shhh, he could hear you."

18

"I THOUGHT GEORGE O'CONNER was foolish five years ago and I still think the same," Jenny said. She stood with one foot on the curb, and the other on the sidewalk in front of the drugstore. Under her Navy pea jacket, which was really too warm for the beautiful spring weather, she was wearing her favorite torn cashmere sweater. Jenny loved wearing old torn clothes.

"Why should I like him because we're both Catholic?" she said, annoyed. "I mean, where's the mystery? I don't especially like people who are like me."

"Yeah," Sarah said, "I know what you mean. God, I'm glad it's Saturday and I don't have to work and I don't have to go to school. It's all such a bore. But now I'm hung up here for the rest of the goddamned summer. Just when I thought I was getting out of that bag."

"Well," Jenny said, pushing a long hair out of her mouth and placing it behind her ear, "I'll be here. We can go swimming on weekends. I don't go to Sarah Lawrence till mid-September, or the end of it."

"Yeah, but I'm leaving before then, I hope. I can't make a whole summer in this cesspool."

"We'll both be east, won't that be nice? I'll visit you in Cambridge Christmas vacation."

"I've been thinking, Jenny," Sarah said, unbuttoning her sweater. The spring sun was strong. "I've been thinking, I don't know if I really want to be a rock 'n' roll singer. It might be a drag. If I'm going to study voice I might as well go far out and study opera or something important. As long as you're going to be something, it might as well be good. Don't you think?"

Jenny smiled at her. "I don't know," she said. "I always thought you'd be a good writer. You have such a marvelous imagination."

"Hey, you're putting me on, sugar," Sarah said.

"No," Jenny said.

"No?" Sarah said.

"No," Jenny said.

"I do like to write," Sarah said, "but I'm basically lazy and besides I have nothing to say. I just like to camp around."

"You'll figure it out," Jenny said.

"I will?" Sarah said.

"You will," Jenny said. "Now let's have a Coke. Or a Pepsi. We're in the Pepsi generation."

"Ah shit," Sarah said.

"Definitely," Jenny said, and stepped onto the curb. "The drugstore won't be filled with geeks today," she said.

"No geeks, the local idiots," Sarah said, fluttering her false eyelashes.

19

SARAH DROPPED the change into the box, flashed the bus driver a Miss America smile and made her way to the back of the bus. Two teenyboppers sat gazing vacantly out the window. She sat behind them so she could amuse herself with their wild conversation, if there was any. The second week at work and she was still on time. She glanced at her brand-new and shining watch with an enormously wide vermilion band. It was a good record for a girl who was constantly and perennially late. No one could say she hadn't become conscientious, and her watch would help her keep up the good record.

The teenyboppers were being very silent, gazing blankly out the window at the passing parade. They were too young to work, probably. Sarah sat back in her seat with a lovely feeling of superiority. All was well with the world. She had the new watch, charged to her mother at Crowley Milner's, which if she were clever would be paid by Mr. Green without ever a comment from Mrs. Green. This was something important to think about. Sarah had to save every penny so at the moment of Mr. Green's emergence from ill health, she could instantly fly off to Cambridge.

One teenybopper said something to the other in a low voice. Sarah leaned forward to listen and noticed the teenybopper on the right was wearing a wide-band watch similar to her own. Sarah's watch said twenty to nine. The teenybopper's said something different. Sarah couldn't quite see, but the hands were definitely in different places. She leaned closer. The watch was precisely the same color as hers. What thirteen-year-old brat could afford such a watch? It must have been a gift. She looked at the other teenybopper. Was she, too, wearing an expensive watch? The girl's hand was hidden behind her waist-length hair so Sarah couldn't see her wrist. Finally she moved her hand and Sarah saw that, she, too, was wearing a wide-band watch. And on the fourth finger of her left hand a gold wedding band was prominently displayed. Was it possible? They were mere children, just little brats in junior high.

Sarah craned her neck to study their profiles. They were even younger than she first thought. They couldn't be more than eleven. The wedding band was obviously a fake and the watches, too. That was it. They were faking it.

"Where did you get the watch, kid?" She spoke gravely to the little chick on the right who turned around and gave her a steely stare. "Crowley's," she said, lifting her wrist to show Sarah. It said ten past nine.

"Well, dig this little scene, it doesn't work properly. Must be a copy of mine," Sarah said, holding her arm forward.

"Oh yeah," the teenybopper on the left said, "mine says ten past nine, too."

"Your watch is wrong, lady," the other one snarled viciously, "and looking at you no wonder."

"You think you're smart," Sarah said, getting up to move her seat.

"Drop dead," they both said. "Butt out."

Sarah walked to the last row of seats and pretended an interest in something on her lap. Where did they get off being so fresh-mouthed, anyway? She looked up to where they were sitting. They had pretty hair. It made her angry. Why weren't dummies as ugly as they were dumb? It no doubt fit into the fitness of things. They had almost ruined her day. The one on the right surreptitiously lit a cigarette, turned and blew the smoke in Sarah's direction.

Was she anything like those two creepy teenyboppers? They were all wearing identical watches. Their hair was long, and they were smoking. But it was here the similarity ended. She really wasn't anything like them. They were toughies, and probably never had a thought in their heads outside of what clothes they would wear and what boys they could force to notice them. They were jerks.

She looked at them again. The brat on the right looked the

teeniest bit like herself. Of course, only in profile. When she turned her head she had a mutt face, a silly, stupid mutt face. Anyway, they weren't going anywhere in this world. They would probably spend their lives riding the bus on Woodward Avenue, up and down, down and up, quite aimlessly, whereas she had a destiny. Perhaps not yet known, but certainly to be discovered.

20

AS SARAH RACED by the switchboard at the Michigan Insurance Company, she noticed a new girl vigorously filing her nails.

"Morning," Sarah sputtered. "Where's Fatty? I have permission to arrive at this time. I'm a personal friend of Miss Abercrombie's. In fact, she's my cousin."

"Fatty's out sick," the new girl said as Sarah darted off to Sam's cubicle. He was seated at his desk, nibbling at his lunch.

"I was sick in the ladies' room. Some trouble," she said in a loud conspiratorial tone. "Know what I mean?"

"My wife didn't bother to fix breakfast this morning," Sam explained, smiling apologetically. "Thought I'd eat lunch now." He chewed the edge of a meager peanut butter and jelly sandwich.

"It has a lot of flaws," he said, picking up a mottled, twisted carrot and cramming it into his mouth.

"It's a carrot?" Sarah said, sitting down at her typewriter and putting a fresh sheet of paper into it. Poor Sam, he was such a lump. A lump of a man. So sexless with his lump face and his poor, sloppy lump body. Perhaps he had a childhood disease that tore the life out of him. There must be some explanation.

Sarah knew such diseases could affect people in odd ways. Mumps maybe, yes, mumps. He must be a lump mump. Or maybe a mump lump. This must be the explanation for his present decayed condition. She tried to imagine him in bed, stretched out under stained sheets. Such a mump lump surely could not get it up. Surely. A lover? Impossible. He had to be sterile. Sterility and impotency were different. But he must be impotent as well. It was too bad. He wasn't such a bad boss. There were worse sorts. He demanded very little, didn't even seem to notice whether she had done her work or not. The first day he had been silent. Ocasionally she looked up to find him smiling kindly.

After all, it wasn't such a terrible job. Who knew but perhaps she would stay the whole summer at this one job. If they wished, they could promote her. Miss Abercrombie's job didn't appear to be so complicated. Why couldn't she do it?

If she had Miss Abercrombie's job, she might consider staying in Detroit. Mr. Duncan Bones lived in Detroit. They could move to Grosse Point to a mansion and invite Motown Records over for far-out Pot parties and freak-ins. They could have a human be-in, too.

Sarah made a typing error and swore.

"Here," Sam said, handing her an eraser.

"Thanks."

"I want to ask you something," he said, drooling on his shirt and trying to keep his voice low.

"Sure," Sarah said and swiveled her chair in his direction.

"Do you like older men?" he said.

Sarah considered the question for a moment. "I adore older men, they're a groove," she said in her best bass.

"Men over fifty?" he said.

"Love them," she said.

"Sixty?" he said, beaming. He must remember to thank Miss Abercrombie for hiring this beautiful, efficient girl, who smelled of soap and perfume. She must bathe every day. She was smart as well as beautiful. She could be in a movie magazine, easily. He looked at her legs. Her dress was short. It was hard to avoid her thighs, young and strong. The first day had been rough. He could barely extract his glance from her legs, staring wildly, hungrily from her ankles to her hip bone. He didn't want her to catch him, knowing full well how frightened and needlessly skittish virgins sometimes acted.

He nibbled the last hard crust of the peanut butter and jelly sandwich and spit into a tattered tissue.

"I often eat my lunch in the morning. I read on my lunch hour," he said.

Sarah shouted, "How nice!"

For ten years he had been sending mail-order magazines to the

] 128 [

office for fear his wife might discover them at home. She wouldn't understand.

"You're a good worker," he said.

"Thank you," Sarah said, raising her voice and wondering if peanut butter could be safely removed from an old silk tie. Sam wiped his mouth on his hand and sighed. He would have one whole joy-filled hour to pore through the latest magazine. His habit was to read in the men's room. In there he could read undisturbed.

He looked at Sarah's ankles, so young, so alluring. She was a dish. If only she would speak clearly. She had an annoying habit of speaking softly, swallowing her words so he had to strain to hear her. They ought to teach public speaking in the schools. It should be a definite part of the curriculum. Fortunately, it wouldn't be long before he could read his magazines. When he was finished with them, they would be pressed into a folder marked PER-SONAL, where they wouldn't get him into any trouble. They would be quite safe, exempt from prying eyes, nosy, probing eyes and the eyes of Miss Abercrombie. She had a tendency to be sharp-tongued.

"It's too bad you have no children," Sarah shouted sympatheti-cally. She handed him a poorly typed letter, and the smell of her exotic perfume wafted its way into his half-closed nostrils. She thought if he had children, he would clean himself up. Children have a way of getting on their parents' asses, the same way parents have of getting on their children's asses. The idea of having such an unkempt, dirty specimen for a father made her feel faintly sick. But even if he cleaned up, what then? Poor creepy Mr. Cox made her own father look like David McCallum and Don Juan rolled into one. Poor Mr. Cox with his bleak, empty, futile, disorganized, unsanitary life.

Sam began to laugh, his jelly face flopping and slipping around like a dessert she had once seen decaying on a shelf in a Greek restaurant. He laughed till the tears squeezed out of his eyes. She waited politely for him to stop. Had he suddenly gone bananas?

"I have five brats," he said, clutching his stomach, "five mon-sters. Egbert tried to stick a knife in my back last week."

"Really?" Sarah said.

He smiled.

"Egbert, who's fourteen and a rotten egg, tried to stick me with a knife. In my back," he said with pleasure. "And Candy is a moron. She's the second oldest. Delphina, the youngest, is lovely. A lovely child. She has muscles in her calves."

Sarah watched in disbelief. He must be lying. He couldn't have five children. He just couldn't. He couldn't even have one child. She studied his face for a sign of virility.

"I've been with this firm for forty years," he said, a crazed gleam coming into his eyes. "Someone has to support these bastards. I'm elected." He knew if he could only pass through the morning and get to his lunch hour in the men's room everything would be hunky-dory. But somehow something had gone wrong. He felt a terrible ache over his right eye.

"They hire these girls like Delphina all the time," he said excitedly, "and then they're good workers."

"I understand," Sarah said.

"They have muscles in their calves," he said, "usually."

"Yeah, I understand."

"Girls like you," he said nervously, "with short dresses."

"Now, Sam, don't get all up-tight," she said, beginning to stack the papers on her desk in a neat pile.

"Forty years I've been here," he said, "and what do I have? Five bastards and only one of them good enough for movie magazines."

"Right," Sarah yelled, putting pencils into the drawer and closing the cover on the typewriter.

"And this Abercrombie with her tongue quacking. I had to listen to that for the past year."

"She's been here for a year? Isn't that interesting?" Sarah said, getting out of her chair. She stood by the door with her hand on the knob.

"And they have nosy, prying eyes," he said, edging over to her.

"Yeah," Sarah said, "sure, Sam. Now try not to be up-tight."

"Where are you going?" he asked and put his hand on her arm.

"Isn't it lunchtime?" Sarah said, shoving his hand away, opening the door in preparation for flight.

"It's not time," he said, "it couldn't be. Please, please, don't go. Stay here. I'll be good. You're such a good worker. So speedy." He

] 130 [

was standing close enough so her perfume made him quite dizzy. Something was spinning. If he could only clear his head. What had gone wrong? What?

"Please stay a little longer, please. Miss Abercrombie will be very cross." He grasped her elbow. She seemed to be sliding away from him. "You'll get a raise," he screamed.

Sarah stared at him. He was standing directly behind her, breathing peanut butter fumes into her face and dribbling an undetermined substance on the back of her dress. Is this rape? she wondered. Evidently real rape was nothing like her fantasy. This buzzard was grubsville all the way. There was no getting around it. Where was the handsome, strong, masculine, dark rapist she had always imagined?

Blindly, he pinched the skin over her elbow and began to drag her back into the room. With one hand she flung the door wide and with the other adroitly slammed her greenbookbag into his flabby, puzzled face. A strange smashing, cracking sound was heard.

"Eeeeeeeeeee!" he shrieked as she bolted down the hall past the new girl at the switchboard. "Eeeeeeeeeee!" he shrieked like a police siren. "Eeeeeeeeeee!"

"Call an ambulance," Sarah mumbled, streaking through the reception area. "Mr. Cox stuffed a rusty paper clip up his schnozz and broke his nose."

Having run nonstop down five flights of stairs, she was breathless and panting when she reached the street. She paused for a moment to settle down. It was the end of The Michigan Insurance Company. She wouldn't bother to go back. She'd be God-damned if they'd see so much as her little finger in that banana farm. She looked around.

Now what? The street was crowded with mid-day shoppers, the dull, gray faces of the middle-class, the dull, brown faces of the lower class, cluttered up the street. Angrily she drifted through the throng of people, watching their faces and their bodies moving listlessly, boringly, slowly by. What would she do? Certainly none of these slow wits would give her a job. What would she do? Couldn't a dashing, clever knight who looked like Duncan Bones give her a job? She passed a store window and peeped in. Not much business in there. Still, perhaps she might happen upon a sign in a window reading

WANTED BABYHIP
good salary

She wandered to the corner of the street, stopped and decided to go into a coffee shop to sit and think out her problem at hand.

"Coffee and a sugar donut," she said to a cute Latin type behind the counter. He smiled, touched the cleft in his chin self-consciously and went to pour the coffee. She felt sick. What a fucking freak of a pig Mr. Cox turned out to be. Probably spent his leisure masturbating to Lawrence Welk. She tapped her fingers in irritation against an ashtray. How could she go to Cambridge? How? John never had any bread. Never. It was so discouraging. At least if she were with someone who had a little bread, things were possible. Not that she was such a rank materialist, but having no money meant being trapped at 10117 Cherrylawn. She had the same trouble with Moses. He never had any money either, and he wasn't very responsive to the fact she wanted it.

"Why do you want to go out with me?" he said. "I don't have any money. You probably want to drive your parents crazy. I won't be used, Sarah. You're a gold digger."

"But I like you," she had protested. "You're my big brother."

"That's why you should stay away," he said. They were sitting on the lawn in front of the Green house, playing chess.

"But I like you," Sarah said, checkmating him.

"Listen, girl," he said, "I like black women or blonds, and nothing in between."

"You're a lousy chess player," she said.

Moses was no help at all when you got right down to the nitty gritty. He had lots of advice but when it came to action, he copped out.

She pulled out the cigars and offered one to the counterman, who shook his head no. She frowned. She lit the cigar. What a bore, money, money, money. She looked at the counterman. He probably didn't make much bread. He wouldn't be of any use. The crucial question was the richness of Mr. Duncan Bones. He would, no doubt, be willing to come to her aid. He looked rich, he

] 132 [

talked rich, he smelled rich. But was he actually rich? He might have family money if he didn't have his very own. She would make it a point to know.

"Here it is," the counterman said, smiling, and set the coffee down. Gray, gray, his eyes were gray. Green, green, how much I want you green. Wasn't that a line from Garcia Lorca? Green, how much I want you, green money. Her face brightened.

"Where's the phone?" she asked. It was interesting how brilliant schemes occurred from the blue. A beautiful flash, a vision, a dream had popped into her head. And it was the perfect solution to the dreary problem at hand.

She could sell Pot. Who would suspect a nice, Jewish girl from a nice, Jewish family? No one. It was a first-rate groovy idea. She could trot around to Highland Park High School and deliver it to the hippies hanging in. They were forever turning on in the john, so why not buy it from her? She was doing them a fantastic favor, like Johnny Appleseed in a way. She looked into the greenbookbag for change.

"Back there." The counterman pointed to the phone. She dug the change out of the greenbookbag and headed toward the back. With all her savings, some twenty-five dollars she had managed to collect from a combination of frugality and theft, she could go into the Pot business immediately.

The first person to contact was Jenny. She would want an instant opinion from her. Wouldn't Jenny be surprised and enchanted?

She dialed the school, pretended to be Jenny's mother and asked the principal, an apple-cheeked nun, to fetch Jenny to the phone. The principal sounded annoyed but went to take her from Shakespeare class.

"This is the second time you've done this in a few weeks, Sarah," Jenny whispered into the phone. "I'll be in trouble. Sister is standing right here beside me."

"But I had a fabulous idea, just listen for a second," Sarah begged. "It's great! I just had a new flash of genius. I left my job and I need bread."

"So?" Jenny said.

"I need bread. I thought I'd sell Pot like around school. I'd make a fortune and we'd have free stuff, you dig?"

] 133 [

"Please," Jenny said, "not on the phone."

"Oh nonsense, they don't know what Pot means," Sarah said.

"Please," Jenny said.

"Oh, crap."

"They know what crap means," Jenny said.

"Listen," Sarah said, "can't you get it for me at a discount or wholesale, even?"

"Not on the phone, Sarah," Jenny said. "I've got to hang up. They're watching me. They think I'm evil incarnate. Please, I can't talk. I'll call you at home. Please, don't call me again here unless there's an emergency."

"But this is an emergency," Sarah said.

"You're turning into some kind of sociopath," Jenny said. "You better go to church and confess."

"I'm unhappy," Sarah said. "My boss tried to attack me."

"That's no emergency," Jenny said. "Nothing is unless it's an immaculate conception. Call me later, I've got to scurry back to Hamlet."

Sarah stood by the phone thinking. Jenny was in a peculiar mood. She put another dime in the phone and dialed her own number. It rang three times and Mrs. Green, rasping, answered.

"Hello," Sarah said, disguising her voice to sound Southern, "Carmine there?"

"Just a minute," Mrs. Green said, flinging the phone down. Sarah could hear her heavy steps ploughing through to the kitchen.

"Hello," Carmine said, hesitantly, "who's this?"

"Carmine, listen," Sarah said, "don't blow your cool and fink out on me, this is Sarah but pretend it isn't, okay?"

There was a pause. "Okay, child," Carmine said, "what's the matter? Is something wrong? I'm in a hurry. Your mother's waiting on me to go to the hospital."

"Shhh," Sarah said, "don't talk so loud. Here's what's happening."

"Uh-huh," Carmine said, "go on, I'm in a hurry."

"Everything's cool, you better believe that, but I need your help. Please, you must help me."

"Uh-huh," Carmine said, "you in trouble?"

"No," Sarah said, "I've got to buy some Pot, that's all. A large quantity and I've got to put my hands on it right away. Like today."

"What's that, child?" Carmine said. "You want pots?"

"Look, I need to buy some Pot right away. Where do I buy it? I thought since you lived around Eight Mile, you'd know. Isn't Eight Mile the place?"

"Uh-huh," Carmine said, "I suppose you could buy pots on Eight Mile."

Sarah groaned. "Where do I go exactly?" she said.

"Well, child, it might be better to go downtown to Sam's Cut Rate. They got 'em cheaper."

"For Christ sake," Sarah said. "I don't mean pots, I mean P-O-T, Pot."

"They got nice cheap ones there," Carmine said, "or the dime store, Woolworth's on Livernois."

"No, no, please shut up, please listen, I said Pot. I need money, Carmine, money, m-o-n-e-y. I've got to get bread right away."

"Money? You need money?" Carmine said, incredulously. "Well, child, you sure come to the wrong person. I ain't got money. You want to talk to your mama? Maybe she got some."

Sarah breathed heavily into the phone. What was the matter with Carmine? "Listen," she said, "I want to buy some Pot, you get it? Marijuana, grass, the weed, stuff, Maryjane, Boo. I want to sell it to make money. Don't you dig?"

"Don't you sass me," Carmine said, outraged. "Don't sass me, child. I ain't taking any nonsense. I don't know what you're up to but it ain't no good. I'm glad I'm getting out of here this summer. You sure got to be something-else around here."

"You won't help me?" Sarah said.

"Child, you come here and I'll wash out that sass mouth with soap. That's how I'll help." Sarah heard a sharp click.

"I better put more bread into the phone," she said. "Hello?" There was no reply. Sarah put down the receiver and stared at the wall, her cheeks flushed in anger. She had been betrayed by one of her dearest friends. How could she do such a low thing? Carmine, the fink, and after everything she had done for Carmine. How quickly people forget.

At first Mrs. Green had been only too eager to fire Carmine. Carmine was there two weeks when Mrs. Green discovered she was afraid of earthworms and wouldn't go into the backyard on rainy days. But Sarah had come to the rescue and demanded she be allowed to stay. How else could she play with the marvelous son, Moses? Every day she would ride her bicycle over to Moses' house, which was a mile away in the dark section. They would climb trees in the park, and run around, playing make-believe. Even then, Sarah remembered with distaste, Carmine had finked out. In fact, maybe Carmine was never ever much help. She simply gave the illusion of being a friend.

Sarah stood tapping her fingers on the pay phone, thinking about Carmine. She had loved Carmine. Carmine would slip her pieces of raw potato, strictly forbidden by Mrs. Green, but deeply adored by Sarah. But actually when she had gone to her at a moment of deepest trouble, she had finked out.

She and Moses had been playing chicky on their bicycles when he suddenly blurted out, "I'm black and you're white. I'm black and you're white. You're nothing but a white girl, a paleface."

Sarah was eight years old and had never given the subject much thought. She got right off her bicycle and inspected her hands and arms. She held them out in the strong summer light and had a long look. "No," she said, "no."

"Oh yes," he insisted, "yes."

"No," she said, "I'm more yellow."

"You're a paleface."

"You're a liar," she said, "I'm yellow."

"Huh!" he grimaced.

She pedaled off, feeling miserable. Something wasn't right. "You're mean," she shouted, beginning to cry. "I'm going home."

"I don't care," he said. "You're white"—he laughed—"and you didn't even know it, stupid."

"I hate you," she shouted. "I hate your guts, it's not true." She dropped her bicycle and ran into the house where Carmine was dreamily folding sheets.

"Moses is a bad boy," Sarah said, "he's a mean wild Indian."

"What?" Carmine said.

"He says I'm white and he's black and it's not fair," Sarah shouted, her body shaking with rage.

"He's teasing you, child," Carmine said. "Want a cookie, or a piece of raw potato? Stop all that fussing and whining, child. Right now!"

"He's a liar," Sarah said.

Carmine put her large, square hands on Sarah's cheek.

"It's the God's truth," she said. "You sure are white."

"It's true?" Sarah said, the tears splashing out of her eyes.

And now Carmine had done it again.

Sarah paid for the coffee and donut and walked outside. Crap, there must be an easy way to make money, aside from sweating yourself into bananas fever over it. She strolled calmly through the midday crowds. The best thing was to take a nice, slow walk, cool down and think clearly. She could always work as a salesgirl in a store or even as a junior model. She stopped and gazed at her small, shapely body in the window of a record store. She looked rather well. She pressed closer to the window to see whether her eyes were green in the reflection. They weren't. The thought of working as a model made her want to scream. Everyone knew models were insipid, vacant-minded, off-the-wall, sort of, like waitresses. Somehow the category couldn't contain her. One could do better than that. She'd rather work in a record store, where, at least, a few hippies might come in to exhibit themselves. It might be vaguely amusing.

Sarah looked through the window. Inside the well-stocked store were numerous tables covered with albums. In the middle of the room was a jazz table. One of the albums said BIRD in large letters.

"Charlie Parker," she said. If she bought a Bird album she would be minus five dollars, which she could ill afford to be minus. Nevertheless, drawn to the cover, she walked into the store.

It appeared to be empty. "Anyone home?" she said, peering under one of the tables. "Hey!" she called, "where are the gnomes, the troglodites?" There was no response. She shrugged her shoulders and began to shove the album into the greenbookbag. Why bother paying for it? Who would know the difference? Before she could manage to push the album all the way, the door opened and a kid came in. Hastily, she threw it back on the table. Stealing was no good if you were caught.

The kid was wearing a striped red-and-black trousers suit with a white turtleneck sweater. The jacket was covered with medals and the trousers were bell bottom. Who did he think he was?

"Yes," she said. She might as well impersonate a salesgirl. What if he had seen her boosting the album? "May I help you?" she asked. He did have a nerve going around the way he did. It was a wonder he wasn't arrested. His black hair fell in soft ringlets to his shoulders. His appearance was designed as a sheer put-on.

"What are you gaping at?" he said rudely. He was an outrage.

"Nothing," Sarah said, "it's just, you sort of match this album cover." She pointed to the Bird album, which was done in a red-and-black stripe motif. "See?" she said.

"Well," he said, "I'm looking for The Boss Pornographers record if you don't mind. And could you find it quickly. Just give it to me and I'll leave. I came all the way down from Huntington Woods to get this record so my group can listen. They're waiting outside for me. We're going to do a record date this afternoon so could you find it quickly?"

He was certainly long-winded for a little kid. A record date? This kid was doing record dates?

"It's under religious music," the kid said, noticing Sarah wasn't moving, just standing there looking at him with a funny look in her eye. "The Boss Pornographers," he said. "It's LSD music to wig out by. I mean that's the full name."

Sarah began searching through the table marked RELIGIOUS and after a few seconds dragged out the album. "That'll be five dollars exactly," she said. She handed the kid the album.

"What's LSD music?" she said, annoyed she sounded square. The kid jiggled his identification bracelet around self-consciously. "I couldn't say," he said huffily and gave her a five-dollar bill.

"I see you're wearing a skull-and-crossbones ring," Sarah said. Why hadn't she noticed before?

"Yeah," he said, "so?"

"Here, I'll give you a paper bag for the album. What is that ring?" she said as pleasantly as possible. If she were sweet to him, could she wring some information out of him? The ring glittered on his little finger, the red eyes sparkling seductively.

"What does it mean?" she said, putting the album in a bag she found behind the counter.

"It's from my school," he said. "I'm in the ninth grade at Country Day School. A lot of us have these rings."

"Oh," she said, "did you know a Duncan Bones?"

"No, and I know everyone at the school."

"He was there a long time ago, I suppose," Sarah said. There was something very irritating about this kid. "Didn't you ever hear of him?"

"No," he said and reached into his sweater to extract a triangular-shaped pendant hanging on a chain.

"Rich boys go there," he said. "Is he rich?"

"Yes," she said, "he's very rich."

"It's a pretty *In* school," he said. "It's hard to be admitted. You have to take a test."

"What is that ring?" Sarah said, casually.

"I can't tell you," he said. "It relates to school."

"Okay, okay," she said, "but if you tell me, I'll give you back your five dollars and you can just trot your little self right out of here and only you and God will know the difference."

The kid was distrustful. "I don't know," he said.

"Come on, sugar," Sarah said, "don't be afraid. I'll give your money back and you still have the album."

The kid looked down. "It represents virginity," he said. "I don't like telling you. It's supposed to be secret like that society for boys with high I.Q.'s, the Mensa society."

"No kidding," Sarah said. "I should have known. Virginity? This isn't a put-on is it?"

"No, it's the truth," the kid said. "I wouldn't lie."

"You mean you're still a virgin?" Sarah said. "How can you admit to it? How can you wear such a silly ring, that sillyass ring?" He didn't look too stupid, but he had to be a moron if he agreed to wearing it.

"I'm only fourteen," he said. "It's a club, a secret club. But I can't tell you any more. I have to go."

"Gee, everyone's in a mad hurry today. Anyway, fourteen isn't so young. You're old enough not to be a virgin. You ought to be ashamed."

The kid twisted up his face in an ugly way. "Yeah, well if I met a chick who wasn't so hostile, maybe I could change that."

"Hostile?" Sarah said. They were the same height, which annoyed her. "Hostile?" she said. "Bostile, schmostile, where do you come by such jerky words?"

"My father's a psychiatrist," he said, "and are you going to give me that money back like you said or am I going to punch you right in the teat?"

Sarah handed back the money. "All right," she said.

"Thanks a whole big bunch." He ran out, holding the paper bag tightly.

Virginity? In other words, John had been a virgin when they met? Is that why he wore the ring? This would explain George's sulky, bad-tempered moods. Any virgin over seventeen must be a nervous wreck. Virgins were irritable people. But it was hard to believe John was a virgin. Hadn't he told her otherwise? Maybe the wearing of the ring simply meant the person wasn't getting laid. She would have to ask him for an explanation.

She watched the kid dart down the street toward a car parked nearby, spilling over with awful teenybopper types. As she stood at the door, a man appeared and looked in. He gazed at her and then opened the door. "What are you doing here?" he said. "I thought I locked the door before I went to lunch." He had a soft voice and graying temples. Handsome for an older man. She smiled. "Oh!" she said, "are you the manager?"

"Owner," he said, going behind the counter and checking the cash register. "I guess I left it locked," he said, absently.

"Were there any customers besides you?"

"No, there weren't," Sarah lied coquettishly.

"I've been at the other store," he said, wondering whether the painters were doing any work or sitting on their bottoms drinking beer. "I'm expanding," he added.

"Oh," Sarah said, "you'll need someone to work here if you're at the other store, won't you?"

"Yes," he said, "I guess so."

"Well, I came in to apply for a job. I know all about music, it's my field. I'm at Wayne University at night. A music major."

He looked at her. "How much do you want? I can't pay much."

"Eighty-five," she said. "It would do."

"I don't come in till ten in the morning," he said. "I have to walk the dogs."

"Dogs?" Sarah said, "how many?"

"Five dobermans and a cocker," he said, unbuttoning his gray tweed jacket. "It's warm in here."

"Yeah," Sarah agreed. He wasn't too bad. He was attractive in an older way with his graying hair and his nice tweedy jacket. He looked like a professor.

"I have a cat named Clytemnestra," she said. "She eats furniture."

"Hmmm, a good name," he said and reached into his back pocket to take out a pipe.

"I have good references," she said.

"Could you come in tomorrow," he said, "and we'll try you. I don't know if there's enough work."

"Good," Sarah said. "What's your name, Mr.?"

"Green," he said, puffing on his pipe. "Jack Green."

"Jack Green," Sarah said. "That's my name, I'm a Green. I'm Sarah Green."

"A coincidence," he said. "A good name, too." He seemed a little distracted, kind of a Mr. Magoo type, but sweet. She felt a curious excitement. Wasn't she just the luckiest lady alive! Here she was in search of a job and suddenly out of the blue Jack Green appeared to give her one. And in a record store, which wasn't too disgusting. She could forget about the betrayal by Jenny and Carmine, completely forget about it, and go on loving them in spite of their rotten behavior.

"What a groovy coincidence," she said. "Are you Jewish, too?"

"No," he said, "sorry."

"Oh, don't sweat it!" she said.

21

SARAH SAT on the steps outside Lawrence Tech waiting for the sartorial figure of Mr. Duncan Bones to come through the door and change her life. She had phoned John and informed him he was not to pick her up after classes. She was determined to have her rendezvous with Mr. Duncan Bones. No one and nothing was going to interfere. John seemed put out, but she convinced him she had to go straight home due to utter exhaustion. John was a dear in his way, his straight-arrow way. Fortunately, she could dominate and control him so he didn't give her much trouble. It was one of the really nice, charming things about John that she could manipulate him.

Mr. Duncan Bones came liltingly through the door.

"So kind of you to wait," he said. "I was detained with Mr. Leeway."

"I dig your shoes," Sarah said, touching the well-polished pointed toe of his left shoe.

"Last year in Florence, you sweet thing," he lisped.

"I'm not such a sweet thing," she said. "You should know what you're dealing with. I hate illusion."

"And so grown-up and smart," he said, "so terribly grown-up." He bent down and patted her head. "Where have you been, you darling girl?" Sarah looked up at him. He did have a wonderful aristocratic face with his finely chiseled nose, the high forehead, the intelligent eyes.

"Did you go to Country Day School?" she said.

"Country Day School," he said. "No, why do you ask such a passionless question? I'm not even from these parts."

"I thought you might have gone there, that's all," Sarah said.

"Let's go right this minute to my apartment and have a refreshing drink," he said, helping her up. "Would you like?"

"I'm not sure," Sarah said.

"Have no fears," he said. "I shan't rape you."

"Okay, let's go," Sarah said, feeling faintly disappointed. She knew undressed he must be divine, a god with lean muscles, a magnificent waist and strong, well-shaped legs. It might be necessary to seduce him.

"A few days more and high school is over," she sighed.

"A turning point," he said, leading her to the car, which was parked in front of the school. He held the door open for her. "It's an old Chrysler," he said.

She moaned. "Elegant, ooooh, elegant."

"I suppose you're excited about graduating and going on to college?"

"No," Sarah said, "it's all a bore. I'm not going to college. I can't wait to get it over. The teachers, present company excluded, of course, are dolts. We're on different wave lengths."

"Yes," he said, "it's important to be on the same wave length." He smiled at her, his warm, brown eyes flitting over her delicate upturned face. "You're not a Marxist, are you?" he said.

"No," Sarah said, "I don't think so. What do you mean?"

"Nothing, my pet," he said, turning on the ignition, "nothing. Sometimes, you sound like a Marxist."

"I don't even know what it is," she said.

"You'll love my apartment," he said. "I live in a lovely new building on the river."

"Umm, crazy!"

22

"YOU'RE RIGHT," Sarah said with admiration, "it's beautiful. I've never seen a pad like this!" She stroked the red flocked wallpaper in Mr. Duncan Bones' vestibule, then walked into the large living room, where vases filled with blue flowers were everywhere, their sweet fragrance penetrating the air.

"Oh! Louvers!" she exclaimed, rushing to the big bay window and touching the shutters. "It's like a New York pad, isn't it?"

"You have a superior awareness," Mr. Duncan Bones said. "What an aesthetic girl you are."

"Do you mind fresh air?" she said, parting the shutters and pulling up the window.

He inhaled, stretching his arms and expanding his chest. "Fine," he breathed. "The weather is becoming summer, isn't it, my pet? I hope we may see each other this summer. Where will you be?"

"I don't know. I'm saving money to go to Cambridge, maybe." She picked up a newspaper. "*Women's Wear Daily?* What's this?"

"Oh," he said, taking the paper out of her hand. "My sister, Greta, is in the business. She's a buyer. A clothing buyer."

Sarah walked across the living room and stood in front of an antique desk. "I like lithography," she said, examining two lithographs hanging over the desk. She sighed. Everything surrounding Mr. Duncan Bones was beautiful. Was she in love with him?

He touched her back. "Shall we sit over here?" he said. "It's so snug." He took her hand and led her to a white brocaded satin couch.

"Here," he said, gently pushing her into the couch. Surreptitiously, she tugged on her red silk micro skirt so it wouldn't expose the tops of her fishnet stockings, which she had caught up with ridiculous rubber bands so they couldn't fall.

"First, a drink," he said. "In my eagerness to sit next to you and stroke your beautiful hair, I forgot."

He patted her hair. "Come," he said. She arose and followed his graceful form into the kitchen, where numerous gleaming copper pans were arranged on the wall.

"Gorgeous," she gasped. "What taste you have! It's too much!"

Mr. Duncan Bones began to laugh, tossing his head back and clapping his hands together in what she observed was a strangely feminine gesture. But oh well, it fit into his beautiful side. Men with sensitivity were a little like women.

"You sound like a transvestite I know," he said.

"Trans what?" Sarah said and ran her finger down a pan making a scratchy sound.

"Transvestite," he said, taking a tray of ice cubes out of the freezer. "I'll make you a lovely drink, trust me." He poured gin into a glass, stirred in something green and tossed in a cherry.

"I'm not much of a drinker," she said, "but I love cherries."

Mr. Duncan Bones turned and looked at her, amused.

"Sweets to the sweets," he said.

"Shakespeare," Sarah said, wondering what he meant. "Do you have a maid?"

"My sister cleans." He took a long swallow. "It's good," he said and handed her the glass.

It seemed odd to Sarah his sister cleaned the pad. It was her observation sisters and brothers usually didn't get along very well. When would a career girl find the time to clean a pad? It was funny. Did she make a special trip? Why would she be bothered?

"Your sister comes here to clean?" she said. It was possible, of course. Maybe she was crazy about him and liked doing favors. He was adorable.

Sarah's only direct experience with brothers and sisters and the intricacies of their relationships was with her mother's first cousins who lived in Louisville.

Mr. Duncan Bones chewed the cherry. "Yes," he said, "she comes to clean for me." He leaned against the cupboard with his hand on his hip, scrutinizing her.

Sarah saw her cousins on the average of once every two years. If she saw them in the street she wouldn't recognize them. Gretchen Samuels was a year younger than her brother Paul, but she was almost a foot taller, and regularly beat the crap out of him. At sixteen, Paul enlisted in the Army and was sent immediately to Vietnam, where he flourished in the mud. Anything, as long as he was away from the sadistic Gretchen. He was in Vietnam for one year and was sent home with a psychiatric discharge.

The only letter Sarah ever received from a relative was from Gretchen. How could she ever forget it? It said:

> Dear Sarah,
>   I hate Paul's guts. He's a prick.

This was before Paul enlisted. Sarah showed the letter to her mother to find out what prick meant, but Mrs. Green didn't know.

Of course, brothers and sisters were rotten to each other, as were relatives in general. Aunt Ruth and Mrs. Green were a perfect example. Battling sisters-in-law. Mrs. Green had always been suspicious of Aunt Ruth and when she was on her second divorce from the Seventh Day Adventist milkman, finally Mrs. Green wouldn't allow her to enter the house.

"You must have a close relationship with your sib," Sarah said. Family relations were such a monumental drag, so tedious, so unrewarding. There ought to be a special list for the really dullass, insular members of the family. Mrs. Green would be at the very top. She hadn't spoken to her younger brother, Milton, in twenty years. The Raunchy Drag Relatives List seemed to fit, or maybe The Rancid Drag Relatives List.

"The bedroom," Mr. Duncan Bones was saying, "would you like to see the bedroom?"

"Sure," Sarah said, "why not?" She followed him obligingly out of the room. The bedroom was black as a crypt with no light coming through the windows. He stood for a moment in the darkened room, then, dramatically as an actor in a play, switched on the light to reveal an immense bed covered in an elaborate fringed peacock-blue bedspread.

"Pretty," Sarah said, looking around the room. The walls were mirrored.

"Oh!" she said. "There are ten thousand of me, what a splendid idea!"

"We thought so," Mr. Duncan Bones said.

"We?" Sarah said, surveying her ankles in one of the mirrors. The micro skirt looked rather good and the fishnet stockings were gorgeous.

"My sister and I," he said. "She did most of it, actually."

"Really?"

"Yes, the interior design," he said, finishing off the drink and setting the glass down on an elegant antique table. "She's good in interior design."

"An interior decorator?"

"No, dear girl," Mr. Duncan Bones said, "interior design. There's a vast difference." He smiled. "I could teach you so many things, dear girl, if you would only let me."

"May I see your clothes?" Sarah said skeptically and wondering what prompted men to say such cornball things. Did they think it was an obligation of some kind? She moved her hips slightly in a mild frug motion and stuck her tongue out at Mr. Duncan Bones.

"Don't, dear girl," he said, "not in that skirt. It's not fair."

"Okay, Dad," she said, walking toward the closet. "I want to see your clothes. I like them. They're interesting for Detroit. Did you ever notice the way people dress here? It's so boring. I've seen pictures of the way the mods dress in England and it's absolutely refreshing. The men wear flowered shirts and wide op ties and long hair and the chicks wear flowered shirts, wide op ties and long hair. I dig the scene. New York too, of course," she said knowingly, "and I do want to see your things."

Mr. Duncan Bones posed himself like a film idol in front of the closet mirror. He put one polished hand on his hip. "Now my dear girl," he said, "why such a silly thing. I think it's a bit *petit bourgeois*. Besides they're in the other room."

Sarah felt insulted. *Petit bourgeois?* Certainly not she. She was anything but bourgeois, petit or grand. It seemed rather unfair, especially since he didn't know her terribly well. Couldn't he tell automatically she was classless, stateless, homeless, establishmentless, schoolless, moneyless, etc. etc. etc.?

"Now come away my pet, come away from such mundane materialistic things as clothes. Let us sit upon the cozy couch and

I'll tell you beautiful stories about love. I'll even recite the *Arabian Nights*."

"You're super, Mr. Bones," Sarah said seductively and smiled at herself in one of the mirrors. She popped the cherry into her mouth and chewed vigorously.

"Call me Duncan, we're not in academia now, we're standing in my bedroom."

Sarah felt a surge of excitement pass through her body. He was so attractive, so sexy. Her kneecaps were shaky. Was he going to kiss her? When was he going to hold her in his lovely swimmer's arms?

"Another drink?" he said politely, touching her arm. "I see your drink is almost finished. Let me freshen it up for you."

"Not yet," Sarah said. She was beginning to feel tipsy. "What's in this closet?" she said and flung open the door. "Hey, what's this? Your sister's clothes?"

"I told you, my sweet," he said, "not to open the door. It's exactly like Pandora's box and all the evil in the world will come flying at you and get hold of you. Come," he said, taking her hand, "this way."

"You mean your sister actually lives here with you?" she said, trying to figure out where she slept. The couch in the living room was not a bed. And since she was standing in the only bedroom with the only bed, it was evident the sister shared it with Duncan.

"Is her name Bones?" Sarah said.

"Yes," he said and closed the closet door. "Now come, dear girl."

"She must get a nice, fat discount on these clothes if she's in the business," Sarah said. "Why this is a Pucci!" She took a dress off a hanger and held it up to herself. "It's a Pucci!" she exclaimed. "Hey there are lots of Puccis. Too bad you're a real friend. Couldn't I boost just one?"

"You wouldn't steal, would you?" Mr. Duncan Bones said in awe.

"Oh no," Sarah said, remembering the time she and Jenny visited The J. L. Hudson Company and went on a shopping spree. It was wintertime and bitter cold and she really felt she needed a couple of warm winter suits. Jenny agreed to go shopping after school and, armed with enormous shopping bags, they descended on the subteen department. Sarah exited wearing an expensive green tweed suit under her dress. Jenny was too chicken to go as far but she managed to slip three pairs of bell bottoms and two cashmere sweaters into the bag.

Everything would have been cool except Mrs. Oliver discovered the clothes and had a conniption. She phoned Mrs. Green, making a fantastic scene on the telephone. Mrs. Green confronted Sarah, a glass of cold water in her hand. They were forced to return the clothes, going back to the subteen department and sneaking all the clothes onto the racks.

"It's exactly my size," Sarah said and put it back in the closet. She had read in anthropology books about incest. It was nothing new. Through the ages people committed incest. She knew it though she had never actually encountered the real situation. And here she was looking at a person who was in the process of doing this peculiar thing. Poor Mr. Duncan Bones. She had discovered his fatal flaw and so quickly. Perhaps he was attracted to Sarah because she was the same size as his sister. What he needed, obviously, was a love cure. Then he could cast away his sister, take his place in the mainstream of civilization and give the Puccis to Sarah.

"I'll fix another drink, you're ready?" he said.

"All right," Sarah agreed and drained her glass.

"Wait, my pet, in the living room. I'll bring you a lovely surprise." He put his arm around her waist for a moment and smiled deep, deep into her eyes. And was he wearing a kind of ambrosia? A faint smell of something interesting escaped his body. She sniffed the air. Chanel Number Five? Impossible! Men didn't wear Chanel, did they? It must be something else, though she could have sworn.

He escorted her into the living room, fluffed up the pillows on the couch, turned on some music and went to fetch drinks. Sinking into the comfort of the couch and settling her feet on the coffee table, she began to feel drowsy and closed her eyes. She could drift easily into a sleep, a deep sleep. The liquor definitely had clouded her brain. She heard Mr. Duncan Bones' soft footsteps and opened her eyes. Resplendent in a red fox fur smoking jacket, he stood there with two gigantic drinks in his hands.

"My," she said, "you're a regular geisha girl." How divine, to wear red fox. It was so seductive, so sexual. How many people would have the imagination to wear fur? And would he wear it to bed? Would he rub up against her with the red fur? Or maybe let her wear it. It would be a fun innovation.

"You are beautiful," Mr. Duncan Bones said. "I love you. We shall be married. You in a long white dress for your virginity and I in a tuxedo for my wisdom."

Sarah watched him uncomfortably. Should she tell him? Did she owe it to him? Why did men always want virgins? They want to be the first. None of his business, to hell with it! She could fake it, anyway. What was such a big deal about being a virgin? It was all a hoax, a fraud parents affixed upon you to scare you away from fornicating. It was jealousy, sheer jealousy. Parents didn't want you to have the pleasure they were missing.

"It's so good being with an educated man," Sarah said. "I've thought about being a teacher but I'm not going to college. It's such a supreme drag. But men should be educated." She could pretend to be a virgin.

"I want my Master's," he said, sitting next to her, "but can't find the time."

"Did you attend college in the East?" Sarah said, imagining him captain of the crew team, flexing his muscles for the young admiring girls.

"No," he said, "I didn't." She wanted to question him further but a cold nasty stubborn expression suddenly appeared on his face. Maybe he went to Georgia Polytech and was ashamed?

"Drink," he said, "drink this ambrosia from the gods."

"No," Sarah said, "not now."

"I think I've failed you in a sense," he said. "Do you want to go home?"

"No," she said, "not yet."

Mr. Duncan Bones put his arm around her and pressed her to him in a great bear hug. The fur brushed against her cheek.

"Allow me to kiss you," he said.

"I don't think so," she said, pushing him away. "Let's wait till we know each other better." In his aristocratic, Henry James manner, he was rather persistent. She would like to kiss him but the sickening image of the sister lying next to him in that immense bed prevented her.

"I don't think so," she repeated.

"And this fiancé of yours," he said, "you're not really going to marry him? You couldn't marry a person who wore blue jeans, could you?"

"Yeah, I could," Sarah said. Did he have to remind her of John? She had succeeded so well in forgetting him.

"Let's not discuss it," she said, "please." If Mr. Duncan Bones didn't go to school in the East, and didn't even have a Master's and wasn't from Detroit, where was he from?

"You're English nobility?" she said. She thought she might suddenly fall asleep like Alice in Wonderland.

"Yes," he said and ripped off the fur jacket. There was nothing underneath. He was absolutely stark naked and across his chest were painted pictures of nude women. He started unbuttoning his pants, one button at a time, very slowly, at the same time rolling his large brown eyes at Sarah. What did it mean? It was scary. He pulled his pants down and let them hang around his ankles and did a funny little dance. Sarah watched with interest. She hadn't expected him to behave in such an unconventional fashion, but it was all right. She didn't really mind. When she saw he wasn't going to do anything to really frighten her, she didn't mind at all.

"You are so feminine," he said, touching her shoulder and winking. Was it joke? Didn't he mean it? She began to laugh. The whole thing seemed terribly amusing.

"Are you asleep?" Mr. Duncan Bones said. "Wake up." He shook her.

"I'm not asleep, I'm not asleep," she assured him and opened her eyes to find a small woman with short blond curls leaning over her and shaking her. Oddly, Mr. Duncan Bones was wearing all his clothes.

"Who are you?" the woman said. Sarah stared around her. Where was she?

"Oh, crap," she said. "I fell sound asleep in Mr. Duncan Bones' living room."

"It seems so," the woman said. Sarah noticed an edge of sarcasm in her voice. Mr. Duncan Bones slipped out of the living room.

"I was visiting," Sarah said, soothing the woman, who must be Greta, the sister.

"I can see," the woman said.

"You're a Bones," Sarah said.

"That's right," she said, "where's Duncan? I left my bags in the vestibule."

"I guess he's in the kitchen," Sarah said, "making drinks."

"No doubt," she said. "And who are you, prithee?"

"I'm Sarah Green," Sarah said. "I'm Mr. Bones' student. An all A student, of course," she said.

"You're a little young, aren't you?"

"To be in high school," Sarah said. What was she getting at, anyway? The utter fucking nerve! Sarah knew she appeared young but not that young. No one ever thought she was younger than high school age.

"Yes, young for Duncan," the woman said, angrily. "Okay, so he doesn't like his contemporaries, it's still pushing it a little."

"How old is he?" Sarah said.

"Forty," the woman said.

"My goodness, lord love a duck," Mr. Duncan Bones said, flying out of the kitchen, holding two more drinks. "Greta, darling, I didn't expect you until tomorrow. Why didn't you phone?" He shoved one of the drinks into her hand. "Take this, my pet, it'll do you good. This is Sarah Green, one of my students. I was helping her with her homework."

"How do you do," Greta said coldly.

"We're the same size. I knew it," Sarah said, surveying Greta's diminutive form.

"Now, Sarah," Mr. Duncan Bones said quickly, "I think it's time to take you home. It's long past your bedtime."

"Bedtime?" Sarah said. "Are you wigging out? I go to bed at three in the morning, sugar."

"Time for children to be in bed," Greta echoed, walking into the hall for her suitcases.

"I'll lift them," Mr. Duncan Bones said with alacrity, springing into the hallway. "Sarah, you wait for me in the car like a good girl."

Was he going to carry the suitcases into the bedroom? Was he actually going to have the brazen nerve to carry them in there in front of her? The truth will out. Had he no shame? Didn't he know every tribe in the world, even the most primitive had an incest taboo? He was a biologist, after all, one would think he'd know such basic information.

He boosted the suitcases into the air and with one well-coordinated gesture threw them from the vestibule into the bedroom where they landed smack in the middle of the bed.

"Did you have to throw them, Duncan?" Greta said annoyed. "I think I've had about enough of this nonsense."

"Greta, love," he said, rushing over to her and kissing her neck, "don't be mad at Duncy. Duncy loves you. Duncy was just having a bit of indulgence, that's all."

"Get this child out of here, will you?" Greta said.

Sarah looked stricken. "Miss Bones," she said, "I'm not a child, and your brother invited me here as his guest. You have some nerve barging into his pad like this, anyway, so you can make your dirty piggies."

Greta wheeled around, her round, blue eyes wild with rage. "Miss Bones, Miss Bones, Miss Bones," she said, her teeth clenched together. "It's not Miss Bones, it's *Mrs.* Bones, and he's not my brother." She made a rapid sweeping movement with her hand, which knocked the drinks off an end table, causing the cherries to spill over the brocaded white couch and the liquid to stream across the pale rose carpeting. "And everything in this apartment is mine, everything, everything, including him." She pointed a sharply filed fingernail at Mr. Duncan Bones who gingerly plucked a piece of lint off his red-fox fur jacket.

23

"I WOULD HAVE given a leg, an arm, anything to graduate from school and this one don't want to go to her own graduation. I don't understand. It's a *schande*," Mrs. Green was saying, perched like a mountain on the edge of Mr. Green's hospital bed. His face was turned to his pillow so his audience, Sarah, John, Tilly, George and Mrs. Green, couldn't see the melancholy that had, only ten minutes before, seized him.

"A shawnda?" Tilly said.

"A shame, she means," Sarah explained. "It's Yiddish or Lower Slobovian or something."

"I see," Tilly said. "They send you the diploma in the mail, don't they?"

"So?" Mrs. Green said, "it's not the same. She don't know what she's missing, my crazy daughter."

"*Mishugenah*," Sarah said.

George looked at his watch. "I have to go," he said sullenly. "I'm meeting Connie at her house. And I'm never late. That's why I'm a good driver."

"So go?" Sarah said, noticing the skull-and-crossbones ring was gone from his finger. Connie and George must have made it since she had seen them last.

"I guess you're not a virgin anymore," she said, wondering whether they had tied Connie's thick red hair back before they did it. Was her pubic hair red, too?

"Huh," George said.

"Never mind," she said. "I'll tell you later."

"Bye, Mr. Green, hope you feel better," he said.

Mr. Green grunted.

"Speak up!" Mrs. Green said, "he don't hear you."

"Good-bye," Mr. Green said, turning over to confront them, tears in his eyes.

"What's the matter, Mr. Green?" George said.

"Daddy, what's the matter," Sarah said. "Should we call the doctor? What's wrong?"

"I don't know, I don't know," he said weakly, the tears running down his face. "I wanted to go to my daughter's graduation but no, God in heaven won't grant me this one favor, this one favor to a poor old man."

Sarah looked at John. "But, Daddy, I'm not even going, I'm not going, either. Don't be sad, you'll come home soon and then John will go away to Cambridge."

Mr. Green smiled. "When is he going?" he said.

"In a week, I think," Sarah said.

"He's right here in front of you, Mr. Green, he can tell you," Tilly said.

"I'm going in a few days if anyone is interested," John said, glancing at Sarah, wondering why she had been so inattentive recently.

"And leaving me to the wolves," Sarah said.

"I've got to go," George repeated. "Bye, Mr. Green, hope you feel better." He ran from the room into the hall, where they could hear him colliding with someone.

In a moment the nurse marched into the room, her cap askew but nevertheless a starched and glistening white smile plastered on her face.

"Temperature time," she said, "it's our temperature time." She waved a thermometer around like a wand. "That boy nearly impaled me."

"I think we should leave Mr. Green to his privacy," Tilly said, dropping the veil of her hat over her eyes. "Let's have tea in the cafeteria. Won't that be fun?"

"Yes," Mrs. Green agreed, "tea."

"A bundle of fun," Sarah said. "Hey, Dad, where's Mr. Ginzberg?"

The melancholy expression gripped Mr. Green's face again. "He got out," he said. "He don't know what hit him. He got out for good."

"Now, dear, don't be morbid," Mrs. Green said, putting a fat arm over his stomach to comfort him.

The nurse hovered, eager to do her work.

"It's rectal, folks," she said, waving the thermometer.

24

"HURRY UP," TILLY said to John, who was walking behind with his arm around Sarah's waist. "Hurry up, we'll have a bite in the cafeteria, then we can visit Mr. Green again."

"Okay, okay," John said. "It takes five minutes to have a cup of tea."

"No sweat," Sarah said.

"Sarah, is that some nice talk in the hospital," Mrs. Green said sharply.

"It seems cool to me," Sarah said, poking John in the ribs. She gazed down the long silent hall.

"I hate gloom," she said, "hate."

"It's not so bad," Tilly said. "You should have seen the hospital the boys' father died in. It makes this place a heaven."

"We don't believe in heaven," Mrs. Green said, pressing hard on the elevator button, "or hell. Maybe you'd like to go to Temple some Friday night."

The elevator door opened and a thin, snaggle-toothed bald man scowled out.

"All right, who's been pressing the damned buzzer? In, in!" he ordered. "Get in! I ain't got all day." They crowded into the elevator and stood quietly.

"Yes, I'd go," Tilly said finally.

"Go where, Mother?" John said.

"To Temple," she said. The elevator operator frowned. "This elevator goes to the first floor and the basement," he said, stopping at the first floor, "and that's all."

"Is there a neighborhood bar?" Tilly said.

"A bar?" Mrs. Green said suspiciously. "What kind of bar?" She scratched the mole on her cheek, and felt a severe hunger pain tear through her intestines. Dr. Kantrowitzsky had put her on a crash diet. All she ate the entire day was two eggs, three pieces of toast for breakfast, a pear salad and jello for lunch and then a mid-afternoon snack of melba toast, honey and cottage cheese. And dinner was at least an hour away if they were going to return to Mr. Green's room. Could she maintain herself? A bar? Would they have something to nibble in a bar? She remembered there used to be hard-boiled eggs and pretzels in bars, but everything had changed so rapidly, it probably wasn't true anymore. In her day only men went to the bars, and usually only lower-class worker types. No businessmen ever went into a bar. Ever.

"What kind of bar?" she said.

"A bar bar," Sarah said, "a regular bar, a bar where people are loaded."

"I thought a bit of sherry would be nice," Tilly said, "just a smidge. That's all I want. To get the smell of the hospital out of my nose."

"Don't you want tea?" Mrs. Green said. "They have good tea in the cafeteria. And jelly crackers."

"Groovy," Sarah said, "but we all want a drink. You can come, too, Mom. It's okay, they'll let you in. It'll do you good."

"Put hair on your chest," John whispered in Sarah's ear.

"It's already there," Sarah said.

Mrs. Green gave a long hungry sigh. "They're *schikurem*," she said, "they're all *schikurem*." They led her outside, down the hospital steps and across the street to a bar.

"Let's sit at the bar," Sarah said. "I'd like to try it." She slung her purse over the shoulder of her lace blouse and hopped onto the stool. Mrs. Green looked around furtively. The bar was long and narrow and filled to capacity with various shapes and sizes. Everyone was thin. Even the middle-aged female bartender seemed thinner than Mrs. Green. How had she allowed them to bring her here.

"What'll you have?" the barmaid said, eyeing Sarah who had unfastened her hair and was twining it in and out of a brown wood ring she was wearing.

"Four sherries," John said.

"I'd like Scotch if no one minds," Tilly said.

"Three sherries and a Scotch," John said.

"That's a good-looking ring," the barmaid said to Sarah.

"Hopi Indian," Sarah said, lighting up one of her imported cigars.

"Not in here." Mrs. Green was urgent. "It's not good manners, Sarah."

She ignored her mother and dragged on the cigar.

"You got some crackers?" Mrs. Green said.

"Yeah, lady," the barmaid said and threw a greasy packet of crackers across the bar. Mrs Green tore open the packet and shoved the crackers into her mouth.

"I'm starved," she said, "starved. Dr. Kantrowitzsky is a good man but he don't know about diets."

"Oh, you poor thing," Tilly said, crossing her thin arms on the bar, "you poor thing, how terrible! You must be starving."

"God, what I wouldn't do for a piece of matzo and chicken fat right this second," Mrs. Green said. "Or a steak wouldn't be so bad."

The barmaid put the Scotch and three sherries down in front of them. "Good-looking blouse," she said to Sarah. "But ain't you kind of young to be in here? They sure start young, nowadays," she said, chuckling.

Sarah touched the sleeve of her lace blouse. She had run out that very day and charged it to Tilly. John had slipped her the charge plate and told her it was all right to use it for a while. He would owe it to his mother. Sarah looked at her reflection in the dimly lit mirror. She was pretty. Mr. Duncan Bones had thought so. She sighed. The fucking nerve of that crass, insolent woman crashing into the pad and breaking up the nice relationship she had established with Mr. Duncan Bones. He ought to get rid of her. It was such a pity that such a fascinating man was with such a nothing woman. All she had, really, were clothes. She wasn't gorgeous, brilliant or even sexy. Too bad all the wrong people had all the beautiful original clothes. They would have looked so much better on her.

"Ain't you kind of young?" the barmaid insisted in her gruff voice.

"I'm of age," Sarah lied. "I've proof." She reached into her purse to drag out her identification, but the barmaid reached out a square heavy hand. "No, no," she said, "no, I mean young for this place. This is a bad joint, it ain't the Ritz."

"I'll have another teeny weeny Scotch," Tilly said, "just a smidge more."

"I mean ain't you in the wrong place?" the barmaid said, pouring Scotch into Tilly's glass, her eyes focused on Sarah. "I can see these other broads in here, but not you," she said.

"I'll have another sherry," John said. He had been thinking about the summer in Cambridge and not paying any attention to the barmaid. Everything had been worked out to his liking. He got the program he wanted, the right hours, his apartment was walking distance from campus. It would be fine. There was only one rub. Sarah. The idea of leaving her to the local wolves could upset his summer. What would she be doing? She wasn't going to sit around like Penelope waiting for Ulysses, that was certain. Her job would keep her occupied during the day, but how about the evenings, the long, hot summer evenings? Her parents had no control over her, she could con them easily. "Give me another sherry," he said. Unfortunately, he didn't have the time to devote to her. It was either get through the degree and ignore her or devote himself to her and flunk. He had put too much effort into his education to give it up for anyone. At least Suzanne Belier knew when to keep her mouth shut. Sarah was a full-fledged pain-in-the-neck, strong-willed creature. But he still would worry that she might be with another guy.

"Another sherry," he said.

"All right, all right, keep your pants on," the barmaid barked.

"Three?" Mrs. Green said, "three sherries? You'll turn into a drunkard." She sipped her drink reluctantly. It tasted bitter. What did these *goyem* see in drinking? She looked around the room. At least there were no soiled, dirty men using dirty foul language. The room was filled with women, all standing around yapping like it was a Hadassah tea. A large, heavyset figure with gray hair caught her eye. She had a familiar *punim*. Who was she?

"Who's this?" she said, poking Sarah.

"No one I know," Sarah said, staring in the direction her mother was pointing. "My, my."

"I know the face, I know the face," Mrs. Green said excitedly.

"It's the lady doctor from your school. Remember? And see how *zoftik* she is." Mrs. Green felt pleased she had spotted someone overweight.

"I don't see anyone who fits your description, sugar," Sarah said.

"I know the face, remember? She was the one at your party wearing the *schmutzik* suit. The funny one."

"I'd like a quick one," Tilly said, holding out her glass.

John looked at his mother and shook his head. "That'll be your last," he said. "You've had enough." He looked at the barmaid. "This is her last," he said, "but I'll have another, please."

"No, son," Tilly said.

"At least there are no truck drivers in here," Mrs. Green said. The woman with the gray hair moved behind a pillar so her face was hidden.

"These are truck drivers," the barmaid said, her voice, a drill hammer.

Mrs. Green watched the barmaid with interest. She had a neat way of pouring the drinks. "How do you keep your weight down?" she asked, leaning over the bar so she could get a good look at just how fat she actually was.

The barmaid looked at her with hatred. "I keep away from you bull-daggers, that's how," she said.

John began to laugh. Sarah giggled. Some of the women, standing around in clusters, glanced up.

"What?" Mrs. Green said. "What did she say?" John clamped his hand to his mouth to keep from laughing.

"Tilly, what did she say?" Mrs. Green asked.

"I wouldn't mind another small one," Tilly said.

Mrs. Green chewed on a finger. "I don't understand," she said. The barmaid wasn't nice. There was something nasty about her. "Let's go back to the hospital," Mrs. Green said. "We don't want to miss your father."

"There's time," Sarah said. "Let's not freak out about it. Let's sit here and relax like civilized folk for two minutes, for Christ sake." It was disturbing to see Miss Crenshaw hiding behind that pillar. Old eagle eye Mrs. Green had spotted her right away. And she had spotted them. She was talking to a tall, mousy chick with tangled hair when their eyes connected. It looked as if she were drinking beer. Poor Miss Crenshaw, the school paid her so little she was reduced to drinking beer.

"The barlady, John," Tilly said. "I'm thirsty, and don't say you won't, son."

"No more," he said. "You've had enough." His mother's cheeks were purple. Was it a new kind of lipstick? She looked ill. Her eyes were bloodshot as though she had been weeping for months. It was probably all the alcohol in her system.

Tilly smiled sweetly at the air. John was such a dear, sweet boy, just like his father. He was so smart, so tolerant, much kinder than George. George was the bad-tempered one like her miserable side of the family. She hadn't even invited her miserable relatives to her own wedding for fear their bad tempers would embarrass everyone. Poor Arthur, dead before his time, shot by a burglar. It was all so absurd. It didn't seem possible.

Tilly reached up and straightened her veil. Poor dead Arthur. When the policeman came to the door and took her to the hospital, she prayed the entire way. It didn't do a God-damned bit of good and the next day she disavowed her religion, threw away her crucifix, and cursed the Church.

"Oh, don't be stupid, give your mother another drink," Sarah said.

"Isn't it time to leave?" Mrs. Green said, shifting hopefully on the stool. "The cafeteria is still open, maybe," she said. The bar was becoming noisier, and noisier, filling up with various shapes and sizes, all female.

"I want another drink, that's final," Tilly said to the barmaid.

"She doesn't want to go, are you blind?" Sarah said. "Leave her alone. Don't censure her."

"Yes," Tilly repeated, "leave me alone, don't censure me."

"Mother," John said, stubbornly, "we're leaving. Now get off that stool." He began to pry her loose.

"Let me go," she cried, pushing him away.

"I wouldn't mind some hot soup," Mrs. Green said.

"Shut up," Sarah said. Her voice rose above the din and prattle of the other women. They began to be aware of a fracas at the bar. And the room suddenly became quiet.

"Shut up," Sarah said. "And you," she said, grabbing John's arm, "let her go. Order her another drink. Right now!"

"Look here, you little bastard," the barmaid said, "what do you think you're doing in this joint? I ain't having this fuss, you get that through your thick head. And I'm the bouncer."

"Let's go," Mrs. Green said, "to the cafeteria."

"Yeah," the barmaid shouted, "get out, get out of here before we throw you out."

The women quieted down and listened to the little dramatic scene taking place.

"Fine," John said, angrily, "we're going. Here." He threw down a five-dollar bill and began to yank Tilly off the barstool.

"Don't let him take me," she said.

The barmaid glared. "It's six dollars, you little bastard," she said, "six dollars. I'll call the cops."

"One more, one more," Tilly said, "one quick one."

The women started to gather around, their mouths silent, their hands gripping cans of beer. Miss Crenshaw lurked in the background, her hand to her face.

"Get out of here," the barmaid shouted.

"Yes," a voice yelled, "get out of our bar." Three of them came forward. "Get out!" they chorused.

"This is plain nonsense," Mrs. Green said. "What do you mean get out? Do you think you own this place, maybe?" She stood on her elephantine legs and confronted a slender girl wearing a yellow raincoat. The barmaid picked up a bottle, smashing the neck off.

"What are you doing?" John said. "Come on, let's go."

"Okay, you broads," the barmaid said to the women, "the show is over. Start those mouths moving and move away. I'll take care of these customers with this." She held up the broken bottle. The women moved speedily away to the far corners of the room. Miss Crenshaw resumed her place behind a pillar, her cheeks aflame.

Sarah smiled. The adventure of the month. The sheer gorgeous fitness of things.

"Let's make it to a discothéque," she said, "there's action there, possibly." She yawned. "I think there's one around the corner. Like I think they have electronic piano and sitar."

"Are you leaving?" the barmaid said, walking around the bar.

"My God in heaven," Tilly said, finally observing the broken bottle. She pulled the veil over the top of her hat and burst into raging sobs. "My God," she wept, "the smell, the smell of that miserable hospital. Like your father. They didn't even send one rotten flower to the funeral. Nothing. The rotten devils! Was it my fault I didn't tell them where the funeral home was?" She buried her head in her son's chest and wailed. "Your aunts, your uncles, all no good!"

Mrs. Green ignored the hysteria and moved out of the vicinity of the broken bottle. "The cafeteria has kosher chicken," she said.

"Go home," the barmaid said, "go home or I'm ramming this in your faces. And you," she said, looking at Sarah in lovesick despair. "Go home before I cut you into little pieces."

Mrs. Green stretched her legs, shot the barmaid a murderous look and waddled to the door.

"We know when we're not wanted," she said.

John and Sarah supported Tilly to the door.

Outside, Tilly pushed them away.

"Leave me alone," she said.

"It wasn't so bad, not so noisy, till the end," Mrs. Green said.

"I wouldn't mind going to an orgy," Sarah said, looking around the dark street. Poor Miss Crenshaw was a little thinner. She really ought to die that frazzled hair. At least she seemed to have developed a life for herself.

"I don't have time to do anything but pack," John said irritably, hands shaking from the encounter with the barmaid. There was nothing like having a bit of broken glass in your face. He looked at Sarah with annoyance. Situations of the most bizarre kind always developed when he was with her. Maybe it was good they would be separated for a few months. It would give him time to figure out what hit him since they met.

"I'd like to go to an orgy," Sarah said, "where everyone is stark naked."

"Sarah," Mrs. Green said, "what a *pisk!* Sometimes I think you were adopted when I wasn't looking." Her stomach growled.

"What's that noise?" Tilly said, sadly.

"My brain," John said, "my brain."

25

MOSES STOOD IDLY BY the fake fireplace, resting his hand on the mantle.

"If I had known you weren't going to your own graduation, kiddo, I never would have made the trip," he said. Sarah was sprawled over a chair in an old bathrobe.

"You should have written," Jenny responded. She was cross-legged on the floor in front of the television set.

They had sat, stood and sprawled around the living room for an hour, waiting for Carmine and Mrs. Green to come from the grocery.

Jenny placed her long legs in a double-lotus position and inspected Moses' face. No wonder Sarah had kept him in the background, had refused to introduce her. He was a fantastic, beautiful specimen like an Ethiopian king. His skin was dark brown and smooth. His hair was thick and very curly and long. He was lean, with long fingers moving in delicate arcs as he spoke.

"Isn't your mother mad?" Moses said.

"Yeah, I suppose," Sarah said. She didn't like the idea of Moses and Jenny meeting in such a random way. In her fantasies, she had thought repeatedly of exactly how she would plan their meeting. She didn't want them to know each other too well. She loved Jenny and she loved Moses, but the idea they might actually dig each other filled her with pain. Moses was her property, after all, and had been since childhood. It was maddening. She had thought that someday she would have a dinner party, and everyone would dress formally. She would invite ten or twelve people to fancy private rooms at a hotel. There would be a large table and she would be at the head of it. On either side would be Jenny and

Moses, but she would be in between. There wouldn't be much opportunity for them to communicate. It was better this way. She could keep them, each, for herself.

She watched the two of them talking. It was maddening. They seemed to have a lot to say. Moses was available to her, for advice, for suggestions, and sometimes, for helping expedite wild schemes. She didn't want to share him, not with anyone.

But perhaps Jenny hadn't noticed how special he was. She seemed interested, but not fascinated. So it might be all right. They would have their little talk. Perhaps they were just socializing, and in a day or so, Moses would head back to school. They would never meet again.

"How far do you have to go?" Jenny was saying. She unfastened the top button on her blouse.

"Why did you do that?" Sarah asked, leaping off the chair.

"What?"

"Unbutton your blouse."

"I don't know," Jenny said. "I wasn't aware of it."

Moses cleared his throat. "If I stay in Chicago, I'll have two more years. But I may not stay. I might transfer to New York. I'd like to be in a more urbane city."

Jenny smiled and reached into her leather shoulder-strap purse and took out something.

"What's that?" Moses said.

"A reefer, so to speak," Jenny said. "Want one?" She offered him the cigarette.

"No," he said, "no. Are you serious? Let me see it." He took the cigarette out of her hand.

Sarah watched, knowing Moses was shocked. "Don't panic, sugar," she said, "creep out of that middle-class bag for one second, it's all right. No one's around."

Moses began to unwrap the thin paper, letting the contents fall into the ashtray. "Where can I dump this?" he said. "Listen, my position in this house is precarious enough."

"In the toilet," Sarah said.

"What do you mean your position is precarious?" Jenny said. "I thought you were the king of Cherrylawn."

"Do your pale-faced parents adore niggers?" he said. He took the ashtray and threw the contents into the pocket of his jacket.

Jenny looked blank. "My, but you're touchy," she said. "As a matter of fact my parents like everyone but Protestants. They especially loathe Baptists. You're not Baptist, are you?"

"No," he said.

"Well, then it's just fine. I think my mother would like your hair. She likes curly hair."

Sarah walked to the window. "Where the hell is John? He was supposed to be here. So where is he? John is very crazy, lately," she said, turning around. "He told me I was selfish. Imagine?"

"Well," Moses said, taking a stale piece of candy out of a candy dish.

"He comes on like an old man at times," Sarah said. "Oh, crap, why does Dad have to be sick? Laying up in that hospital, and then he'll be laying up here and I'll be the one to fetch and carry, carry and fetch. It's so lousy." She flopped into the chair and stuck her feet over the arm. "It's lousy," she said. They were looking at each other for too long. She wouldn't have it.

"Didn't you say you had to go home, Jenny?"

"No, I didn't," Jenny said.

"I like your new scooter, Jenny," Sarah said. Why alienate Jenny? Moses would be gone soon, and then who would be left? She and Jenny could ride to the beach on the motor scooter.

"Yes, it's a good one, isn't it?"

"We could have ice cream," Sarah said, "it's in the freezer. I'll get it in a minute. I'm tired and bored, bored, bored."

"Mummy said if I have the scooter I have to give away the rabbit."

"You've got a rabbit?" Moses said.

"All kinds of animals," Jenny said, "but I'm not giving any of them away. I adore them. But I have to find a hidden place for the rabbit so Mummy doesn't find it."

"That's our summer project," Sarah said. Finding a place for a rabbit was a summer project? What kind of insane summer project was that? It was all Mr. Green's fault. If he hadn't fallen on his ass and split his hip, she would be going away with John to Cambridge, one step closer to New York. One step closer to her dream. In New York she would be something. In New York she would groove.

"I do have to go," Jenny said. She shook hands with Moses.

"I'm glad I finally met you." She pushed her hair out of her mouth and went outside.

"Bye," she called through the window. She waved at them, straddled her motor scooter and disappeared down the street.

Moses stared after her until Sarah touched him on the arm. "Hey," she said, "I'll find ice cream." She pulled him into the kitchen. "It's a month old, you know how my mother keeps things."

It was wonderful to be eating ice cream with Moses again. Hadn't they known each other under all sorts of special circumstances?

"I hope I'm not drafted," he said. "It would be to my advantage if I were married."

"Oh," Sarah said, terrified, "don't marry. Who wants to be married, it's such a corny, middle-class thing to do."

"Don't worry," he said, sitting down at the kitchen table. "I don't have any interest in getting married. It's the last thing I want to do. Only, as soon as I get out of school, I'll go into the Army, I guess. It's a good thing my grades are up."

"I think Mother is pulling up. I hear something," Sarah said.

"*Oy vey is mir!*" Mrs. Green squealed as she came into the kitchen through the back door. "It's here. Like that TV commercial, Eric is here. Remember that?"

"Hello, Mrs. Green. How's everything?" Moses said, noticing Mrs. Green had burgeoned to gigantic proportions. She could qualify for the fat lady in a circus.

"Hello," she said, glancing suspiciously from Moses to Sarah. "John ran down to the store," she said.

"I'll miss John," Sarah said to Moses and handed him a plate of half-melted vanilla-fudge ice cream. She frowned at Mrs. Green.

"It's still good," she said, tasting the ice cream, "but, Mother, you don't get any. There's not enough."

Mrs. Green scratched her head. "A Mr. Duncan Poems called today," she said. "Who's that? Another one of those boy friends?"

"He did? He did?" Sarah moaned. "Why didn't you tell me? It's a very important call. I won't be seeing him, since I'm not going to graduation. What time?"

"I don't know," Mrs. Green said, "he said he was going away

and wouldn't be back until the end of summer and wished you good luck."

"His name is Bones, anyway," Sarah said.

"Bones?" Moses said. "That's an unusual name. I think there's a writer, an expert in Negro Literature with the same name."

"Impossible!" Mrs. Green said, slamming the refrigerator door.

"Mother," Sarah said, "how can you be so dense, so really stupid? What would you possibly know about it?"

"Be quiet," Moses said. "Don't talk to your mother that way."

"Will you shut up?" Sarah said, flashing angry green eyes at him.

"Don't start," Mrs. Green said, edging toward the cold water.

26

SARAH'S EMPLOYER, Jack Green, tucked his summery striped shirt neatly into his pants, took a fleeting look at himself in the cash register hidden adroitly behind the counter and said, "My nephew's coming later, entertain him. I've got to go to the other place. I'll be gone there most of the afternoon."

"Sure," Sarah said, bending over her first letter from John. Everyone had left, which was something of a pain. Moses was in Chicago. Mr. Duncan Bones had disappeared, to some exotic place with his witch wife, and Jenny was discussing going to Europe with her mother for a month. Everyone had deserted her.

"Good-bye," Jack murmured and closed the front door, melting into the overheated throng like a drop of water.

Sarah picked up the letter and began to read. She wasn't certain she understood the tone of the letter. The meaning yes, but she discovered a certain subtlety of tone, which she couldn't interpret. She would read it out loud for clarity.

Dear Sarah:

I have found a really terrible apartment. It's cheap and I'm in penury so what can I do? I thought it would be much better than it is when I heard about it. It has one bedroom, empty and lifeless, a living room crammed with someone's paintings, which I'm supposed to guard with my life, and a kitchen great for cooking if only I knew how.

There's a sexy stained-glass window in the bathroom and I would like to be here with you right now taking a shower.

Try not to use swear, curse, profane language in your letters. They might fall into the wrong hands.

Can you call Tilly and check to see if she's okay? She's lonely too, and probably would like some company. I think Michael Hare left her.

Sarah, I don't know what was the matter when I left. You were cold. I hope you straighten it out before your arrival on this side of the world. Have you told your parents when you're leaving so they'll be prepared? We have to organize this. And don't forget to save as much money as possible as I am going to be poor for the next two years. I don't have time for a part-time job.

I just finished a novel by C. P. Snow.

Found a place for you to work. It's an espresso café near Harvard square called The Café and Radcliffe girls work there as waitresses. They look like you, but don't care about clothes exactly and they never comb their hair. The place is filled with folk singers, and motor scooters, fast cars, the disaffected, the disenchanted, disassociated and depersonalized. It's time for David Riesman to do another study.

Except for Eloise State Mental Hospital, The Café is the quietest place I ever saw. Sometimes the customers sit there for an entire evening and don't say a word.

You'll like it if you leave most of your clothes at home and forget about being stylish. There's more of an emphasis on academic stuff than anything else, although I've heard on good authority that it's very different here when the summer school people clear out. Most of them are ugly girls from NYU and Hunter trying to learn German. A lot of teachers, too.

There's little room in these ivory towers for romance.

I'm thinking of doing my thesis on D. H. Lawrence.

It's a long way off. I wish I had the degree now and could start earning money.

A New England girl owns The Café. She's intelligent except she talks about psychoanalysis. She's from Mary McCarthy by way of Flannery O'Connor, on the fat side with pre-Raphaelite hair. You'll like her, I guess.

It's hot here, hotter than Detroit. I met two Indians in the Coop (The Harvard Cooperative where you buy (or steal)

books, housewares, clothes, or anything). One of them a
prince and the other an untouchable.

I'm not much of a letter writer.

love,
John
P.S. Keep out of museums.

"Museums?" Sarah repeated.

She smiled and put down the letter. Why couldn't she be in
Cambridge right this very minute? Instead, she was languishing
with a dummy job selling records to cretins. And what had Jack
said as he fled to the other store? He did have a tendency to
mumble and withdraw. It was something about a visiting imbecile,
wasn't it? Something about someone he knew dropping by. She
wished she could remember.

But Jack wasn't too bad. At times he was nearly groovy. She had
tried to squeeze him onto the Foolish Over-Thirty Hipster List,
but she found it couldn't be done, not in good conscience. He
couldn't really help the fact that he loved Coleman Hawkins,
Billie Holiday, and Frank Sinatra and had never progressed beyond them. She studied him in detail for other imperfections,
defects and serious tragic flaws, but that was the only one she
could dredge up and there was no honest way of discrediting him
so he passed the tests. He was tolerable.

His pattern was to mumble and withdraw in the morning and
communicate in the afternoon, when he finished tallying up the
previous day's accounts and could think freely. He would begin by
asking a question or two in the Socratic method.

Why do young people show such an avid interest in drugs?
Why do teen-agers desperately yearn for marriage? Why do twelve-
year-olds buy diaphragms? He asked these questions seriously. At
first she thought he was putting her on. They were the most unhip
questions, but then she realized he was actually interested in an
answer. He was interested in her mentality, her sensibility, her
point of view, her *raison d'être*. She spent whole afternoons
babbling happily. He was a good attentive listener.

"What do you think of LSD?" she asked him.

"LSD is to man what dreams are to beasts," he said and then
hurried away to see if the electrician was botching up the plumb-

] 172 [

ing in the other store. Sarah pored over this cryptic pronounce-
ment. What did it mean? She decided he must be a mad genius.
He was the best combination of surrealism and practicality.

Nevertheless, it was true, the job itself was a dummy job. He
couldn't make up for the sheer boredom of standing in an empty
store hours on end, waiting for idiots to buy idiot records. However, Mrs. Green was visibly impressed when Sarah showed her the
first week's salary. Respect from Mrs. Green was hard to come by.
It was not to be sneezed at but did it compensate?

"Our child makes a good take," Mrs. Green said, proudly
shoving the check under Mr. Green's nose.

Mr. Green swung his great cloudy eyes from side to side. "She
don't need parents, anymore," he said. "She's grown-up, look at
her, look at that grown-up *punim*. This child, ach, she'll throw us
away." Mr. Green was thrilled coming home to his own little
house on Cherrylawn, but after two weeks of confinement he
began to grow restless, weary of the loneliness. It wouldn't be long
before he was up and about, but in the meantime he must create
an interest in himself or he would be forced to lie there alone and
unattended while his wife and daughter battled beneath him in
the kitchen. Any opportunity to start an upheaval was welcomed.

"Shut up," Mrs. Green ordered and finished off the last spoon
of tapioca lying like a squashed rat in Mr. Green's lunch tray.

"Don't tell me to shut up," Mr. Green said, weakly. He found
there was a certain strength to be gained from weakness.

"That's right, Mom," Sarah said, "don't tell Daddy to shut up.
He can't fight back. He's too sick. Wait till he's well."

Mr. Green smiled. "More tapioca, Bertha," he said.

Once in a while a person worth noticing came into the store,
either an outstanding freak or a fantastic bore wandered in. It
broke up the day. Sarah glanced at the door. As a matter of fact,
three vaguely interesting people were about to enter. They looked
like a musical comedy team from some other world. Two chicks
and a cat. An Oriental chick with sleek black hair and Jesus
sandals tied up her knees, a big girl about six feet wearing a long
Tahitian dress and a big guy with thick red curls in a safari jacket.
They opened the door.

The girls ignored Sarah and began searching through the
albums. The big cat smiled.

] 173 [

"Hello," Sarah said.

"Hello," the cat said.

"We're just looking," the Oriental chick said.

"Look your heart out, sugar," Sarah said. Was the redhead with the Oriental or the big chick? She looked at the big chick. She had a definite horseface and large hazel eyes the color of a polluted stream.

"Grosse Pointe's slumming," Sarah said.

"What?" the Oriental said.

"Nothing," Sarah said. "Are you all friends?"

"What? Oh yes, I'm Mitsuko," the Oriental said, "and this is Larry. He's looking for his uncle."

"Yeah, and I'm looking for Lenny Bruce," Sarah said, watching them. They were a funny threesome. "Are you related to Consuela, a chick with red hair? I can't think of her last name. Italian."

He shook his head. "No," he said, "I'm Larry, Jack Green's nephew." He pulled off a crazy green knit cap, revealing the incredible density of his hair. It was thick with huge curls that climbed down his face like roses on a trellis.

"Wow," Sarah said, "a full freak-out hair scene."

"Where's my uncle?" Larry said.

"I'm Elsa," the chick said. "Larry's fiancée."

"How do you do," Sarah said. "Uncle Jack, how silly of me. He didn't say you were coming or I would have been more charming. Is there anything you want?"

"Koto music?" Mitsuko asked.

"Oh yeah, I dig it. They're all blind," Sarah said. She came around the counter and walked past Larry. He was big, maybe six feet one and with big arms and legs. Hefty. Muscular. Very cute. "I'll find the album for you. I think there's only one."

She began sorting the albums, all the while surreptitiously digging Larry. He was wearing groovy clothes, a safari jacket with epaulets and shiny gold brass buttons and tight corduroy pants that hugged his legs. A canteen was strapped around his neck.

"Aren't they hot?" she said, looking at his heavy black boots, and slipping her graceful fingers through the cutouts in her dress.

"Nope," he said, his sea-blue eyes darting over to where Elsa was nervously surveying the scene. But what was that *klutz* of a girl doing in a ridiculous long dress on such a warm day? She must

] 174 [

be roasting. Perhaps Sarah ought to turn off the air conditioner and drive her out?

"Where's the skull-and-crossbones ring?" Sarah said. "Don't you belong to any secret society? I should think you would." She grimaced at Elsa.

"What's that?" Larry said, pulling the canteen over his head.

"When you're not getting any," Sarah giggled.

"Getting any what?" Elsa said. She walked closer. "What do you mean?"

"I dig your costume," Sarah said to Larry. "It's so campy!"

Elsa tugged herself. "I don't like *your* dress," she said. "It's naked. Why, you're almost naked. I don't like this new look, do you?"

"Elsa!" Larry said, "maybe you should wait at the cleaners, next door."

"I'm not waiting at any cleaners," Elsa said.

Sarah's dress was sleeveless, backless and with elaborate flowered cutouts along the waist so that any onlooker could peer through and see her soft olive skin.

"Yeah," she said, "I'm almost naked. But it could be topless and it isn't, so I really didn't go too far." She pushed out her chest so the outline of her round, high breasts was pressed against the thin material. "How does that grab you?" she said.

Larry looked confused. There was a certain roughness about him she admired. He had a large head and a large body and a crudeness of movement that gave him the appearance of an extinct animal. A dinosaur?

"There's something marvelously juvenile delinquent about you," Sarah continued, knowing Elsa was watching, horrified. The big *klutz* must have a few missing marbles.

"I'm a painter," he said, removing the top of the canteen. "Want a drink?"

Elsa stepped quickly forward. "I do," she said and grabbed the canteen. She swigged from it and gasped. "Ugh, strong," she said, coughing. "Mitsuko does graphics and I'm an artist's model," she said rapidly.

"Oh yeah," Sarah said, "it might impress me if things like that impressed me, but they don't." This Elsa was slightly bananas.

"I don't need money," Elsa said. "My family is rich. But it's a way of giving something to art."

"Your body?" Sarah said. Elsa looked at her, unable to think of an answer.

"Do you swing with drugs?" she said, turning to Larry. There was no point in pursuing disagreeable subjects, so why not get on to something cheerier.

"We don't believe in stimulants," Elsa interjected, smacking her lips in self-satisfaction.

"Who asked you?" Sarah said. "Here's the Koto record." She handed the album to Mitsuko and pointed to the record player in the corner. "Go ahead," she said, "it's easy to use."

"No," Larry said, "I never tried drugs. But I'm open to things." Elsa looked angry, her horseface tightening up like the top of a Congo drum.

"We don't need stimulants," Elsa said. Larry watched Sarah's armpit. Elsa reached out and put her big arm through his. "We don't need anything," she said again.

"For goodness' sake," Sarah said, "half of America is turned on right this minute. Don't you read the papers? It's happening as you stand before me with your big arm linked through his. And, believe me, they're better off for it. The point is to get the hard-core Establishment middle-class finks to try dope. We would never have had the stupid freak-out in Vietnam if the middle-class dug such things. I'm for love myself!"

"*My* father is an admiral," Elsa said, hate popping out of her eyes.

Larry licked his lip and moved his arm away. "Why do people always think I'm a juvenile delinquent?" he said. "I'm not tough or anything." He flexed the muscle in his right leg to draw Sarah's attention away from his girl friend. He spent two days a week in the gym. An artist didn't have to be a spineless slob, or a mousy, manless, passive toady.

"Maybe when I meet a new person I should say in a loud voice, Picasso, Rembrandt, De Stael, De Kooning, Lichtenstein, Youngerman, so they know I'm not a hood." He began to unbuckle the safari jacket. "It's hot in here," he said. Sarah saw he had mounds of thick red hair on his chest like a fur carpet. She could take off her shoes and run through it.

"Oooooh," she said, appreciatively.

"You can't do that in here, Larry," Elsa said, looking toward the door. "Not in here."

"Why not?" Sarah said, taking the jacket. "I'll throw it behind the counter, and you can get it when you leave." Sarah had never seen so much hair on a human body. He was like a groovy wild animal. But the *klutz* was crazy.

"I never saw anyone like you," Sarah said. There must be a quicker way of shaking loose the chick. She was a parasite, a slimy snail clinging to a hermit crab.

"Thanks," he said, shaking his mane of curls self-consciously. By lifting weights all year he developed large muscles in his arms, back and chest. It had helped in the preparing of heavy assemblages. It had also helped in attracting a certain type of visual female. He looked at Sarah's firm little body. The arc of her armpit connected beautifully to her arm. It was a perfect shape for an abstract.

"How old are you?" Sarah said.

"Twenty-nine," he said taking off his shirt.

"Twenty-nine?" Sarah said. She was thrilled. Twenty-nine. He was a man. He wasn't in Jack Green's or Duncan Bones' category but he was delightfully older. "And how old are you?" she said to Elsa. She wasn't going to let a nut-cake bug her.

"Twenty-one," Elsa said, glaring.

"But you're a gorgeous animal," Sarah said, staring. "You're a gorgeous beast. A red lion, a super red lion." He stood beaming in front of her, naked to the waist.

"More like a bird, I think," Mitsuko said from the corner. "It's the big nose. Like an eagle."

"He doesn't look like a lion," Elsa said, "not at all."

"Yeah, definitely lion," Sarah said.

"No," Elsa said, "no."

"Yeah," Sarah said.

"But lions are fierce," Elsa said. "He's gentle." She put out a hand and stroked the hair on his chest. "Very gentle," she said.

"Quite fierce," Sarah said. "He comes on gentle but he's fierce."

"Gentle," Elsa said stubbornly, her bottom lip beginning to quiver.

"Fierce," Sarah said.

"Oh, well," Larry said.

"Would you drive me to Cambridge on your motorcycle?" Sarah said, imagining them flying through Michigan on a swinging motorcycle.

"I don't have a motorcycle," Larry said.

"But you don't even know him, what are you trying to do?" Elsa said desperately. "We're supposed to get married."

"Oh, Elsa!" Larry said.

"Fierce," Sarah said, "red hair and freckles like Consuela what's her name, but all masculinity like a boss lion. And I bet you're a little funky, too."

Larry smiled mysteriously.

"Here," Elsa said pushing the canteen into Larry's hand, "take it. You need it more than I do." Her eyes began to fill with tears.

"I didn't know this would happen," Larry said, apologetically. "I didn't plan it or anything."

"Yes you did," Elsa said, flaring up, "and you love it. You love it, you love it. And stop that stupid grinning. I can't stand it. I'm leaving." She walked rapidly to the door, flung it open and flounced out, tripping over the hem of her dress.

"You're an awful person," she called, looking back at Sarah. "I'm reporting you to Mr. Green." She ran down the street. The store was quiet except for the subtle chiming of the Koto music.

"Cambridge, England?" Larry said, patting the hair on his chest.

"No, Cambridge, Massachusetts, where Harvard is," Sarah said, wondering if Mitsuko was going to try to slip an album into the brown paper bag tucked under her arm.

Sarah turned her engagement ring so that the stone faced inward. "Listen," she said, "I'm baby-sitting tonight for the kid across the street. You want to visit? I was going to read Le Clezio and listen to Eric Satie but if you come visit we could have a mad game of chess. Ha ha ha."

"Okay," he said, "but I don't play chess." He tied the canteen around his naked chest and examined his hands. "I'll try to remove some of these paint splotches," he said.

"I don't mind. Don't sweat it," Sarah said. "We'll have Leon, the kid, lick them off."

27

JENNY SAT ON the couch reading *The Village Voice*.

"How did you get it?" she said, glancing up at Sarah, who was brushing her hair in the hallway mirror.

"I sent away for it," Sarah said. "It's interesting, isn't it? Imagine all that going on in one city."

"Well," Jenny said, "New York is huge. When Mummy and Daddy took me there last Christmas, it seemed enormous with throngs of people. Just throngs, like Calcutta."

Sarah watched Jenny through the mirror. Her cheeks were flushed. There was an extra sparkle in her eyes.

"You look different today, what's happening?" she said.

"Nothing," Jenny said. "Nothing." She stretched out on the couch, her feet up, her head resting on a pillow. "It's hot. I can't wait till we go to Europe. London is supposed to be interesting now."

"I wish I were going to London," Sarah said, jealously, "or anywhere. I'm bored!"

"You'll be going soon," Jenny said. "By the way," she sat up, "did you know Moses was transferring to Columbia?"

"Yeah," Sarah said, "he told me." It didn't seem fair Jenny was leaving Detroit for some fabulous place like London while she had to stay behind baby-sitting and lifting Mr. Green. And now what was Jenny saying about Moses, the Moses who had belonged, since childhood, to Sarah?

"How did you know?" Sarah said.

"Oh," Jenny said, "he wrote me."

Sarah turned to face her.

"He wrote you a letter? Why?" she said.

] 179 [

"Why not," Jenny said, opening her purse.

"He's mine," Sarah said.

Jenny began to laugh. "He's not yours or mine or anyone's. He belongs to himself. People don't own people anymore, you know."

Sarah frowned. Jenny and Moses? Moses and Jenny? No. She could not think of them together. She refused to think of them together. She had put such things aside. And he wrote her a letter?

"Want a piece of gum?" Jenny said.

"No."

"I better go home," Jenny said, slipping into her sandals.

"Okay, I'm going to Mrs. Ferentz's across the street in about three seconds. She said to be there at six-thirty."

"It's six-thirty now," Jenny said.

"Yeah," Sarah said. "So he wrote you a letter? What did it say? And why are you forever running home?"

"Ha ha," Jenny said, "it said ha ha."

"A letter, a letter, did you see the letter in your room on your bed?" Mrs. Green said, traipsing into the room, her face a mask of cold cream.

"You didn't open it," Sarah shouted, "did you, Mother?"

"No, no, my God!" Mrs. Green said. "She thinks I'm a *gonif*, already."

"I'm going. See you," Jenny said.

Sarah ran up the stairs and into the bedroom. The letter was lying on her pillow. She ripped it open. Did he have something crucial to say?

Dear Sarah:

I miss you today. I never met such hungry women. Last night in The Café a girl tried to stick her hand in my fly. She was a Radcliffe girl. It's hard to keep my hands (or mind) on my work when such occurrences take place. I can't hope for you sooner.

The girl who owns The Café is around our age, but some older Latin fellow from Argentina or somewhere in South America gave her the money to start her business. His name is Ricardo Waters and he was a movie star in South America. Ever hear of him?

This may sound fishy, but this is a preposterous place. There are four students who drive in an old Rolls-Royce, for instance, to classes, etc. There's a Baron who wears a black cape. Actually, I think he's from Boston and an engineer, but he pretends to be a graduate student. I'll have to stay out of there, it's too distracting.

I never saw so much hair, it's longer than yours or Jenny's. Mine is short by comparison. But they don't comb it.

Could you please tell me the exact day of arrival so I can get a maid to clean the apartment. It's a mess.

I understand from your letters, you're not too eager to come, but it'll be okay, don't worry about it. I'll make it okay. And if I don't???

But I don't know how I can prevent those little girls from sticking their hands in my crotch.

George wrote and seems desperate. Horny (like me), possibly. Was thinking of taking a quick trip up here in his car.

Love,
John

Sarah shoved the letter under the pillow, finished brushing her hair, fled down the stairs, out of the house and across the street to where Leon Ferentz was torturing a toy duck in his front yard.

"Greetings from the underground," Sarah panted. John was turning into a sex freak according to his letter. What a cop out! "Where's your mums?" she said.

Leon paid no attention to her and continued stuffing pebbles into the eternally closed mouth of the duck.

"My birthday is yesterday, did you bring a prize?" he said and nibbled the duck's plastic tail. "I want a prize."

Poor Leon, so spoiled and so greedy. His house was overflowing with expensive toys. He even had a walk-in doll's house.

"No, I didn't bring a prize, "she said. "I'm your prize. How old are you?"

He looked at her with tears in his eyes. "Tree," he said, "but I want a prize. What did you bring?"

"Nothing, but don't cry, Leon. I can't stand it."

Wasn't his birthday last month? She remembered quite clearly she bought him a five-cent red whistle, which proved to be the hit of the birthday party orgy. He ignored all other presents, blowing the whistle until it turned into a full freak-out, with his mother finally taking the whistle away and giving him a spanking.

"Where's the prize?" he insisted and pressed his chubby arms around the duck. "Mum Mum Mum Mum Mum," he said into the duck's eye. "Mum Mum Mum."

"I'll make a giant soda when your parents leave," Sarah said. "Don't go bananas now."

Leon looked at her, stunned. He threw the duck against the front steps, where it crashed into his fire engine truck, and began to shriek. "No," he shrieked, "no, don't let them go. No. No."

Sarah picked up the duck, held it to her breasts and waited for Leon to stop. It was too hot to scream. Much too hot. It was more an evening for quietly humming madrigals, while thinking about what one was to do with one's life. To be or not to be a singer??? That was the question. To be or not to be a writer? That was another question. It all came down to the same thing. She had an urge to "do something." But what? Striving without any apparent goal was pretty senseless, dull-brained. To be something or not to be something?

"It's all right," she said to Leon in an effort to console him. "We'll have a mad eating orgy and then I'll read you a million Dr. Suess stories, some pornographic tales or whatever you want, sugar." She patted his duck. God, was he going to bug her all evening? Was he going to ruin the imminent scene between herself and Larry? She bent over and kissed his wet cheek. "Don't cry, baby," she said, "it's going to be all right. I'll read to you and it'll be a gas!"

"I'm not a baby," Leon sniffled. "I don't have gas."

"Okay," she said. Of course, why did she have to begin with a novel? No one was holding a gun to her head saying write or die. No one. She could begin with a short story. She wrote in grade school and then suddenly stopped in the ninth grade, attributable to the stultifying effects of higher education. "It takes all the creativity out of you," she said to Jenny. "It sucks it right out."

"I know," Jenny agreed, "but it gives you something to hate.

Artists have to fight against something." Yes, she could begin again.

"*Babar*. We could have *Babar*," Leon said.

"Like okay," Sarah said.

"*Samantha's Room*," he said

"Okie dokie," she said.

"*The Cat in the Hat*," he said.

"That's for two-year-olds. That was last year," Sarah said.

"More," Leon said, "we could have more."

"Okay, swelleroonie," Sarah said. She could begin with a short story, maybe even write a number of them with one theme and make a book. But what would she write about? Love? Sex? Fate? Boredom? It would have to be something specific. She knew you were supposed to write about something specific. It was the best way. But did she know anything specific?

"Okay," Sarah said, "but none of those teeny-weeny boring baby books. I refuse." She didn't know much of anything, if the truth be known.

"Now!" he said, realizing he had her in his control. "In my closet," he said. "We'll get Mummy."

"Mummy's in the closet?" Sarah said, giving up.

Mummy was sitting dejectedly on the sofa in the living room.

"Hi," Sarah said, "where are Leon's books?"

"In the closet," Mrs. Ferentz said sadly. "Do you mind putting him to bed?" She mouthed the question so he wouldn't hear. "Do you mind?" Leon was so sensitive.

Sarah nodded. "All right, why not?" she said.

"How have you been, Sarah?" Mrs. Ferentz asked. She was broad-shouldered with cropped, dyed black hair and square horn-rimmed glasses, which made her appear intelligent.

"Fine," Sarah said, "I'm thinking about taking singing lessons. And I'm engaged." She flashed her ring in Mrs. Ferentz's direction.

"Yes," Mrs. Ferentz sighed, "your mother told me. But you're not marrying so young, dear, are you?"

"Oh no," Sarah said, "I have things to do first."

Mrs. Ferentz had been married for seventeen years to Mr. Ferentz, a tall, bony man with a shining bald head. He managed

]183[

to be jobless for most of the seventeen years, eating up her family inheritance and keeping her in a constant state of pregnancy. Leon, the youngest Ferentz, had three sisters at school and one brother, who lied about his age and had enlisted in the Army. Mr. Ferentz talked exclusively about money.

"Yes," Mrs. Ferentz said, "do your things first, dear." Wearily she wiped her glasses on the sleeve of her print dress. Perspiration waited like watchdogs under her arms.

"What's the matter?" Sarah said. Poor Mrs. Ferentz looked dragged, drugged and discontent. "Maybe you need goofballs."

"Oh, I do take pep pills," Mrs. Ferentz said slowly, "but I think I'm pregnant."

"Oh," Sarah said, "pregnant."

"Imagine another one like Leon," Mrs. Ferentz said.

"I can't," Sarah said.

"It's so tiring," she said, "and today is so hot."

"I'll read to him," Sarah said.

"Yes." Mrs. Ferentz pulled at the skin around her elbow. "I've got to meet his father at the airport in a few minutes. We're having dinner at the airport."

"Maybe you'll have a girl, you like girls don't you?"

"I don't want a girl," Mrs. Ferentz said.

"Maybe you'll have a boy then," Sarah said.

"I don't want a boy," Mrs. Ferentz said and wiped her glasses again. She frowned at the floor. Leon wandered into the room, arms laden down with books, and stood quietly behind the sofa listening to the conversation.

"A monkey? How about a monkey?" Sarah said. "They eat bananas and are very economical."

"They do, don't they?" Mrs. Ferentz said. She couldn't very well go to the family doctor for a pregnancy test. She didn't really want anyone to know, not yet, just in case she decided to do away with it. She could fly to Puerto Rico or Mexico. Six children was going too far. They had taken her figure, so she looked like a common laborer, taken her money, squandering it on fifth-rate educations, and taken her gaiety, her youth and her self-respect. Mr. Ferentz had done nothing, nothing at all to save her dwindling inheritance, her dwindling zest for life, her dwindling breasts. Hadn't so much as lifted a finger to set things straight and here she was pregnant again. It was disgusting, and on such a humid day!

"An airplane?" Sarah said. "Maybe you'll have an airplane, I mean you're going to the airport," she said helpfully. Leon began to shriek, throwing the books at the sofa. "Don't go, no," he shrieked, "please, Mummy. Take me with you. Take me." Mrs. Ferentz leaped from the sofa. "Leon," she said, "Leon, I'll be right back. Mummy always comes back. You know that, darling." She grabbed him and hugged him. "And Daddy's coming back with Mummy and tomorrow he'll read to you all day."

"Daddy?" Leon said. He gaped in astonishment. Mr. Ferentz was rarely around. Looking for a job, he explained when Mrs. Ferentz asked.

"Yes, Daddy, your daddy. And he'll bring you a . . . uh . . ." she stammered, searching for a bribe. "An airplane," she said, pleased she had thought of such a good bribe.

"Oh, an airplane," Leon said.

Sarah studied the two square, chubby figures clinging to each other. They were amazingly alike down to the turned-up noses. They were like two Japanese wrestlers hugging each other, except there was nothing delicate about them. Mitsuko, for example, could be an extraordinary dumb little bitch, but to Sarah, she was delicate. She must have a whole network of groovy Zen koans stuffed into all corners of her Oriental brain. It occurred to Sarah that Mitsuko might tag along with Larry, in which case she would surely hate her guts, Oriental delicacy notwithstanding. She would truly hate to have a put-down scene, not after what was done to the poor Japanese at Hiroshima, an event which Sarah brooded over from time to time, even going so far as to march in the Hiroshima parade once a year.

"Take him to the bedroom and I'll sneak out," Mrs. Ferentz mouthed. She patted his bottom.

"No," he shrieked, "no."

"Hey! Let's read this stuff," Sarah said, faking enthusiasm. "Come on tootsibear," she said.

"I'm not tusie bear," he said. "I'm Leon."

"I'm hip," she said. "You're Leon and no one else." She took his hand and lead him to the bedroom.

The bedroom was covered from one end to the other in toys of all shapes, sizes and dimensions. Stuffed animals, dolls, tin soldiers, guns, bats, trucks, games, crayons, chalk, blackboards and puzzles were scattered everywhere. There was even an array of pots and pans stolen from the kitchen.

"Heaven help him!" Sarah said. "The affluent society at its worst."

"I'm going to gun you," Leon said and fired an imaginary gun in her face. "I'm going to gun you so your head's down. Put your head down."

Obligingly she put her head down. In a way it was restful. So if she didn't write short stories, who would know the difference? Would anyone care except her best friend Jenny? Anyway she wanted to do something people would care about. More people listened and loved music than read and loved books. But was that the real criterion? It smacked too much of wanting to please the Others. Maybe it wasn't even a case of the Others. She wanted to please herself. And maybe it was selfish but did it matter?

"Now what?" she said, looking up at Leon's round, greedy face. She was sitting on the edge of his little bed, wondering what the hell to do with her life and he didn't even know it.

"Now what?" she said. She would be willing to play any game he wished to play, make any scene he wished to make, do anything at all, if only he'd disappear without a tantrum when Larry appeared.

"You're dead now," Leon said.

"Aha, is that what dead is?" Sarah said.

"Yep, put your head down," Leon said again. "You're dead."

She'd even let him slit her throat if he would just keep cool and pop into the sack at the prescribed time.

"Head down," he said, pressing down her head so her neck ached.

She tried to remember what she first thought of dead. Dead was going away? Was that what it meant? Was dead being unloved? Dead was alone, certainly, that was why it was so scary. Dead was gone. Real gone. Yeah, that was it. Dead was someone you loved going away and never coming back. They were missing, lost, gone forever. It was hard to love someone who wasn't there, hard to love someone gone and dead. Like John?

"When your mother and father go away, are they dead?" she

asked. Leon looked at her resentfully. "Bang," he said, "bang, bang, bang, bang, bang."

"There was a song like that last year," Sarah mused, "or two years ago. I don't remember." She had loved it and listened to it over and over. Sonny and Cher. Then there was the Eleanor Rigby song. Eleanor Rigby kept her face in a jar. Eleanor Rigby died and no one came to her funeral. It was hard loving someone who had gone away. She supposed she was angry with John for leaving, and yet hadn't she known from the beginning he would leave?

John didn't exist anymore. It was sad, but he was dead. The letter she had left under her pillow was merely an illusion to tease and frustrate her. She had to have someone here and now. But then, had she really loved him? Even when they were together she could feel the love slipping through her fingers like grains of sand. And so what was this silly notion of love? She twisted her engagement ring. It was still beautiful, one solitary stone set in a simple gold setting. But what did it mean? Anything? Nothing? Probably nothing. It had begun to disintegrate when Mr. Duncan Bones came onto the scene. Until then it had worked out rather well. It wasn't just his physical attraction that she welcomed, or the graceful aristocratic forehead, the ascot, the witty dialogue, the warm brown eyes. No, it was more than that. She was enthralled by the fact Mr. Duncan Bones was so incredibly, so remarkably charming. Mr. Duncan Bones was gay. No grave, depressing or heavy thoughts entered his conversation. He was as light and as charming as a French pantomimist. In comparison to John, he was like an aerial dancer, refreshing, oh so refreshing. She hated to admit it to herself but in some ways John was a burden. John was serious. Actually serious. His letters did indicate a certain brand of charm but in person, in the flesh as it were, he was often tedious, heavy. He didn't want her to swear or to smoke Pot and it was essential she go to college. He was trying to control her, rule her life, tell her what to do, instruct her. Mr. Duncan Bones would never have the bad taste to be that way. She did want to be free, unshackled. Wasn't that one of the points in falling in love? To fall in love was to feel free and unencumbered. To fall in love was to soar through the sky, free as a bird.

Mrs. Ferentz floated past the doorway, an apparition gone bananas, waved good-bye and floated toward the living room.

Sarah heard the door gently closing and Mrs. Ferentz climbing into her old Ford.

She picked up *The Mice Who Moved to the Moon* and began to read to Leon, whose mouth was hanging open like a trapdoor. She read slowly, trying to concentrate on the story to give it the dramatic intonations it deserved. It was Leon's favorite story. She had read it to him three hundred and forty-nine times and each time he seemed to enjoy it more.

It would have been fitting, no doubt, if Jenny had fallen in love with John.

"You can't go around falling in love like you go bowling," she said to Sarah as they turned on in the drugstore.

"I can," Sarah said looking for the soda jerk. His back was to her. It was cool to inhale the joint.

"This is good grass," she said.

"Yes," Jenny said, with a thoughtful expression. "Love is a serious business."

"Not for me," Sarah said. "I hate serious."

Leon touched Sarah's face. "Don't fall asleep," he said, "more. Read."

"Yeah, sure," Sarah said. Somehow *The Mice Who Moved to the Moon* had begun to pall. Instead of thinking about all the rotten little mice moving to the moon, she found the image of a little blond slut ensconced on John's lap, pushing itself into consciousness. And he was probably loving it, the traitor. The blond slut was sticking her hand in his crotch. He wasn't saying no. Indeed, in the last letter she detected a distinct happiness that a disgusting cretin slut child was coming on.

"Again," Leon said. "Oh, Sarah, please." She had come to the end of the story and was staring at the wall.

"No," she groaned, "anything else. Mother Goose, anything."

"No," he said.

She looked at her watch. If it were keeping the right time, Larry would be on the scene at any moment. She had to immediately find a way of packing Leon off to the sack without incurring a far-out temper tantrum. He would certainly queer any romantic scene with Larry. He was such a pest. As soon as he saw Larry he would be after him, bugging him to play.

Did people really love their children? She looked at Leon closely. He was so selfish, so demanding. Her parents said you always love your own children.

"More," Leon said, clutching his penis and rocking back and forth.

Sarah jumped up. "I think it's time for beddybye, don't you, angel *punim*? And don't struggle, just go quietly," she said. "When you're all tucked in I'll read this goddamned sickening story again."

"Okay," he said to her surprise. She wouldn't have to bind and gag him, after all. What a relief!

She helped him under the sheet and began to read. On page three his eyes closed. Sarah looked down on his selfish little face.

Could this little monster grow up and be someone? She switched off the lamp and walked into the living room to look through the front window for Larry. To her consternation he was already sitting on the rocking chair next to Mrs. Ferentz's early American piano no one played.

"You're early," she said. She hadn't time to brush her hair or fix her eye makeup. He looked much the same as he had in the afternoon except he had plastered his hair down with a strange, smelly, oily substance. Seeing him so unexpectedly, she was struck once more by his size. He was big.

"I didn't want to interrupt," he said.

He looked so big, so much bigger than John or Mr. Duncan Bones, that she felt embarrassed. What was she supposed to do with such a big cat?

"Are you afraid of me?" she asked. The best defense was an offense. A girl has to protect herself, after all.

"Nah," he said, "I rode boxcars all last summer. That's the only thing that ever frightened me. Women don't bother me."

"We don't frighten you, eh? I noticed you were with that big cow giraffe Elsa. I guess if she didn't frighten you, no one would."

"Well I'm a big cow giraffe, too," he said, swinging backwards on the rocking chair and closing his eyes. The chair moved backward and forward in a regular motion. He rocked for a few minutes then stopped and looked Sarah straight in the eye.

"You didn't invite me here for a joke, did you?" he said.

"Oh no," Sarah said. Was he stupid? A great big dummy? It was always hard to determine intelligence simply by looking at someone and exchanging a few casual remarks.

"I don't dig your chick, that's all," she said.

"Hey, she's a good girl," he said, "loyal anyway. Are you? I see you're wearing an engagement ring. I saw it this afternoon."

"Yeah," she said, "I'm still wearing it. But he's dead."

"Dead?" he said, surprised. "I'm sorry. Gee, I'm sorry. I shouldn't have asked. Put my foot in it."

Sarah rolled her eyes around in what she thought was a soulful, heartrending expression. "He fell out a window last July Fourth."

Larry studied her face. She seemed serious enough. "Maybe you should wear it on the other hand," he said.

"Maybe I will," she said. She smiled into his sea-blue eyes. "I've grieved long enough. I'll put on some sounds." She walked to the phonograph and began slipping a record off the turntable. "I don't really dig André Previn, he's square. How about Dionne Warwick? She's a little passé but I dig the animal thing in her voice."

He nodded. "I spent last summer riding back and forth from Arizona to California. The colors out there are beautiful. It's quiet."

"I've never been there," Sarah said. "I'm going to Cambridge, Massachusetts. Harvard, you know. Pretty soon." She would have to write a letter to John breaking the engagement. Was there any real point in going on with someone long distance? And even when she finally did go to Cambridge, which she fully intended to do, she couldn't really live with John, not after meeting the fabulous Mr. Duncan Bones, whose impact remained fresh and strong. Of course, the letter would have to be written in such a fashion that John would in no way communicate the situation to Mr. and Mrs. Green. They would have to continue to think she was engaged. Otherwise, things could get messy.

Dear John, she would write in medieval script.

Dear Dear John,

I'm too young to be engaged. I know it was my idea but everything has changed for me since then. I had an out-of-sight satori walking near the duck pond in Palmer Park the day after you left. In my satori I found I'm not ready for the responsibility of engagement. Okay? I hope you dig this. You were the first and only man I knew and this isn't enough experience for a girl like me, who hungers for life's adventures. I don't mean to sound like a cornball. But that's it.

We could still see each other on a non-hostile basis, like friends, maybe. I have to trust my own judgment, though sometimes I wish I had a guru to help me through.

Don't think of me unkindly but as Françoise Sagan says, with a certain smile (not a s— eating grin, either).

Fondly,
Sarah Green

It occurred to her as an afterthought that she ought to enclose a sexy snapshot of herself so he wouldn't forget her.

"Would you like to make it to Massachusetts on a motorcycle?" she said, sliding next to Larry. "It might be a gas." She pictured herself gathering fury down Woodward Avenue, pointed directly toward Harvard, astride the huge motorcycle, her arms wrapped snugly around Larry's substantial waist. It was the coolest idea she had in a long time.

"I'm going to Mexico at Christmas," he said, "in a Land Rover. Uncle Jack's giving it to me. It's second-hand. It's a good life for a painter there. Cheap and quiet." He tapped his fingers on the couch and moved his head in time to Dionne Warwick, the curls coming loose, unslicked and covering his forehead like a sheep-dog's.

Sarah looked disappointed. "Oh," she said. There must be a way of getting him to do what she wanted. He didn't seem to be rigid and conventional. Surely he could be influenced in the right direction.

"Elsa bakes her own bread," he said, clamming up.

"So?" Sarah said. "So what? That's so fantastic?"

It didn't seem very polite of him to throw in that bit of information. It was downright rude. You didn't talk about one woman in the presence of another.

"D. H. Lawrence's wife, Frieda, baked her own bread and she was probably frigid."

"Elsa isn't frigid," he said, "and it's good to know how to do things when you're in the wilderness. Gee, it's very important."

"Baking bread is nothing," Sarah said.

"You're a strange girl," Larry said, putting his freckled hand over hers.

"Can't you say anything sweeter than that?" she said, wondering why his hand was shaking.

"If I say sweet things, I get an erection," he said, pushing the hair out of his eyes. The palm of his hand was sweating.

"Another mood is required," Sarah said, jumping up from the couch. She ran to the stack of records next to the phonograph and picked up an album. What was he trying to do?

"Is this all right?" she said, holding up Verdi's *Requiem*. Maybe a little depth music would make him forget Elsa.

"I like silence," he said.

Sarah put the album back on top of the stack of records. Okay, she'd do whatever he wanted. She would please him at whatever cost. The idea of riding triumphantly to Cambridge on the back of a motorcycle grabbed her, seized her imagination like nothing since the advent of Mr. Duncan Bones. But why were there always other women in the picture? Other women who ruined her plans.

She sat on the couch and leaned her shoulder against his. For a long time, neither spoke. As soon as Mr. Green was strong enough, she was, most assuredly, splitting the scene. And why not with Larry?

"It's good, isn't it?" Larry said.

"Uh-huh," she said, listening to the silence. She did want to please him but how long can a human being listen to silence? She glanced at Larry's face. In profile he looked like a Roman soldier. He seemed content enough. Was it a put-on? Was he bananas? She looked at her watch. Ten minutes had passed. She crossed one sexy leg over the other, resting her hands together in what she knew was the Hindu meditation position. Had she found her guru?

His breathing was coming in a regular pattern like the steady drone of radio static. She uncrossed her legs and tried to think of a long stretch of sand. A long stretch of silent sand. She undid her hands, shaking them to unstiffen them and set the blood flowing. It was no good. She couldn't think of a long stretch of silent sand. She could only think of a fifteen-year-old blond cretin slut perched like a bird of prey on John's lap.

] 192 [

"Ever read *You Can't Go Home Again?*" she said, breaking the silence. It was unbearable. Maybe a conversation about books would evoke an interest, a response, get his mind off the nothingness that had crept in. It was positively unhealthy.

"No," he said.

"It's not really you can't go home again," she said cheerily, "it's that you can never get away." She waited for his response. It was a *bon mot*, no one could deny. He shifted his weight, putting his black booted feet up on Mrs. Ferentz's Danish modern coffee table and said nothing.

"I suppose Elsa is a quiet girl?" Sarah said. The query should receive more than a one-syllable answer. You just have to know how to handle the withdrawn one, that's all.

"Yep," he said.

"I thought you were a talker," she said. "You talked this afternoon. I didn't know you were withdrawn."

He looked at her nervously. "The desert is lovely and quiet," he said, closing his mouth into silence.

"It's boring," she said. She could hear the clock in the kitchen ticking. It certainly was becoming one of those silly, dullass, dumbbell situations. She inspected her nails. Maybe she ought to paint black and white stripes on them for a kick.

Larry sat, staring straight ahead. Quietly, she ran a sharp fingernail along the nape of his neck. He shuddered and said nothing. She ran the nail over his cheek, across his mouth and into his left ear.

"Painters don't talk much," he said.

"Why did you try to touch me before?" she said. "Didn't you mean it?" Obviously the only way to have this creature do what she wanted was to seduce him. A full seduction.

"I meant it," he said, "only Elsa . . . we're getting married." Well, she had really read him wrong. He had seemed like Mr. Sensuality himself, but instead he was turning out to be Mr. Creep.

"So who cares?" she said. "Everyone's getting married. What does that have to do with the price of yogurt?"

"But you're a child," he said, suddenly frantically pressing his warm hard body against hers.

"I'm not such a child," she said. "I'm a woman, too." She took his hand and placed it on her knee. "You see," she said, putting up her mouth to be kissed.

Mr. and Mrs. Ferentz slept in different bedrooms, one pink, one blue. Sarah decided Mrs. Ferentz's bed was the desired one as it was tiny, therefore more romantic, much more intimate.

"Little by little," Sarah said soothingly. They lay on top of the bedspread without removing their clothes.

"Could you be quiet," Larry said, "just for a while. I must do this my own way." He held her in his arms and stroked her hair.

Sarah felt something dripping onto her cheek. "You got some stuff on your hair?" she said.

"Relax, quiet," he said. "It'll be all right. But gee, I must run this ship. Don't talk."

She couldn't remember he said Gee so often in the store. It had stolen into his vocabulary like a bad dream. How could such a big handsome male use the word Gee? He was awfully big, gigantic even, and with his heavy body lying on her, she felt crushed. She tried to see his face. He was holding her so close, she could barely see the outline of his jaw.

"I can't breathe," she said, trying to push him away. His large arm lay across her throat. "Let me go." She gagged. He grunted and released her.

"Thanks," she said, sitting bolt upright and yanking her dress over her head. "It's hot in here," she said, "let's rid ourselves of the clothes."

"What are you doing?" he said. "Can't you be quiet?"

"Getting laid," she said, pulling at the buttons on his safari jacket.

"Is that what you want?" he said, tugging off his pants and throwing them under the bed.

"Yeah," she said, "yeah. You catch on, sugar." In the semidark there was something demonic about him. The shadow of his face was silhouetted against the wall behind the bed. Was he a devil? How very strange to be in bed, actually in a bed with another man not Mr. Duncan Bones. Perhaps there was a necessity for starting another list, *The Unpredictable Sex Achievement or Sex Trauma List*. This might be a kind of achievement but it looked as if it were turning into a trauma. Oh. Oh. He wasn't behaving like John at all. Everything about him was different, his coloring, his con-

] 194 [

versation, his manners, his sexual behavior. The main difference, she noted, was that he didn't seem to have an erection. Was he a devil?

"Say something sweet," Sarah said, reaching down. It wasn't going well. He lay with his whole weight on her slim body, crushing her to the mattress. The mattress buttons were beginning to dig into her flesh. She tried to avoid them, to stretch her legs, which were rigidly pinned beneath her but he held her fast to the spot. She jiggled her hips. Her body seemed to be stuck to the mattress, so that no movement, no matter how minimal, was possible. His arm lay solidly over her neck, his mouth fastened to hers. How could such a ridiculous situation come about?

She jerked her hand free.

"Don't reject me," he muttered, "don't reject me." As far as she understood she had been trying her best to seduce him, quite the opposite of what he was telling her. Hadn't the whole bloody thing been her idea? And wasn't it becoming a fucking mess? No wonder he was with a virago. He was a kook.

She felt weak, the air rushing out of her as if she were a rubber toy. If only he would just get his mouth off hers so she could take a breath of air. He was feverishly kissing her, his thick stupid tongue defiling her gums. His rib cage banged into her. It didn't make sense. Nothing was really happening. It was a cop-out, a complete cop-out. A fake. A fraud. A nightmare. His teeth dug into her lip. She would definitely make a place for him on The Nasty Fuckers List. Didn't he know you can't make piggies without a hard on?

She strained to see if his eyes were open. In case they were perhaps she could telepathically transmit a message for him to move his bottom out of the Ferentz house. She stared into the darkness of his face, feeling him thrashing over her like a drowning man. He was a parasite eating her flesh, a ghoul, an impotent nut, twisting and contorting like a contender out for the Russian olympics. If only she could get out from under.

He opened his eyes and looked down at her, his face a train wreck, his eyes blank as mashed potatoes.

"Help," Sarah screamed, breaking to one side of the bed with one lusty burst of energy, summoned from the depths of her soul. She pushed him against Mrs. Ferentz's pale pink wall. He struck the wall with his right elbow, the impact shoving him backward to the floor, where he fell into Leon's dump trucks.

"Okay," she shouted, jumping off the bed. "Okay take your pants and bugger off."

"Huh?" he said.

"I'm sorry," she said, "you'll have to go."

"Yes," he said, getting up and pulling his pants from under the bed. "Yes, you're right."

He put on his pants and started buttoning the safari jacket. She watched him. He must be crazy.

"You don't like men at all, not really," he said.

"Maybe," she said. He was going to tell her off and put her down. She was going to get a tongue lashing.

"You don't like men," he said, backing out of the room. "If you did you'd be different. You don't know about romance or affection or loyalty."

"How could a kid know about love? I should have known when you acted so know-it-all today. They're the ones to keep away from. Here I've got a woman, not a girl, a woman who knows how to love, so what am I doing with you?" He stood by the front door, stunned.

"The knob is right behind you," Sarah said.

"Who needs someone like you, anyway?" he said. "What's it called? I may not be educated in the ordinary way but I know about certain things. Castrator?"

He looked at her for an answer.

"Please," she said, her voice trembling, "the knob. It's the way out."

He opened the door slowly. "Yep," he said, "castrator."

Dear John:

The days go like fish in an aquarium. Slow. Boring. Nothing whatsoever is happening. I could scream. Jenny is in Europe with family and I am here as on a darkling plane. Ugh. Crap. Anyway, I'll be arriving in two weeks, just about. Will send the exact time when I figure it out. Dad is well enough, so I can leave.

There's still a few weeks left of summer, maybe we could go to the Cape. I hear it's beautiful.

I'm sorry I don't write often but I'm too depressed. The store has been dead since July. No one comes in, not even any beatniks. Clytemnestra caught a summer cold and is in the hospital.

I got a letter from Moses, the first one all summer, the rat, and he's getting an apartment near Columbia University in New York. I guess he'll work part-time or something. I think he's as poor as you are.

I've saved money, mostly because instead of spending my own money for clothes, I've been charging it to my mother and hiding the bills. She'll flip out when the bill comes.

Moses told me that I'm a psychopath. I don't think so. Psychopaths have goals.

Love,
Sarah

28

SARAH FELT ASHAMED as she carefully arranged herself in the seat. Up ahead the No Smoking–Fasten Your Seat Belt sign flickered and lit up. She reached for the seat belt and began to fasten it tightly around herself. Had anyone heard Mrs. Green's words as she delivered one final wet kiss on Sarah's cheek?

"Careful, you know you've never been up in a plane before," she said.

"For Christ sake," Sarah said.

"Here," Mr. Green said, handing her an envelope. "You'll need this."

"What's this?" Mrs. Green said. They were standing at the entrance to the runway saying good-bye. Mr. Green had put on new shoes for the occasion and shoved his weakened leg into his trousers with hardly a complaint.

"The toilet business is back on its feet," he said, smiling.

"Oh, Daddy, thank you," Sarah said and gave Mr. Green a hug. In a moment she was gone, running down the runway out onto the field and up into the plane.

"You've never flown, remember," Mrs. Green shouted, the words ringing in Sarah's ears even as she fastened the seat belt around her tiny waist.

The idea of flying filled her with excitement. Of course, no one must know it was her first trip. It was too dull, too out-of-it, too mundane. She adjusted her body to the seat and sat up straight in an effort to appear urbane. Urbanity was all. No one in his right mind would be caught looking like a hick, a square goose from the sticks.

"Is something the matter, Miss?" the stewardess said, bending over her.

"Oh, no!" Sarah said quickly.

"Maybe you better lean back, it's more comfortable," the stewardess said with a mechanical grin. "Just sit back, dear, you'll be all right." She walked down the aisle, checking on the other passengers and wiggling a round posterior practically in their faces. Nothing interesting about being a stewardess, Sarah thought, it's more like a glorified maid. Ho hum. Big deal.

Sarah saw a head bob through the door and then the door was slammed shut and bolted. They were taxiing down the runway, the pilot explained. Sarah craned her neck so she could see down the aisle. Where had the head she had seen gone? She was positive she saw a small figure, the last passenger to board the plane, emerging through the entrance.

"Good day, madam," a funny squeaky voice said. "I'm sorry to be late."

She looked around. Where was the voice coming from? She looked behind her. There was only a man asleep with a lit cigar poking out of his fat mouth.

"Over here?" the voice said. It seemed to be questioning the stewardess, whose head and shoulders were clearly visible to Sarah. But where was it?

She unfastened her seat belt, leaning away from the window and stretching her body so she could see directly down the aisle.

"Pardon me, would you move over, please?"

She looked up. A small creature about four feet tall at the most was looking into her face.

"Oh!" she said and squeezed across the seat and into her own.

"I'm Count Rivers," the creature said. "I'm a midget." He patted her arm and climbed into his seat, placing his elegant little feet under him.

"How do you do," Sarah said. He had a lovely face with round eyes, a pug nose, and a red mouth like a baby's. Sarah stared at him.

"A midget, not a dwarf," he said. "There's quite a distinction." His collar-length hair looked soft. It was graying at the temples, a rather ridiculous thing to be doing in view of his size. He leaned

] 199 [

his head into the seat and closed his eyes, his lips moving in some kind of incantation. She leaned closer and peered into his face. He looked familiar. In some weird kind of way, he looked wildly familiar. Had she seen him somewhere?

He opened his eyes. "Young lady," he said politely, "you're gaping at me. Do you think that's polite?"

"Polite," Sarah said above the noise of the plane, "polite. Who cares about polite. I'm just interested in you. You look familiar."

"Really?" he said, folding the seat belt around his waist four times. "We can smoke in a minute," he said, looking up front. "And then we'll order drinks."

"Yeah, sure," Sarah said.

"I'm an actor," he said, "perhaps you saw me on television."

"I don't watch the tube," Sarah said, "but maybe I saw your picture in the paper. I read the paper. I like to know if there's anything happening."

"There usually isn't," he said.

"Uh-huh," Sarah said. She had missed the takeoff by paying so much attention to him. He did have a funny squeaky voice that made her want to giggle. If only Jenny could be present to dig the scene.

"Two martinis," he said to the stewardess, who was pointing her mechanical grin at his nose.

"Now," he said, turning to Sarah, "you are a beautiful child, a mere babe." He touched her hand. "Aha, and some other child has given you a bright shiny ring."

"I'm eighteen," she said. "That's not a child any longer."

"A woman is always a child." He reached into his pocket for a cigarette.

"That's what I always say about men," Sarah said, accepting a cigarette from the Count.

"The reason I say I'm a midget and not a dwarf is important," he said, lighting her cigarette. "My body is in perfect proportions. Dwarfs have large heads, you know. My body is perfect."

"Yeah, sure," Sarah said.

"Except for one part of it. And it's not my head."

Sarah watched him. He was a fascinating little creature what with his neat, expensive little suit, his little wrist watch, his pug nose, but what the hell was he saying?

"Uh-huh," Sarah said. The stewardess returned with the drinks, tilting to one side of a tiny little tray that looked as if it were made for a midget. Sarah giggled and took a sip of her drink.

"Strong," she said. She made a wry face. So this was a martini? It tasted like poison.

The midget polished off his martini with one gulp and waved to the stewardess for another.

"You're not ready yet," he said.

"No," Sarah said.

He pulled his legs out from beneath him and let them hang down, the feet barely touching the floor.

"I'm three feet, ten inches," he said, "and perfectly put together except for one part of me." He smiled at Sarah and touched her shoulder. "I'm not a dwarf, you understand."

"Right," Sarah said, feeling dizzy. Was he going to attack her? Did people get raped on airplanes? She had heard all kinds of gossip from Mrs. Ferentz's cousin, Jody, whose friend was a stewardess. The friend said all kinds of things of a sexual nature went on in airplanes, particularly in the cockpit, so aptly named. Sometimes, the friend said, the automatic pilot flew the entire trip.

"There's a universe of difference between a dwarf and a midget. And midgets don't have to marry other midgets. But dwarfs always married dwarfs."

"Uh-huh," Sarah said. "Are you married?"

"Well," he said, rubbing his pug nose, "sort of."

"What sort of?" she asked.

"I'm engaged," he said.

"Oh," Sarah said. She couldn't think of anything else to say. She could tell he was a little weird but what difference could it make? Just as long as he didn't come on too peculiar, as long as he stayed on his half of the seat and left her alone, everything would be all right.

"We'll be in Boston soon," he said, "and you didn't even ask me what the big part was."

"No," Sarah said, "I didn't."

"It's my behind," he said, tittering. "I'm perfect but for that," he added.

"Yeah, I bet."

] 201 [

Suddenly she felt quite drunk. The plane seemed to be jerking around, moving awkwardly up and down, down and up. At times it moved sideways and then in circles. She shut her eyes. She opened them. She shut them.

"Sorry to cop out this way," she said, opening her eyes wide and staring at the Count. He looked amused and wrinkled up his pug nose in a self-conscious circus-clown gesture.

"I need a tiny nap," she said, closing her eyes then opening them.

"Okay for you," he said.

She turned her back to him and rested her head against the window, her cheek against the pane. Life was the best dream of all, she thought, as her eyes closed into blackness.

29

SARAH HAD BEEN in Cambridge for what seemed centuries before she received a letter from Jenny. She tore open the envelope and groaned.

"It's not long enough, only three pages," she said to John, who was sitting at the typewriter.

"What does it say?"

"I don't know, haven't read it yet," Sarah said, beginning to read.

"If you were more quiet I could think of something to write," John said sadly. "As it is, you've been mouthing so long, my mind is in another dimension."

"Be quiet," Sarah said, "I'm trying to read this letter." She sat down in a broken chair in one corner of the room. "I wish this lousy light was better," she said. "I can't see properly." She looked over at John. "Did you hear?" she said, "it's lousy, dreary and dull. Like guess who?" John ignored her and slowly began to type.

"Did you hear?" Sarah said, standing up and moving behind him. "Did you hear?" she repeated and put her hand in front of the typewriter.

"You've been strange for weeks, ever since you arrived," John said, trying to grab her hand. "It can't be your period. It doesn't last that long, does it?"

"I know. I'm bored."

"I'm busy, Sarah. Go to The Café. Find a job. I've work to do. I told you, I warned you, but you didn't listen. You thought it would be one continuous party."

"I thought it would be better than it is."

"What does Jenny say?"

"I don't know," Sarah said. "I hate her."

"You hate Jenny? What do you mean?" John said. "You love her, she's your only friend, isn't she?"

He got out of the chair and went to peer through the window. It was dark out, though only four o'clock.

"My only friend," Sarah said, standing beside him at the window.

John turned to face her. "Couldn't you go to The Café or something? I have to do this work. Everything depends on it."

"She's in love with Moses."

"I could flunk out, you know," John said.

"I hate her, hate hate hate."

"She's in love with Moses?"

"Yeah," Sarah said, "she's going to New York at Christmas to marry him."

"I don't understand. They're getting married? Is that what you said?"

"Yeah," Sarah said. "Imagine. She's taking the only person I ever truly loved away from her best friend. Some friend!"

John peered into Sarah's eyes. The pupils seemed to be tiny pinpoints, tiny pinpoints of selfishness. How did he ever become mixed up with such a girl?

"You don't love me anymore, of course," he said.

"Of course," she said, "I don't."

"Did you?" he said. "Did you ever really love anyone?"

"I told you. I love Moses."

"Sometimes my hand itches to slap you," John said, "but I'm too polite."

"Good Irish breeding," Sarah said.

"Are you warm enough in that blouse?" he said. "It's cold outside!"

"Yeah, I suppose," she said. It was damp and chilly in the apartment. What must it be outside? But why should she allow John to tell her what to do? She would put on a sweater and trek over to The Café. A job could be useful. She could take a walk, take her time, there was no rush. It might break the incredible monotony of a dreary Cambridge afternoon.

Sarah looked around the room. It was dismal.

] 204 [

"See you later," she said. "I think I'll go now." She ran to the bed and picked up her yellow angora sweater and flung it over her shoulders.

"You need a coat," John said. "It's cold."

"No," she said, pausing at the door.

"Listen," she said, flicking hair out of her eyes. "Listen, don't take me seriously. Don't tune in to everything I say so seriously."

"Uh-huh," John said. "I'll take fifteen pounds of salt and swallow it."

"Yeah," Sarah said, "and a grain."

She walked along Massachusetts Avenue in the direction of The Café. There would be no need to hurry. The Café would be there for a long, long time. Like Harvard, like Cambridge. Cambridge was old, one of the oldest places in America. She gathered her sweater tightly around her. It was cold.

Yes, Cambridge was old, but wasn't it also something of a bore? Weren't most things that were old, boring? This included people, places, events. There was something unfathomably boring about the past. So far, Cambridge hadn't impressed her. It was different than she expected. The students, for instance, didn't look exceptionally brilliant. It was difficult to tell the supposed dumbbell townies from the students. The drop-outs looked like the drop-ins. Everyone was alike. Everyone had long hair, dark glasses and came on cool. The girls wore short skirts, Dr. Zhivago shirts and had fixed, vacant, expressionless eyes. Everyone was camp. And doesn't it make me rather commonplace? she thought, as she kicked a stone lying in her path. She was just a face in the crowd, an ordinary, non-kinky, nonexciting, silly face in the crowd. At least in Detroit she had been something of a celebrity. In Cambridge, she was a girl like so many others walking along Massachusetts Avenue kicking a stone.

She pressed her hands into the sweater. For an instant she had the feeling she was on the wrong block. She stopped. Was she going in the right direction? She looked at the street sign. It said Massachusetts Avenue in freshly painted letters. Everything was in order.

"Aye," she said out loud in her best down-east accent, "aye, aye!" Where did she get the impression she was going the wrong way?

Possibly she had been going the wrong way for some time. Lately, such thoughts had occurred to her. Particularly in the mornings when she awoke and found John's face next to hers. What did it mean? Here was this male lying next to her. It was all so intimate, yet it wasn't. First, his face was there and then his body and then his soul. Did she have everything mixed up? Maybe the soul should come first? It was a pity Cambridge wasn't a better scene. It might have compensated for the lack in her love life. The only part of Cambridge that turned her on was the visual charm. Perhaps this was its saving grace. In truth, most of Cambridge was a vast slum, but an interesting slum and somehow the slum was more exciting than the best residential section of Detroit. A good all-out slum was more appealing in its way than a well-planned bunch of shit. The Cambridge slum was a delightful example of the fitness of things.

Boston was another story. She wouldn't mind living in one of those groovy Beacon Hill pads, high up, overlooking the rooftops. Even the fog was aesthetic. And then, Louisburg Square did lend itself to the most amusing fantasies. No one ever saw anyone enter or leave a house in Louisburg Square. The elegant people were snug inside the buildings, drinking Scotch and going insane. They were the fashionable abodes of the old rich who lived with their homely, nymphomaniacal daughters and their addict sons. It was more colorful than Detroit.

Sarah shivered and stopped to catch her reflection in the window of a pawnshop. She drew out John's comb and pulled it through her thick hair. Standing close to the window, in order to have a clear picture of herself, she thought she saw someone inside smiling shyly out at her. Who could it be? She pushed her nose against the window and peered in. It was dark, so she was unable to make out what was inside. She swung open the door. An old man with white hair and a bristly red beard was sleeping at a desk. He belched as she tiptoed past.

She could have sworn she saw a young, handsome face smiling at her. Was she having a psychotic episode or was it her usual state of bananas fever? Perhaps she had been daydreaming?

"These are gorgeous coats," she said to the old man. "I dig them." She began to thumb through a rack of old chesterfields. "I don't know if they fit." She pulled one off the rack and began to put it on.

"Where's the bloody mirror?" she said.

The old man continued to sleep, emitting tiny gaseous sounds.

"Where's the mirror?" Sarah said loudly.

"Over there, I think." She looked around. A young man stepped out between the racks of clothes. He smiled shyly.

"Venus rising from the sea," Sarah said. She looked at him carefully. He was extremely handsome, with a broad high-cheekboned face, dark hair, fantastic, sad violet eyes and a slightly long, deliciously fine nose like a Greek sculpture. She stared. Nervously, he returned her gaze. His hands were beautiful with long tapering fingers made for some important task. He might actually use his hands for something. What a superb idea! Hands were, after all, made to be active.

"Ohhh," she gasped, "Mr. Wasp, Aesthete, Adonis."

"I beg your pardon?" he said, shifting his large, unhappy violet eyes away.

"Nothing," she said. "Do you dig this coat?" She made a quick ballet movement in an attempt to model it. "I mean does it fit?"

"It's splendid," he said, "simply splendid. You should have it."

"Yeah," she said, "I think it's good but I don't have any money to buy it. I have enough to buy two pecan tarts at St. Claire's." What in the world was she saying? Nothing but drivel was coming from her mouth.

"I'll buy it," he said. He reached into his back pocket and pulled out a five-dollar bill. "I'll buy it for you. You must have it. You look splendid."

Sarah scrutinized him. He certainly didn't look rich. He was wearing faded levis, a torn sweater and funny contraptions on his feet.

"I'm Sarah Green," she said. Was she making a total ass of herself? She stuck out her hand. Gently he held it.

"Bobby Trees," he said sadly. "Bobby Trees." He stood uncomfortably before her but for a moment something lifted in his violet eyes. A flicker of happiness?

"What are those?" Sarah said, staring at his feet.

"What?"

"Those, on your feet."

"Shoes," he said.

"Shoes, yeah, but they're queer, aren't they?"

"Queer?" he said. "No. I like them. They're for the opera. Opera pumps they're called."

"Oh yeah, pretty wild," Sarah said.

"You see," Bobby explained, "I always wear them. You can slip in and out so easily." Immediately he took them off, pressing his well-shaped bare feet against the dirty wooden floor.

"None of dat," the old man said, suddenly coming to life. "We'll have none of dat in dis shop."

"Yes," Bobby said, offering him the money. "We'll buy this coat. The young lady will wear it, thank you."

The old man took the money, stuffed it into a crowded drawer and put his head back on the desk.

"All right," he grunted.

"It's terribly nice of you," Sarah said.

He held the door open. She glanced down. Was something crawling on her leg? She felt a creepy, tingling sensation swiftly making its way from her kneecap to her pubic hair. Was it guilt? Lust? She looked at Bobby's handsome face. He was terribly serious, the poor darling was terribly serious. Oh, Dear Lord, not another heavy, not another drag!

"Where are you going?" he said.

"I'm drifting over to The Café to try to find a job," she said, wondering if it were possible to have two affairs at one time. Was it possible to sleep with two men in the same day?

"Do you know Patsy?" he said, avoiding her eyes.

"No," she said. She slipped her arm through his. The sudden contact made him jerk his arm back. The poor dear seemed to be rather afraid. What could be the matter?

"We'll go together," Bobby said. "That's where I was going." The touch of her hand made his flesh goosepimply. If he held her in his arms her head would come just to his shoulder. "That's where I was going, anyway."

"But not for a job."

"Oh yes, by all means," he said. "I'd like to be a dishwasher."

"I knew you used your hands for something," Sarah said.

Bobby slowly smiled. "I like the idea. There's a certain integrity in being a dishwasher. I admire people who do manual labor. Sometimes, I make dolls' houses out of plexiglass."

"Imagine," Sarah said enthusiastically, thinking of the shoulder strap patent-leather purse slung over her neck. All she had to do was reach in and bring out the last stick of Pot Jenny had given her before she left. Would he share it? It did seem quite correct, quite within the fitness of things that she should share this last joint with her new-found friend.

"*Oui, oui, vraiment,*" Bobby said.

"You speak French?" Sarah said, reaching into the purse and searching around for the Pot. She hadn't felt such fervor in months.

"I lived in Paris for a year. I dropped out of school. But I'm back now." He sighed. "Often I wish I were back in Paris, but if I don't finish school, I'll be disinherited."

Sarah pressed his arm. "You could always wash dishes."

Bobby laughed in a restrained way. "Perhaps you and Patsy would like to go to Patisserie Gabrille for a sweet," he said. "She likes sweets."

Sarah fished the Pot out of her purse and held it between her fingers. Was it still fresh? This was the crucial question.

"Do you have a thing for her or something?" she said.

"A thing?" he asked.

"Like a great, super love interest."

"No," he said sadly. "I don't get along with women, not at all. I just don't get along with them."

Sarah clung to his arm. What a dear, mad, kooky creature!

"Sometimes I wish I were back in Paris. The people seemed realer."

Sarah dug her fingers into his arm. It felt very strong.

"I'm real," she said.

Bobby stole a glance. "Yes," he said, "good."

Sarah stopped and held his arm tighter.

"Hey," she said, "do you want to turn on?"

Bobby looked at her, his face breaking into a happy grin. "Splendid," he said, "right on the street?"

"Yeah," Sarah said and lit the joint. "I've been saving this stuff from the great unwashed for a couple weeks. There's nothing like the present moment to make things happen. Maybe I'm an existentialist."

Bobby took the cigarette and inhaled deeply. She watched him closely. He knew all about it. What incredible luck! Where had he been for the last two weeks?

"We used Hash in Paris. Do you know it?" he said, handing the cigarette back to her.

"Just vaguely," Sarah said. She didn't wish to appear naïve, but she had never smoked Hash.

Silently, they resumed their walk, handing the cigarette back and forth until it disappeared into a tiny ash.

"Want it?" Bobby said.

"No, you have it," Sarah said. She couldn't remember ever being so congenial, so absolutely congenial. What was happening? Bobby took the ash and popped it into his mouth.

"*Pas mal,*" he said, "*pas mal.*"

Sarah began laughing. "My best friend is marrying a black," she said.

"Black what?" Bobby said. She gazed up at him adoringly. It was too dark to see the color of his eyes, but she knew they were violet.

"Man," she said, "man, a black man."

"I like black," Bobby said. He touched her hair. "You would come to my shoulder if I held you in my arms," he said.

"Why don't you?" she said.

"I don't know," he said. "I don't get along with women. It never works."

"Try," she said encouragingly, "you could try." They turned down a small narrow street. Bobby said nothing. He began to walk in the gutter, holding her hand in his, and humming under his breath.

"You could try," Sarah repeated.

He stopped, still in the gutter, and stood in front of her. Gently, he pulled her toward him and held her in his arms.

"I can't," he said. "It's impossible." He pushed her away.

"Yes, try," she said. She nestled against him and put her face up to be kissed. Hesitantly, he placed his mouth over hers. His lips felt moist. They parted. She could feel the tip of his tongue poking its way toward her. He might be a bit slow, a trifle unsure. Is that what's worrying him? This wasn't such an enormous problem, after all. She could help him. Just as long as the problem wasn't in the category of Larry Green's hangup. She put her arms around his back and grasped him to her as firmly as she could with such a thick chesterfield between them. He probably had damned good teeth. Anyone on an Inheritance List would surely have the very best of teeth. Mrs. Green might even approve.

She touched his tongue. How beautiful when tongues touched, how truly beautiful. She felt a lovely kind of ecstasy filling her body from her fingers to her toes. It wasn't premature, was it?

"You'll be disappointed," he said, pushing her away. His lips ached from the intense kissing, his tongue felt as if it had been burned from his throat with a blowtorch. He coughed acidly.

"No," she said. How was she to broach the subject of bed? Obviously, he hadn't much experience. This was probably the reason for his reluctance. The best things were spontaneous. Perhaps he didn't know.

Swiftly Bobby moved up on the sidewalk and pushed her against the side of the building. "You're beautiful," he panted.

"Come to my room, Eliot House."

"Eventually," Sarah mumbled into his chest. She felt something pressing against her. Did he have a chunk of steel in his pants? She edged away from him and twisted her body around until she was in a better position to pet him.

"No," he said, forcing her hand away. "No, I can't stand it. Don't." He held her hand fast so she could not touch him.

Sarah gazed into his face. "All right," she whispered, "let's go." He released her hand. Embarrassed, they leaned against the building trying to catch their breath. Finally, Sarah began to straighten her coat. She reached for her purse, which was lying on the pavement. They could try again.

"Well," she said, searching for something to say, a way to help this creature. He probably wasn't nearly as backward as he imagined.

"Have you tried LSD?" she said, clearing her throat and trying to sound like a mature woman. Perhaps LSD was the answer to their particular predicament. She had been told when you took

] 211 [

LSD with another person, unless you were altogether crackers, you would instantly, irretrievably, fall in love.

Bobby shook his head. "Yes," he said, his voice receding into his moist lips. "Yes. In Paris. I wandered the city for twenty hours. It was frightening and fascinating. I was alone, of course. I was mostly alone in Paris."

Was he serious? This gorgeous trick was alone in Paris? Sarah stroked his hand. "We'll do it together," she said wisely. He could be devastating in an actual bed, a veritable dream come true. And wasn't this what she wanted? He was clever and he spoke French and he was rich. His physical beauty was almost secondary to these other qualities. And what difference did fidelity make? Mentally she had moved out of John's apartment and out of his life a long time ago.

"We'll do it together," she repeated. "It will be fantastic." She touched Bobby's waist. It was unusually small for such a tall, strapping lad. She threw her arm around his waist and squeezed hard. The only other man she knew with such a small waist was Moses. She sighed with pleasure, thinking of her Moses, her interesting, intelligent, dignified Moses. Moses of the lean, the dark, the slightly protruding, adorable buttocks.

"We'll see if we love each other," she said. "It could happen." He licked his lips.

"You'll see," she said. "I won't be disappointed. Not me."

He kissed her hand and proceeded down the street in the direction of The Café. He felt able to hum the entire Beethoven *Fifth* if someone asked him.

"You'll see," she said, noticing in the occasional light from the street lamps his lips seemed to be mutely forming words.

They reached the end of the block and stood on the curb about to cross.

"My genitals are a peculiar shape," he said suddenly in a startlingly loud voice, the echo reverberating along the street and bouncing off the buildings like tennis balls.

"Plural," Sarah said, grasping his hand. "Why do people say genitals. Is there more than one?"

"I don't know," Bobby said.

"It felt fine," she said. "I think you've gone bananas. There's nothing wrong with you physically. It must be your mind that's blown."

"Bananas?" Bobby said nervously.

"I mean maybe you're a little psycho. Everyone is bananas in New England, aren't they?"

"It's like a banana?" he said.

"No, no," Sarah said, "it's exactly like what it's supposed to be like in my limited experience. Where did you get such a kook idea?"

"I don't know," he said. "I don't know. My mother, I think. She made comments about me, about my body."

Sarah looked at the shape of his eyes. Definitely an aristocrat.

"Well now, sugar, think of me as your mother. I'm your mother substitute from now on, you dig?"

"A surrogate?" Bobby said, his voice throbbing. "A surrogate?"

"Call it what you like," Sarah said.

30

SARAH HURRIEDLY yanked her purple turtleneck sweater over her tousled hair and got down on her hands and knees to look for a hairbrush. She had spent an hour painting her nails silver and drawing tiny silver dots on her eyelids. Everything was complete except for the head. If she could find a hairbrush, hers or John's or anyone's, she could do her hair up on her head in a kinky African hairdo.

"What are you doing?" John said, opening the door from the kitchen and walking rapidly into the room, a sour, disapproving grimace on his face.

She turned. There was no reason to aggravate him further, was there? She would have to exercise a certain amount of self-control. Since she didn't intend to be home until very late in the morning, when surely he would be in a fury, it would seem the best idea was to avoid any present antagonism.

"I wonder if I should wear my purple tights," she whispered as if they were conspirators, "or is it too much?"

"Where do you think you're going," John said, "to a Bar Mitzvah?"

"Very funny," she said, "very droll." She began searching through the top of the chest of drawers. It might be smashing to be entirely garbed in purple. She would be the only one at the party in purple from head to toe. Of course, she had no intention of telling John that she and Bobby Tree were *schpatziering* at midnight to a party on Beacon Hill, escorted by Patsy Capri.

"Why are you pawing through my underwear with such abandon?" John asked.

] 214 [

"I told you," she said. "I'm looking for my purple tights." She might even wear the long silver earrings Jenny had given her as a going away present. It would further enhance the African look.

"I'm going to work," she lied. If only Moses could see her tonight. Would he still choose the skinny, pale Jenny? "Just going to work," Sarah said. The idea that Jenny might kiss Moses, put her thin tongue inside his pink mouth made her flesh crawl. And then would they make piggies? Would they have the unmitigated nerve to make piggies? Or had they, already?

"I'm going to work," she said irritably. She looked at John. In a funny way he was beginning to remind her of Mr. Green. He was hanging in the doorway just as Mr. Green had done for seventeen years.

She smiled at John. Why start a whole big scene with him when a Greek god awaited her?

"Wipe the phoney grin off," John said unpleasantly, moving closer to her.

"Okay," Sarah said.

"Well, should I meet you after work? Should I pick you up?" John said. There seemed to be a stain on his bathrobe. It was infuriating. He was turning into Mr. Green.

"No," Sarah said, her lips freezing falseness, "no. It won't be necessary. I'll be home late."

John shrugged his shoulders. "Good," he said. "I've mountains of work to do." He rubbed his temples. He was tired. "I think I'm acquiring mono," he said, walking across the room and flopping down on the bed.

Sarah shot a cold, vicious look across the room, which he failed to see. "No," she said, stamping her foot so he swerved his head around. "No, impossible. You can't be sick."

"What?" he said, watching her kicking her foot on the floor. "What? Are you screaming at me? I don't feel well but it's no reason to have an attack. I'm not asking anything of little selfish you."

"Well, I hope you're not sick," Sarah said, envisioning all freedom of movement suddenly suppressed. If she had to take care of him, when would she see Bobby?

"Come here," John said, unfastening his robe.

Sarah looked across the room and didn't move. "Why didn't

]215[

you tell me Patsy was such a nice, fat girl? Why didn't you? I like fat ladies."

"Come here," John repeated.

"I think I like her," Sarah said. "She's so nice and fat."

She couldn't deprive him forever, could she? After all she was a guest in his pad. He had been good to her even though she no longer felt there was anything between them. Why did men catch on so late? Didn't he realize she didn't dig him?

"Come," he ordered.

Obediently, she marched to the bed. Since she hadn't as yet been to bed with Bobby, she could still afford to go to bed with John. She had decided that going to bed with two men in one day wasn't really appetizing. It could be confusing. Her heart really was in Bobby's hands though her body was still in John's bed. And what difference did it make? She could close her eyes and imagine Bobby making love to her.

She lay down beside John, shut her eyes and waited.

"You look as if you're waiting for an injection," he said disgustedly. He reached out and took her by the shoulders. "Is this the girl I knew?" he mumbled. He tugged on the bottom of her sweater, pulling it over her head.

"You once liked this," he said, looking at her closed eyes.

"Well, sugar, I don't anymore," she said, opening her eyes. It was no good. It wasn't Bobby. It was John. And where were those fucking purple tights? They could be at the laundry or they might be buried under one of the mounds of rubbish strewing the pad. There was a lot of junk around since she had ceased cleaning the place.

John sighed. Maybe he should try to make love to her a new way? Maybe on the floor? Is this what she wanted?

"I've got work to do, anyway," he said, giving up and turning away. He'd be damned if he'd beg for it. Suzanne Belier was a fairy princess compared to this little bitch. How could he get mixed up with such a bitch? Since Sarah arrived in Cambridge his entire world was upside down. If he passed his courses, it was a miracle.

Sarah laconically moved from the bed and picked up her

sweater. "You don't think the purple tights are too much?" she said. If the sex scene was finished between them, at least he could be her fashion consultant.

"I may start masturbating," John said. "A man has to have sex. I've work to do. How can I concentrate?"

Sarah stared down at him. Poor John, lying with his bathrobe open like some type of pervert. Poor John. He's gone around the bend, as they say, too much studying has turned him into a freak.

"I don't have much time," she said, lying on the bed, and pushing her round, soft body at him. "I shouldn't be late to work, they count on me."

John held her breasts in his hands and thought of the easy comfort of Suzanne Belier. Her breasts didn't fit into his hands so perfectly as Sarah's but she knew when to keep her mouth shut.

"Turn off the light," he said.

Sarah switched off the overhead light, plunging the room into darkness. She could hear John breathing into her ear. It was all too boring, too incredibly boring.

"I'm ready," she announced.

"Oh, Christ," he said, "you're what?"

"Ready," she said.

"I've barely touched you, what do you mean?"

"I'm ready," she said, feeling for his face. Didn't he like his face stroked? Perhaps she ought to encourage him so he would do it quickly.

John switched on the light. "Forget it," he said and gazed forlornly at the ceiling, which was cracking in a thousand places. Certainly he deserved more than this? How had he allowed himself to become engaged to this child-monster, allowed himself to be tortured and tormented by her and then violently teased by his brother? It was a surfeit of torment. Why hadn't he listened to George? He seemed to know from the beginning she would sap his energy and cause him to do poorly at Harvard. He had warned him. George had been right all along.

"It's the map of the inside of my brain," John said, thinking that Finley Brown, the student who sat next to him in Shakespeare 14B, would receive an A in the course and he, John, would

] 217 [

receive a B— if he were very lucky. Finley wasn't even an intellectual.

"Oh, oh," Sarah said, nibbling her wrist, "I must find those tights."

"Make a whole busload in tips," John said, pulling the sheet over his face. "You'll need it."

31

"THERE'S A BOY out there," Sarah said, "who wants a vase for flowers he brought. He has three dozen tulips."

Patsy was bending over the stove, deep into a sauce pan. Her plump arms grasped the edge of the stove for support.

"Give it to him," she said. "There's one in the front in the cabinet." She looked at Sarah, who was standing in the doorway, her silver eyelids sparkling.

"They bring their own atmosphere, the pigs," Patsy said. "Give them what they want. We try to please these pigs." She wiped her greasy hands on an apron.

"This is my Japanese apron," she said, smearing grease on it. She tied the apron around her thin transparent blouse.

"No," she said, quickly removing the apron and unbuttoning her blouse. "I think it's better without the blouse." She hung the blouse over a peg on the wall and wrapped the apron around her so her dirty pink underwear could be seen from the sides.

"Yeah." Sarah nodded agreement. She would be pleased to give the customers what they wanted providing the tips rolled in. What difference did it make that Patsy's red strands of hair fell into the coffee or that the pastry was three days old? The customers seemed to dig the place. Was it actually necessary to take pride in one's job?

As she passed through the front room on her way to the cabinet, she noticed the person Patsy referred to as the Baron sipping black espresso through a large, silver funnel. The funnel was something new. She hadn't seen it before. Of course, since he was a close friend of Patsy's he was allowed to do anything he wished, even though the espresso dripped down the tablecloth, leaving dark stains and onto the floor, leaving a dark puddle.

The Baron was a kind of spoiled brat from somewhere or other. He sat on his flaccid bottom for hours drinking coffee until he shook. Rarely did he pay a bill. His tips weren't worth mentioning. He waved self-consciously as she passed. She stuck her nose in the air, ignoring him. Because he wore a crazy black cape didn't mean he could impress her!

The Café was busy for so early in the evening. She hoped it wouldn't continue, not wishing to be too exhausted for the party.

"Hello," the Baron called out in a friendly manner. "Hello."

"Hello," she said coldly. Was this idiot going to be at the party? Probably. Where Patsy went, so went her friends.

The vase was on the top shelf of the cabinet. It was a shame Bobby hadn't arrived yet. She would have to drag the vase down by herself. She pulled a chair over and climbed up on it, balancing herself so she wouldn't crash to the floor, joining the many fools already present. She stood on the chair and surveyed the room to make certain none of the customers who might be lying on the floor could look up her skirt. In the far corner she saw part of a leg and a foot sticking out from beneath a bench. It must belong to Carl Corsica, the New York poet. It was his particular corner. From eight to ten he lay there, writing poetry on toilet paper. No one bothered him as long as he remained in that spot. It was reserved for him. Patsy enjoyed encouraging poets and writers to frequent her place. She thought they lent an authentic note to an otherwise disgusting, filthy hole. Occasionally some unsuspecting dolt would attempt to sit at Carl's bench over his head, as it were. His face was stepped on about twice a week on an average.

Sarah grabbed the vase and jumped neatly off the chair. It was a damned good thing she was wearing her tights.

"Sensation," Carl called from under the bench. He poked his head out and gaped, his enormous, vacant eyes glimmering like Christmas decorations. It was incredible he could write poetry. According to Bobby, who had been supporting him for six months, he was barely literate. Bobby had found him during the summer and taken pity on him. He allowed him to sleep in his room at Eliot House, and borrow money, and eat his food, and wear his clothes. Carl had begun to go to all of Bobby's classes, sitting in the back row and throwing spitballs. He never thanked Bobby for anything. The world owed something to poets.

Sarah brought the vase to a balding, bleary-eyed boy who sat at a table biting his fingernails. He was young, maybe about twenty-two, but his hair was falling out in great tufts, giving him the appearance of a much older man.

"I want mineral water," he said, pulling at a curl, "please."

"No got," Sarah said, setting the vase down and picking up the tulips. "I'll just plop these in," she said.

"Okay," he said. He was tall and badly put together. "I'll ask Patsy myself," he said, lumbering toward the kitchen. She wouldn't get any tip from him, that was clear enough.

The boy was pinching Patsy's rump when she walked into the kitchen.

"Excuse me," she said.

"Never mind," Patsy said, "it's only Terence. Terence, this is Sarah."

Terence bowed. "I want mineral water. Perrier, please."

Sarah made a wry face. "Are you stoned?" she said. "You act it. I don't think it's too cool when a man is out of control. You're supposed to be in control."

"A drunkard," he said, giving her a watery stare. "Patsy invited me to a party just now. Will you be there?" He tottered toward her and leaned into her face. His breath smelled of beer.

"Yeah," Sarah said.

"Keep away from him," Patsy said. "He's English and has a drinking problem. My analyst says I should keep away from him because he has a drinking problem and is too dependent on motherly women like me."

"Mother, Mother." Terence giggled and slapped her hard on her plump rump. "Don't be an ass!" He giggled. He turned away from her and paused as if a brilliant idea had suddenly sprung into consciousness.

"Let me wait on tables," he said. "May I?" He looked at Sarah. "May I?" he said pleadingly.

"Go ahead," Patsy said, "out there with those pigs."

"Go ahead," Sarah said.

Patsy pushed his uncoordinated body out the kitchen door and into the front room.

"What incredible pigs," she said. "It's something out of *Marat/Sade*. I could have a castle in Spain, instead I have this. My psychiatrist says I'm a masochist." Beads of perspiration appeared on her upper lip.

"It's my downfall," she continued, bunching the arpron around her expansive stomach. "Intellectuals are my downfall." She glanced at Sarah for a reaction.

"Yeah," Sarah said dreamily, touching the African earring. "Yeah." But wasn't it Patsy who was the pig, some kind of red-haired pig? She had a pig's complexion, and a kind of pig look around the nose. Sarah examined her face. She had a snout for a nose. She was turning into the Red Queen.

"What's the matter?" Patsy said. "Tired?"

"Oh no," Sarah said, snapping out of her introspection, "no, everything cool, here."

"Terence," Patsy called, putting her head through the doorway, "wait on those two, over there." He was stumbling around, searching for customers as though blind.

"He's sort of a dummy, isn't he?" Sarah said, watching him.

"No, he's very smart," Patsy said. "He's drunk."

"He is something of a dummy, I do believe, drunk or not." She watched him. He had strange sloping shoulders and long arms like a chimpanzee.

"Maybe," Patsy said. "Help him, I've got the filthy coffee to make."

Sarah walked back to the front and leaned against the wall to survey the scene. Terence was standing, facing a couple who looked around in confusion.

"What is it?" the girl said. Her hair was fluffed around her face like a cheerleader's and on the fourth finger of her left hand was a tiny diamond engagement ring. She wore a powder-blue knit dress, edged stiffly in navy.

"It's The Café," the boy said. "I told you."

"It's beatnik," the girl said finally, coming to grips with the environment. "It's beatnik," she said, making a discovery.

The boy was embarrassed. "I think the coffee is good," he said.

"We better go," the girl said, taking her purse off the table. "It looks weird to me. And look at the waiter."

They looked at Terence, who rocked sideways, waiting for their order.

"Let's go," the girl said.

"No, two hot chocolates," the boy said.

Terence weaved back and forth uncomprehendingly. Sarah listened. Perhaps it was sensible to observe this little intrigue. It would give her good practice in handling customers. As long as she was having a career as a waitress, it was a good idea to find out what the dynamics were.

"I have to be home soon," the girl said. "Listen, I have to be home." Her tiny engagement ring flashed and sparkled, reflecting the fake crystal chandelier hanging above them.

"Two hot chocolates," the boy said firmly.

The girl got up, holding her purse.

"Sit down," Terence ordered. "Down." He took her by the shoulders and pressed her back into her chair.

"Do you see what he's doing?" the girl said in horror.

"Yes," the boy said, very embarrassed. "Now, we'll have two hot chocolates, please. You'll like them." He looked at the girl. "You'll like them."

She sat there shocked, saying nothing.

Terence smiled and dangled his tongue.

"Sweet girl, sweet thing," he said and lumbered toward the kitchen.

"Who's that?" the girl said, hostilely looking at Sarah, who was leaning over a table. "What's she doing here?"

"I don't know," the boy said. "You'll like the chocolate. You'll see."

"I don't care," the girl said. "I'd rather leave this beatnik joint."

From the kitchen the garbled tones were heard pronouncing the words hot chocolate. Suddenly Patsy's sweating face appeared at the kitchen door.

"We don't have chocolate," she screamed. "This is a coffee house. Tell the pigs." Sarah glanced around the room. She must be talking to her.

"Let's go," the girl said. "Did you hear?"

"No," the boy said.

Sarah lifted her elbows from the table. Ho hum. She supposed she would have to tell them about the chocolate, even though it was quite audible from Patsy's mouth. They didn't seem to understand.

"No chocolate," she said to the boy, "none."

] 223 [

"Did you hear?" Patsy said, running to the table, the sweat spilling over her lip and onto her chin. "We don't have chocolate in this filthy place. We have thirty different kinds of coffee all from the same pot."

"I'm going," the girl said, standing up.

"You're not," the boy said, grabbing her arm and pushing her back into the chair. "Two Hungarian coffees," he said, looking Patsy straight in the eye.

Patsy wiped the sweat from her face. "We don't have Hungarian," she said. "Czech, Outer Mongolian? Maybe Italian?"

The girl rubbed her arm where his fingers had dug.

"Italian," the boy said firmly. "Italian is fine."

"Get them Italian," Patsy said to Sarah, "and tell Terence to leave my customers alone. He doesn't know what he's doing. You see? I took care of everything quite nicely."

Sarah watched Patsy's face in talk. She could be much more attractive if she lost about twenty pounds and went to a health club for a year.

Terence was standing in the kitchen over the stove, stirring an ugly black mixture with a dirty spoon.

"I'd like to give that bird something," he said.

"Bird?" Sarah said, looking around. She didn't hear any chirping.

"Bird, you nit, a bird is slang for chick, girl, you know."

"Oh yeah, sure," Sarah said. There was a certain sexual depravity among the Harvard students, she noticed, directly in proportion to their intelligence. The really smart ones seemed to be the most depraved.

"Are you in the Honors Program?" she said.

He nodded. "Yes, or Mummy would force me to leave and attend Oxford."

"Force?"

"It's all *queer*, you know," Terence said, madly stirring the black substance.

"You're not?" she said and put two cups and two saucers on a tray. Carefully she poured the three-day-old espresso.

Terence tittered, leaping over to her, and in one drunken movement lifted her high into the air.

"No, put me down," she yelled. "No, no, stop you idiot."

] 224 [

Slowly he put her down, holding on to her buttocks, and loosening one silver African earring so it swung off into one of the espresso cups.

"See what you've done, you dummy," she said, and shoved her fingers into the espresso cup. She fished out the earring and put it on the counter.

"Hands off," she said, holding the tray, backing out of the kitchen into the table under which Carl lay. Strange sucking noises were coming from the floor.

"What is it?" she said to Terence, who had followed her from the kitchen and was standing with inebriated lust in his eyes. "What is that crazy noise?"

Terence put his head under the table and inspected. "Look," he said, "an inchoate form."

Sarah quickly set down the tray, and peeped under the table. Carl's enormous vacant eyes were closed, his head was crushed against the wall and the two middle fingers of his right hand were pushed into his mouth. In his sleep he was busily sucking his fingers, like a slobbering child.

"Sucking," she said, "he's sucking."

"Aah, you wouldn't put a bloke on, would you?" Terence said, lurching at her, trying to find her rump.

"Go away," Sarah insisted, "let's not make a scene for nothing." She picked up the espresso tray. So this was Cambridge? One dunce lying on the floor driveling poetry into paper napkins and another dunce believing he was something sexy out of *Tom Jones*.

She carried the tray to the table, where the boy and girl silently waited. The girl twisted her hair through her fingers, gritting her teeth.

"Right here, I think," the boy said, emerging from a daze.

"I know," Sarah said, removing the cups from the tray.

"It's cold," the girl said.

"No," the boy said, "mine's hot."

The girl shook her head.

"I say it's cold," she said. Sarah bent across the table to touch the cups.

"Having a bit of an argument, eh?" Terence said, stumbling over.

"We don't need you here at this moment," Sarah said. After all, how many people were needed to serve two lousy cups of coffee to two cretins?

"I'll handle this," she said. "Come on now, this is excellent coffee. Shibuyi, as they say." Shibuyi? Shibuyi?

Terence gagged with laughter. "You pretentious thing, you," he said, slapping her on the rump.

She turned around quickly. "Would you mind not doing that? I don't think I like your mitts on my ass, if you don't mind."

"Let's go," the girl said.

"Sit," the boy commanded, "just sit there." He reached out and grabbed at the well-cut navy-blue edge of her knit suit and yanked her back.

Tears welled up like great fountains in her eyes and she began to weep, burying her face in her hands.

Noncommittally, Sarah observed the scene. Wasn't it something of a bore? Is this all the excitement The Café had to offer? She looked around. Thank God Bobby was pushing the front door open. He had arrived to witness the denouement. She smiled at him across the room. He seemed to be holding a massive piece of equipment in front of him. Was it a camera? What was Bobby doing with a camera? Maybe he was a movie producer, a secret movie producer? Her heart palpitated. She knew there was something quite special about him. Was this it? He was really the son of a Hollywood mogul and was discovering her for the movies. Sarah patted the girl's coffee cup with compassion. It might very well be cold.

"If it isn't Bobby the Trees as they say in Wales," Terence blubbered, "part-time dishwasher, part-time creator, part-time queer."

"If we don't leave this minute," the girl said, weeping into her hands, "you can take this miserable engagement ring back." She drew her hands away from her face, ripped off the ring and threw it on the floor.

"Here," Bobby said, putting the camera aside and bending down to retrieve the ring. "Did you drop this?"

"You came in too late." Sarah smiled.

Bobby nodded. "And for you," he said, glaring at Terence, "I'm not queer." From behind his back he produced a large fist and thrust it straight into Terence's long, red, English nose. The unexpected impact sent him reeling drunkenly into the table, spilling the boy and girl to the dirty floor. The girl sobbed, clasping her face with her ringless hands.

"Maybe it's time to go," the boy stuttered. Her nice, navy-blue dress had splotches of coffee all over it.

"Here," Bobby said, putting the girl's hand away from her face and pushing the ring back on her finger. He patted her on her fluffy hair.

"Hey, wait a minute," the boy said, getting up. "Don't touch her."

"What?" Bobby said. Was he going to have still another fight? He hadn't had a fight since he was ten years old and suddenly there were two fights in two minutes.

"Yes, put the bloke down," Terence said, rubbing his large, flabby hands together.

"Never mind," the boy said, hastily sitting in the chair.

"Listen, don't go," Patsy said. She stood behind Terence and held him by the waist. "It's okay. I'll make hot chocolate, special for you." She put out her hand and pulled the girl to her feet. "Sit here, I'll be right back." The girl sat uncertainly in the chair, watching Patsy move quickly to the kitchen.

"She means it," Terence said.

"What's that?" Sarah pointed at the camera. Thank God Bobby had come.

"I'm doing an underground movie here, I've decided," Bobby said.

"I'm the co-producer, actually," Terence said and drifted toward the kitchen. "No reason to hit me, though."

Bobby picked up the camera. "It's heavy," he said, "but it's very good. You can be in the film. I think you have the right quality." He glanced at her, his violet eyes shining. "Yes, I think you'll be splendid," he said. He began to set up the lighting equipment, putting the lights in all the corners of the room. "I'll do the dishes later," he said.

He was handsome in his opera pumps and his washed-out levis and torn sweater.

"Have you seen Carl?" he said. "I'm worried about him. He

didn't have supper. I went to the dining hall and no one had seen him." He stepped out of his pumps and shoved them under a chair.

Sarah took a paper napkin and began to mop up the coffee that had slopped around when the boy and girl were knocked over.

"Never mind," the girl said.

"Please," the boy said.

"Carl is in his usual nook," Sarah whispered and stroked his back. Was tonight the night? She was damp with anticipation. And where was it to take place?

"Well," Bobby said, snatching her hand. "I saved some food for him. It's in the room. He can have it later."

"Aren't we using the room later?" she said. The purple tights made her legs feel uncomfortably warm. Perhaps it wasn't such a keen idea to wear them, knowing she was to see Bobby. He made her flesh hot. Was there something wrong with the dye?

"It's against the rules," he said sadly. "Women aren't allowed after a certain hour."

"It would be an uncertain hour," Sarah said. There must be a way to get him to come through. He wasn't all that strange. He was a male, after all, with the necessary apparatus, no matter what his opinion was.

"Carl isn't supposed to be there, is he?" Yeah, the boy and the girl could be in the film as two dummies.

"No," Bobby said.

"So? What difference?"

"Yes, perhaps you're right. We could sneak through the passageway." Sarah smiled at the girl. The girl could play a dummy but Sarah would be the star.

"Passageway?" she said.

"Yes, there are passageways hidden beneath some of the houses. Didn't you know? They connect the houses that have no kitchens. It's a way of getting food to the dining halls. We could slip you in through the kitchen door and down into the passageway of Kirkland House and then over to Eliot."

"Yeah, I dig." Sarah shivered, imagining hordes of sleek Clytemnestra cats roaming the passageways in search of delectable rodents.

"You're beautiful tonight," Bobby said, standing on one foot and then the other. "You're beautiful. Your hair is so luxuriant, I can hardly look at you. Are you cold?"

"No, hot," Sarah said. "I mean I had gooseflesh because I thought of Clytemnestra down in the passageway sneaking up on rats." Three tables down, Sarah could see the Baron snapping his fingers at her. Ignoring him, she decided to let him wait. He wouldn't leave a tip anyway. Why should he ruin this exquisite mood?

"Clytemnestra?" Bobby said. "Yes. Like Agamemnon, you mean?"

"Uh-huh," Sarah said.

The girl was whispering in the boy's ear. They looked as if they might get up and run out without paying the check. Of course, any tip from them would be a dream come true.

Bobby gazed at her petite form, her clear green eyes, her olive skin, her glossy, thick hair, her butterfly mouth, her straight Egyptian nose. "But I think it's impossible," she heard him say.

"What?" she said. The Baron was rising, funnel in hand.

"You'll be disappointed. It's peculiar, I tell you. The wrong shape."

Sarah turned to the Baron, who was making a lewd gesture with the funnel. She tugged at her sweater. Her armpits felt awfully warm. She reached out and touched Bobby. She could feel the round, hard outline of his bicep. He flexed it.

"Do you believe me?" he said.

The Baron was elbowing his way around and past the tables, jostling the other customers, accidentally clipping the girl on the shoulder.

"See?" she shouted into the boy's confused face. "See! Did you see what he did?"

"Do you believe me?" Bobby repeated.

"Yeah," Sarah said. "But let's move to the kitchen before the Baron whacks us with his funnel!"

The girl put her face in her hands and began, once more, to weep.

32

THE PARTY HAD already begun when Patsy, Terence, Bobby and Sarah arrived, looking exhausted from the night's work. Bizarre and far-out types floated through the red-carpeted Beacon Hill apartment in various, striking stages of decay. New England was improving.

"I hope the police don't come," Carl Corsica whispered from behind a closet door. He had hidden in the closet for an hour, protecting a cache of LSD.

"Well!" Sarah said, smiling at him for the first time.

"You have to buy it from me," he said.

"How much?" Bobby said, unwinding his long plaid scarf and tossing it over the doorknob.

Carl looked doubtful. "Five dollars?" he said.

Bobby handed him ten dollars. "Give me the change later," he said.

"The same pigs who come to The Café," Patsy said, pushing Carl to one side of the closet.

"Get out of here," she said, hanging her fake fur coat on a hanger. "Get out of here. Go in the bathroom or something." She looked around. A number of people were gathered in front of a roaring fireplace, throwing glasses into the flames. The crack and crunch could be heard throughout the apartment. Through the hallway she could see the bathroom, where still another party seemed to be in progress.

"The same pigs," she said. "Should we start washing the dishes, Bobby?"

"Don't bother," Sarah said, feeling to see if her earrings were still anchored to her ears, "they're breaking them all."

Patsy shrugged and wandered off with Terence toward the bedroom.

"Let's have a lot of drinks first," Bobby said, giving the sugar cubes to Sarah for safekeeping. "We'll have this later. We have the whole night, haven't we? An eternity."

They shut the closet door on Carl. "I'll find the drinks," Bobby said, leading Sarah to the couch. "Stay here." At the other end of the couch a chick with long, straight white-blond hair was sitting alone, laughing to herself.

"Bananasville!" Sarah muttered, moving to the edge of the couch. She would like to be in a fairly flexible position, so if the chick decided to blow her mind, she wouldn't be in the path of destruction. The chick seemed to be having an uproarious time all by her lonesome. She was pretty, too. In fact there were too many pretty chicks at the party, and all dressed in the latest Anti-Mod. The kook was garbed in a super, gorgeous, bright pink angora sweater and a mouth to match. And still she was laughing to herself, all the while sticking her little pointy breasts through the softness of the sweater.

"A full kink," Sarah said.

"I'm sorry," Bobby said, putting the glasses down on the coffee table. "Scotch, okay?" he said. He looked at the girl and nodded hello.

"The French girls wear sweaters like that," he said admiringly and sat down between them.

"Did you make piggies often when you were in Paris?" Sarah said.

"They wore angora sweaters and black stockings, I like it."

"Did you make piggies often, I repeat," Sarah said, turning his head away with her hand. "Did you?"

Bobby watched her with his sad, violet eyes.

"Have affairs, I mean," Sarah said, "you know, like with women. Affairs. Sex. Lust. I call it making piggies."

Bobby flushed.

"With prostitutes," he said, "mostly with prostitutes."

"Oh."

"I was queer in prep school," he said.

The girl in the angora sweater moved slowly off the couch as in a dream in the direction of the bathroom, which was overflowing.

] 231 [

Sarah could see somewhere in the middle of the fracas, the Baron was shoved, his black cape pinned to his sides, giving him the appearance of an unhealthy penguin.

"Maybe the chick has taken L," Sarah said. The chick was trying to squeeze herself into the bathroom.

"I was queer in prep school, I repeat," Bobby said. "I'm not interested in that girl at this particular moment."

"Oh, then Terence was right!" Sarah said. "I don't dig that chick much or many girls come to think of it. I did like Jenny Oliver, my very best friend, but she's rapidly joining the Nasty Fuckers List. She is a betrayer, a definite betrayer. Most people have betrayed me at one time or another." Bobby was gazing across the room, eyeing the chick who had squirmed her way into the center of the bathroom throng.

"You don't mind about prep school?" he said.

"No. Is this all Scotch, no water? It's very strong." At least he had torn his mind off those silly pointy teats, that was something.

"It's strong, yes," Bobby said, draining the glass.

Patsy and Terence emerged from the bedroom, their hands clasped together, and went to sit in front of the fireplace.

"The fitness of things," Sarah said to herself as she saw Patsy and Terence throw their glasses into the flames along with everyone else. Perhaps she and Bobby ought to do the same. It was like a Jewish wedding.

"Too bad I didn't bring the camera. I could fit all of this into a great underground film." He slipped off his opera pumps and put his well-shaped bare feet on the coffee table.

Sarah groaned and frowned. "I don't think it merits much attention." She had seen better freak-outs at K.C.'s carriage house near Wayne University. At least K.C. always had a steel band and dancers from Jamaica to entertain his guests. This was just a self-conscious anti-scene as far as she was concerned.

A sharp scream came from the interstices of the bathroom and in a moment the twenty-odd people inside parted to allow the girl in the angora sweater to rush forth brandishing a scissors.

"Ah, shit, she's going to kill us," Sarah said, leaping on the couch. But the girl simply stood laughing near the fireplace. When a sufficient number of people fixed their attention on her, she began to thwack away at her gorgeous, super fine, white-blond hair, leaving long strands spread out across the carpet like autumn leaves.

"Maybe we should collect it and make a merkin," Sarah said.

"Don't bother," Terence said, setting his clumsy frame on the floor next to the couch. "It's just Goody Rockefeller, she always behaves like this. Fortunately, the bird's hair grows fast. Ignore her." He looked at Goody and yawned.

"Oooooooh," Goody screamed hysterically. "Ooooooh wonderful! Now I can go back to Bennington reborn." She leapt across the room in a frenzied dance, pushing her pointed teats out as far as she could push. And then she stopped, as though some mechanism deep inside her had run down, and began to gather the long strands of hair.

Sarah swigged down the rest of the Scotch. "It wasn't such a bad idea," she said, "but it's not so fascinating either."

"It's not very interesting." Terence burped. "And where did the whore Patsy disappear to?"

"I'm right here," Patsy said, running from the kitchen with paper cups in her hand. "We're out of the filthy glasses," she said bitterly, "and don't talk about me. I'm not a whore." She handed Terence a cup.

"Slut?" he said.

Goody Rockefeller walked past them and laughed, her face a hymn to mental disorder.

"I'll lie here," she said, attempting to lie on the couch on top of Bobby. He gracefully rolled to the floor.

"Well!" Sarah said, "I'm not having any of this weird behavior in my presence," and she stamped toward the kitchen to find something to drink.

The kitchen was seething. A girl was sitting on the ironing board, quite naked, undulating to a Miles Davis record. Carl Corsica was freely passing out sugar cubes and an elderly woman with owl eyes painted all over her face was forcing a bull terrier to kiss her. There was nothing to drink.

"Oh, crap," Sarah muttered and turned to find Bobby. There was no reason to have such a dull party.

Bobby was standing near the door holding her chesterfield in one hand and his opera pumps in the other, a look of acute distress on his face. "Hurry up," he called, "we're leaving." Sarah ran to his side. "The police are coming. I saw them pulling up outside. Hurry, let's go."

"The fuzz?" Sarah said. "What should we do with the L?"

"I don't know," Bobby said, confused. "Throw it away, I guess."

"No," she said, "we can't, it's a sacrilege."

"Let's go," he said, flinging open the door. "We can go to jail. I'll be chucked out of school and disinherited and you'll go to a juvenile home or wherever they put seventeen-year-olds."

"No," Sarah said, standing firm, "let's take it."

"Take it?"

"Yeah," she said, "what if they're waiting for us at the back entrance? They could still find the stuff even if we throw it away." He plucked the cubes from his wallet.

"Swallow it," she said. "It's all right, Bobby." She popped the cube into her mouth and gagged it down. "Take yours," she urged. For an instant he watched her.

"Let's go," he said and pushed her ahead of him into the dim back stairs, at the same time swallowing the cube.

"Oh, Bobby," she said excitedly, "I can feel it taking effect already."

33

THE SMELL OF aging food greeted Sarah as she stepped tentatively into Bobby's room. He turned on the light and glanced around the room. Nothing looked familiar, yet he knew he was in his room. The LSD had pulsed through his body in a great passion, flooding his brain with all kinds of new thoughts.

"I don't recognize it, but it's my room," he said, patting Sarah's face. The room was deep in books. Even the bed was piled high.

"I could dance, I could sing, I could do anything," Sarah said, "but I'm scared." She looked at a picture of an apple hanging on the wall. "I'm scared," she said.

"It's just Magritte, a French painter. He's splendid. Did you see the man looking in the mirror?"

"Yeah," Sarah said.

"But he sees the back of his head. Understand?"

"I dig," Sarah said. "I feel so warm." She dropped the chesterfield to the floor and began to remove her sweater.

"Aren't you going to let me do that?" Bobby said, looking at her mouth. She had a delicious mouth. He would eat her mouth. It was a candy mouth, made of peppermint kisses. He sat next to her on top of the coat and kissed the tip of her ear. He would eat her ear and then her nose, her lovely nose and then he would eat her eye. When that was done, he could start on the other side of her face.

"I love you," he said, feeling her smooth skin brush against his cheek. He had never told a woman he loved her, or anyone.

"Your hands are cold," Sarah said. "Everything is swimming before me. My whole life."

"My feet are warm," he said, sliding his feet up around her head. "They're always warm."

Tenderly, she rubbed the soles of his feet.

"You're a Bernini, a Michelangelo, a gas!" she said. Bobby smiled. He had never been in his room with such a beautiful girl. In fact he had never been in his room with a girl, or anyone.

"A gas," he repeated.

"That which can never be is," Sarah said. It wasn't every day that she had such a mystical experience. She must savor every occult, spiritual and ineffable moment. She must remember it all so that she could give Jenny and Moses a detailed account. Perhaps Jenny had done it? If not, Sarah could turn her on to the wonderful L. She felt magnanimous.

Bobby wrapped his legs around her and squeezed her olive flesh. Her hair was somehow entangled in his toes. Her face seemed to be very far away, the eyes greenly luminous like eyes beneath a mask. There was exoticness, something quite splendid coming across to him.

"When sick for home she stood amidst the alien corn," he said, thinking of the Old Testament and Ruth, a replica of Sarah, standing in the center of a magnificent field, eyes on the horizon, looking, searching, wondering.

"Like I'm Sarah," Sarah said, bending forward. She should take L more often. It had a strangely elevating effect on her and evidently had opened new vistas for Bobby. His legs gripped her neck. Was it a new position? She put her hands behind her back and began to unfasten her pink lace brassiere.

Bobby pulled her over on top of him and began to tear at the brassiere. "I'll do it," he said, fumbling with the snap. Never had he felt such intense desire. He ripped off the brassiere and threw it. Above him he could see her silver eyelids flutter like two incandescent birds.

"You're tearing my underwear," she said.

"No," he said, "you'll have dozens and dozens. You can go right down to Bonwit's tomorrow and charge a million." He had not felt so expansive in his entire existence.

Sarah stretched her neck around. "What is that ghastly, fucking smell?" she said. "It smells like something decayed."

"I don't know," he said, examining her breasts. She was perfect, an erotic fantasy come true. In his maddest dream, he never imagined a more perfect woman.

"I'm having an olfactory hallucination," she said in a frightened voice. "It smells like sulphuric acid. It smells like my mother's refrigerator."

Bobby began to pull at her tights. "It's roast lamb and sweet potato," he said, remembering he had stashed food away for Carl. Gently, he stripped off her tights. It was different from being with the whores of Paris. Gently, he plucked off her bikini panties. It must be the L that had brought him to this point of free expression. He licked her knee, and then slid his tongue along the inside of her thigh.

"I'm cold," she said, clutching at his back.

He lifted her into his arms and carried her to the bed. Could such a marvelous thing happen to him? And why hadn't he ever crusaded for LSD? When he had the opportunity he would write to the president of Harvard. He would even write to the President. He kicked the books off the bed and placed her in the center.

"Yes," he said dreamily, "yes." The LSD had torn him away from a generation of repression. It was worth more than ten years in Paris, better than an education, better than anything!

"Bobby," she moaned.

He heaved his clothes somewhere in the direction of the decaying food. In the back of his head was the vague idea that his clothes would cover the food and erase the hideous smell that was creeping solidly through the room. He lay on her and bit her shoulder. Her skin was soft and sprayed with a mysterious fragrance. If he could just keep his nose close to her skin, perhaps he could blot out the terrible smell of the sweet potato that filled his nostrils. He separated her thighs.

She touched him. It seemed quite all right. It wasn't a funny shape, at all. He must be nutsy to have such a distorted sense of himself, the poor darling.

Fortunately, the LSD had given him a new sense of self. He was a man. She closed her eyes, feeling his tongue in her mouth. It was all so fantastic! No longer did she care where she was. A trance had fallen upon her. Time and place had ceased to exist. She was floating down the Nile on a throne. Everything around her was green and fresh and growing. She was the beloved, the adored, the worshiped. She was Sarah, the great, wonderful, superior Queen of the Cosmos. And he was the King. The King, with his strong legs wrapped around her body holding her tight and his arms around her back, rose above her like a waterfall, a beautiful waterfall. They rocked in eddies, rolled in waves. They moaned, and sighed, and gasped and finally, pulled under by the current, she knew they were drowning.

She opened her eyes. He was lying there quietly.

He kissed her neck. "I love you," he said. "Turn over on your tummy." Obediently she began to move, to comply, to change positions, to do anything he wished. The LSD had transformed her from a vain and selfish child to a warm, receptive woman.

"Where are we?" she whispered.

"In Eliot House," a high-pitched, hysterical voice promptly replied.

"What?"

"I didn't say anything," Bobby said, looking around the room. "It must be the acid, try to relax. This is the real drug experience. The real trip, I suppose."

"Heh heh heh," the voice said.

"I'm frightened," Sarah said. "Hold me, Bobby."

"It's the acid," Bobby said. "Go with it, don't be afraid. I'll protect you."

"Heh, heh, heh," the voice said, beginning to giggle, first in tiny heaving sounds, then increasing to a loud guffaw.

"We're hallucinating," Sarah said, grabbing Bobby.

"Lie still," Bobby said. "It will leave shortly. The books say not to fight it."

Sarah covered her breasts with her hands. "I feel someone is watching," she said, her voice trembling. "Maybe we should call a doctor. They give you an antidote. We should have the *Tibetan Book of the Dead*."

Bobby patted her back. "No," he said, "it'll pass."

"It'll pass," the voice repeated.

"I could swear I see the idiot eyes of Carl over there," Sarah said.

"Where?" Bobby said, sitting up and looking toward the door.

"Right there," Sarah said calmly. Carl Corsica was standing in the doorway, a large, shit-eating grin slopped over his mongoloid face.

"Some nerve," Sarah said, sitting up next to Bobby, who had moved to the edge of the bed. "Do something," she said. "Are you going to let this idiot get away with it?"

Bobby jumped from the bed and ran across the room, seizing Carl by the throat. "Have you gone mad?" he said furiously. "How can you do such a disgusting thing? You were watching, you were watching, you low breed. You're less than a man." He began to strangle him, shoving his fingers into his Adam's apple so the whites of his eyes went totally red like the Apple in the Magritte reproduction. "Less than a man," Bobby screamed.

"Don't kill him," Sarah said, running naked across the room and beating her fists on Bobby's back. "Don't. You'll kill him." Bobby paid no attention and continued pressing on Carl's neck. She scratched him as hard as she could with her long, silver nails, so that the blood sprang to the surface and began clotting.

"Please," she screamed, "stop." She put her arms around Bobby's naked waist and tickled him. If scratching didn't do it, perhaps a tickle would. His fingers slowly came away from Carl's surprised throat.

"It wasn't even L I sold you," Carl said hysterically, panting hard. "It wasn't the stuff. I took all the real LSD there was and sold you sugar cubes." He laughed hysterically. "Just plain sugar. You could buy it anywhere. I took all there was."

Sarah and Bobby, naked as Adam and Eve, stared helplessly at each other.

"Get this slob out," Sarah said, "before I kill him."

"Heh heh heh," Carl said, "it wasn't the stuff."

"You did such a heinous thing," Bobby said, in disbelief. "You did this to me, your friend?"

"Heh heh heh," Carl said.

Bobby took his arm and twisted it behind his back, at the same time fishing under the worn-out levis that covered the food. "And I bothered to get this food for you, for an untouchable like you," he said, wondering what the noise in the corridor might be. It sounded like footsteps. "Get your clothes on," he said quickly to Sarah, "right away."

"You did this disgusting thing to me?" he said, still holding Carl's arm as he looked around the room for his opera pumps. Where were they? They would have to make a run for it. If she were caught in his room, it would mean expulsion. It was one thing to be caught with a girl who was dressed, it was another to be caught with a girl who wasn't.

"Heh heh heh," Carl said for an answer and tried to pull his arm away. Bobby let go and jumped into his levis.

In three seconds Sarah had pulled her chesterfield over her naked body, and hastily stuffed her clothes into the greenbookbag. She ran to the doorway. At the other end of the hall she could see a tall, plump man with spectacles and a look of authority making his way toward her.

"Let's split," she said, wondering why she was so constantly on the run. It must be an astrological sign. In the morning she better consult her horoscope and maybe stay indoors for a while.

"I knew it wouldn't work," Bobby said frantically, running into the corridor. "Nothing is possible."

Sarah had already begun to run down the corridor in the direction of the plump man. Why was she always running? Was this what life was all about?

"No!" Bobby screamed after her. "No, it's Mr. Raven, the tutor, no, no, this way."

She halted abruptly, directly under Mr. Raven's nose. Beneath his spectacles, his eyes glinted coldly.

"So," he said in a voice of pompous authority.

She switched course suddenly, rushing to Bobby, who stood gripping the plate of decaying food in his sculptured hands. But Mr. Raven, not to be at all outdone or confused by the commotion and the disheveled, stricken appearance of Carl Corsica, took a deep breath and sped right after her.

"Bobby," she gasped, "what are you doing with the food?"

Bobby looked at her in alarm. "I know I'm peculiar," he said. "I told you. It never works with women. And you, you rotten, unfaithful friend," he said, glaring at Carl, "this is yours." Whereupon he flung the plate of food straight into Carl's silly face.

"Heh heh heh," Carl snorted, moving aside so the plate whirling past him splashed squarely down the front of Mr. Raven's expensive pinstripe Brooks Brothers suit.

34

IT WAS A LUCKY thing in a way that Carl Corsica had been present to distract Mr. Raven or how would they have gotten out, Sarah mused, as she held Bobby's hand. They had been in the passageway between Eliot and Kirkland Houses for what seemed hours.

"Are we lost?" Sarah said. She was beginning to feel completely exhausted. Overhead, it must be daylight.

"No," Bobby said sadly. "I want to make sure there's no one in the kitchen at Kirkland before we enter."

"I don't understand," Sarah said, taking her tights out of the greenbookbag. "Why couldn't we go through Eliot House? It's the same thing, isn't it?"

Bobby thought for a moment. "No," Bobby said. "I don't know them at Kirkland. If there's someone there, we can just run through as if we're Cambridge thugs."

Sarah nodded agreement and started to pull on her tights. "I wonder where my bra is? It's gone."

"I should have brought a flashlight," Bobby said, looking down at the cement. "I do everything wrong."

"Yeah," Sarah said. She peered down the long, dim passageway. It was very quiet. Evidently, there weren't hordes of rodents swarming around. It was rather anticlimactic. At least there might have been a few roaches, something moving.

"Does the tutor know you?" she said.

"I see him every day," he said, nodding.

"Oh, well," Sarah said, "another day, another freak scene."

"I knew it was impossible," Bobby said, walking along bent with defeat. "I don't think we can see each other anymore. You see what happens. Everything I do turns to rottenness."

Sarah yawned and rubbed her eyes. "I think I've a hang-over," she said, following behind.

"I'll be asked to leave school," Bobby said. "There's no denying it. I know." Gingerly he stepped over a puddle. "Watch out," he said.

"A rat?" she said eagerly.

"No."

"My God, you poor dear, your feet are black!"

"I couldn't find my shoes," Bobby said. "It's the way I do things. I'm peculiar, I tell you. My mother is right."

Sarah licked her lips. They felt very dry. "Maybe I'm pregnant."

Bobby turned to face her with a look of horror.

"Pregnant?" he said. "How?"

"For Christ sake, sugar!"

"Shhh," he said, holding her back, "we're approaching the entrance to the kitchen. I don't think you're pregnant."

"All right, all right," Sarah said and leaned forward to kiss his shoulder blades, first one and then the other. Perhaps they ought to remain in the passageway until normal activity was resumed above them? In this way, they could unobtrusively make a dash for freedom or whatever it was they were making a dash for.

"Make love to me again, Bobby," she said, pressing her naked breasts into the small of his back.

"Now?" he asked. "Here?"

"Yeah," she said, "why not?"

He flushed and put his arms around her. Yes, why not? No doubt he would be expelled, shamed and berated but what did it matter? Since nothing ever worked, anyway, owing to his peculiarity, he might as well enjoy himself.

"You're quite splendid," he said, spreading her chesterfield on the cement, "quite wonderful to put up with someone like me."

Sarah looked into his melancholy face. What was she doing anyway? Here she was down in a hole, more or less, with a poor, lonely, inexperienced child, taking complete advantage of his sweet nature. His violet eyes were so gentle, so naïve.

"Oh, no," she said, tears springing to her eyes, "no, no, no, no, no, what time is it?" Nervously, she clutched his wrist. "What time is it?" Surely she must be a witch to have lured him to her

]242[

lair. She was playing with him, wasn't she? Did she love him? Could she love anyone? John was probably at home waiting for her, frustrated with fury, raving with rage, incensed, crazed, maniacal, and here she was down in a hole under Harvard University hiding out with the poor victim of her perverted, lusting desires.

"No, no, no," she said, grabbing the chesterfield and sticking her arms into the sleeves. "No." Rapidly she buttoned it. "What's the time?" she said.

"I don't know," Bobby said. "I don't have a watch. I think it's about five o'clock. What's wrong? Did I do something wrong?"

"Five? I thought it must be daylight. I've got to go. I've got to go home right this minute."

Bobby riveted his eyes on her, surprised and fascinated by the insistent tone.

"Yes," he said, a sense of duty, of manners, of good breeding pouring through him. "Yes, of course. I hope I didn't cause this change of heart."

"I'm sorry, Bobby," Sarah said, tears of regret streaming down her face. "It's not you who's peculiar. I'm the one. It's me. I mean it's I."

Bobby stood up straight. He wouldn't let her down.

"I'll go first," he said. "Don't worry. We'll get you home."

He was almost disappointed, when he opened the door, to find no one in the kitchen. He fully expected a reception committee.

"We've eluded Mr. Raven," he said. "So far, so good."

Sarah wiped a tear away. Maybe it was her lot in life to have a manless existence? Maybe a great career as a lesbian awaited her? Was it this she had been looking for all along?

"You know," she said, "maybe he didn't recognize you. You look very different tonight. You look kind of wild. He could have thought you were someone else."

Bobby glanced at his bare feet. Where were his shoes? In the excitement he had lost his favorite shoes, in fact his only ones. "Yes," he said, "yes, and certainly Carl wouldn't say anything." He looked at Sarah's tearful face. She was tired, a pathetic weariness on her face. He must get her safely home, and very soon. "Carl won't report me," he said.

]243[

"Yeah, don't bet on it," she said and tiptoed out of the kitchen. "I think I better run now, don't go with me. Just go back the same way."

Bobby cleared his throat. His eyes itched from drinking. His feet ached from walking through the passageway, but he couldn't let her go home alone. It wasn't polite. And even though it would never work out, she was a splendid girl.

"No," he asserted, putting his arm around her waist, "I'll take you."

"No," she said, pushing him away, "good-bye, dear Bobby." She bent toward him and planted a wet kiss on his chin. "Good-bye," she said over her shoulder. "Good-bye, good-bye, dear, dear Bobby." She ran through the empty hall to the door, where she grasped the knob to pull it open.

"I can't get the damned door open, it's stuck," she yelled, trying with all her strength to force it.

"It's stuck," she yelled as the door flew open and Mr. Raven, smeared in sticky slop, crashed into Kirkland House.

35

WHEN SHE RETURNED to the apartment, John was asleep, one pale hand thrown over his face. Outside, the first feeble rays of the sun appeared, promising another dreary, drag of a day.

"Ugh," Sarah said, for the first time in her life wishing she were at home with Mr. and Mrs. Green, snuggled into the depths of her bed. She walked straight into the bathroom and switched on the light. It was time to inspect the ravages on her face. The tears had left ugly, smudgy streaks on her cheeks and little puffy bags like welts under her eyes. And this was the face, the grotesque face, being seen by that handsome Greek god? She groaned, switched off the light and stood in the dark to think about what had happened. It had happened so fast, it was hard to assimilate. And yet she must try to understand. She had gone on for too long without thinking about the events in her life. And now since everything had turned to horse manure, maybe it was time.

It seemed as if Mr. Raven had let her off the hook. He stood, stiff with rage, and delivered a quick, stern lecture about not darkening Eliot House again. Then he let her go. She was lucky. He could have called the University police. It might have been in the newspapers. Mr. and Mrs. Green might have come across the news item.

BABYHIP FOUND IN SOCIALITE
SEX-BED—EXECUTION FOR BOTH

Mr. Raven's mean, cold, tiny eyes glinted evilly under the spectacles, yet he had the incredible kindness to let her go. It was puzzling. It was a definite frightening experience, one she wouldn't like to repeat. She felt an enormous feeling of achievement when he had released her. She ran quickly to the street, the tears staining her face, and looked over her shoulder for a second to make sure he wasn't following. He was standing silently, stiff with propriety, holding Bobby by the back pocket of his levis.

Mr. Raven was, of course, a top member of the Nasty Fuckers List and a charter member of the Idiot List for Academic Slobs. And although he fit perfectly onto these lists and was also the perfect ideal of the fitness of things, she had to concede that now and then a person absolutely stinking of authority turned out to be an anticreep.

Sarah groaned and tapped her fingers on the sink. What did it mean? Would Mr. Raven take pity on Bobby as well? He wouldn't want poor Bobby to be kicked out of school? She rapped her knuckles on the sink until they hurt. She, too, could take pity on Bobby. Wasn't she the one who had caused the trouble? And, wasn't this a portent, a warning she might always be a royal pain in the ass?

"Dear God," she said, grasping the edge of the sink and kneeling on the bathroom floor.

"Dear God, why am I such a fuck-up?" She waited for an answer. "Dear God," she said again, "why am I such a miserable fuck-up?" She lifted her eyes to the ceiling and waited for an answer. There was only the dripping of the faucet and the muted whirr of the toilet.

"I've had it," she heard John moaning in the other room. "I've had it." She rose to her knees and staggered into the other room to see what was happening.

"It's morning, isn't it?" John said, blearily. "Were you praying? I heard you."

"No," she said, "I've never prayed in my life."

"What time is it?"

"I don't know," Sarah said, stalling for time. He might think it was still night.

"Don't lie to me," he said. "What time is it? Look in the kitchen."

"It's seven," Sarah said.

"Well," he said, "you have two days in which to pack your belongings and get out."

"What do you mean?" she said.

] 246 [

"I borrowed money from George and I've a ticket for you. You'll have to leave. I'm sorry. I've given it a lot of thought. The freak show is over."

"You're throwing me out?" Sarah said.

"Yes."

"You can't take advantage of me like this," she said.

John pushed his lank hair out of his eyes and stared at her. She looked as if she had just seen a ghost. The room was chilly. She stood there in the cold, looking terribly forlorn. But he wouldn't give in. He had given in enough.

"Ticket to where?" she said.

"Detroit."

"Detroit?"

"Detroit."

"I'm not going to Detroit," she said. "I'll go to New York but not Detroit. I don't like Detroit."

"You better go home to your parents," John said.

"No," Sarah said stubbornly, "but maybe they'll come here and castrate you."

John sat up in bed. The idea of Mr. and Mrs. Green descending upon him for such a purpose seemed altogether ludicrous. However, did she mean she would tell them something so they actually might arrive in Cambridge?

"I'll report you to the authorities," she said, "and I mean it."

"Authorities?"

"Mr. and Mrs. Green," she said.

"My God," John said, "you're naked!" He jumped out of bed, ran to her and grabbed her arm. "You're naked, you're naked. Where are your clothes?" He yanked her chesterfield open. Indeed underneath was nothing. She was naked as the day she was born.

Sarah pushed him away and ran into the kitchen. "Leave me alone," she shouted. "It's none of your business. You've kicked me out, anyway."

"Where were you?" he said, shoving her against the stove. She could feel the knobs digging into her back. "Where?"

"Stop," she said, "it's bad enough. Everything is bad enough."

He held her with one hand and slapped her across the face with the other. "You're a bitch," he said, tears in his eyes, "a real bitch."

"I don't care," Sarah said tiredly, watching the tears weave a course down his cheeks. "I don't care." She put up a hand to feel where he slapped her. It burned. No one had slapped her across the face, not ever in her life. "I don't care," she said.

"You don't, do you?" John said, releasing her, and standing awkwardly. She really didn't care. He was right when he wrote to Suzanne asking about her plans for the future. He was right when he wrote to George and borrowed the money. He was right when he wrote to Tilly and told her his engagement was over.

"You can't get away from these responsibilities," Sarah said, turning on the oven. It was freezing cold in the kitchen, a damp draft coming through the window. "You can't get away with these things. There'll be a penalty. It's irresponsible."

"Here," he said, putting her chesterfield over her bare shoulders. "Put on some clothes. It's cold."

"I know," Sarah said, warming her bare stomach. "You can't just leave me in the lurch like this," she said. "You have an obligation, you know. We're engaged, e-n-g-a-g-e-d. Engaged. You can't cop out. You owe me something."

He looked at her large, bloodshot, tired eyes. She might have something. Yes, he did owe her a ticket. But hadn't he already told her?

"A ticket," he said, wondering how long it would take to find a nice girl if Suzanne were already married or involved with someone else. He didn't have much time to spend searching for a girl. Yet he had become accustomed to being with a female, listening to the rantings and ravings from that department, and enjoying the funny, odd things females do. He didn't have much time to spare if he was going to save his neck at school.

"I should get what I want," Sarah said.

"What do you want?" he said, his heart sinking. Was she going to say she wanted him? He would be torn. He would have to make a terrible choice. If he continued with her, he would surely flunk the entire semester. His scholarship would be taken away. And then did he really want to live with such an unconquerable bitch? Maybe they were all bitches.

"A ticket," she said.

"I said I'd give you a ticket," he said.

"I want a ticket to New York, you bastard," she said. "Other-

]248[

wise I'm telephoning my parents and they'll be down here in a flash and you won't dig it, you really won't dig it."

"Oh," he said, looking at her chin and controlling the urge to slap her again. "All right," he said and ran into the other room. "Yes," he shouted, "anything, anything." He began to ransack the closet. "Where are my brown corduroys?" he shouted.

"Beats me," Sarah said, bored with the proceedings. She had put on an adequate performance. Indeed, the freak show was over. But she would secure her ticket to New York. She yawned. It was a very, very busy night. She was tired.

"Anything," he was shouting, "here." He whipped into the kitchen. "Take it, it's yours. It's all yours. It's my life savings and George's. And it's for you." He threw the money at her. Quarters, nickles, dimes and dollars fell to the dusty kitchen floor.

"How much is it?" she said, not bothering to pick it up. She could do that later. Or John could do it.

"A ticket to the moon," he yelled heatedly. "Just pack and go."

"How much is it?" she repeated.

"Three hundred dollars," he said, "everything I have."

"Big deal," she said, pushing a ten-dollar bill with her toe. "Big fucking deal."

"And stop using that language," he said. "Please, I can't stand it. I never could stand it. Ladies don't speak that way."

Sarah yawned. It was boring. The show was over. It was time to sleep. She walked to the other room and dreamily climbed into bed.

"You better pick up that money," John warned, pulling on a pair of khaki pants. "I'm going out now. You'll be gone when I return, I suppose."

"I'll leave tomorrow," Sarah said, trying to find the spot John had made warm.

"And keep the engagement ring," John suddenly shouted into her ear. "Keep it. You could pawn it."

"You bet," Sarah said, burying her head under the pillow. "You bet," she said again as he slammed the front door.

36

"HERE," PATSY SAID, handing the tweezers to Sarah. As she bent over, Sarah could see the big hunks of fat above the high woolen socks. Her large buttocks moved like two watermelons beneath her mini skirt. Fat girls oughtn't to wear mini skirts, Sarah reflected as she took the tweezers from her.

"I looked in the drawers," Sarah said. "I've everything, I think." Leave-takings were such a sad thing. She had a lump in her throat since early that morning. It wouldn't disappear.

"Departures are a drag," she said.

"Yes," Patsy said, "separation anxiety." She wiped the table with the back of her hand. "It's too bad about Bobby," she said. "I mean I do think he wanted to stay at Harvard this year. He had a good future ahead of him, academically speaking."

"His future hasn't begun," Sarah said, feeling guilty and wondering why every stupid dullass thing in the world happened to her. It was she alone who was responsible for his expulsion. The dummy, Mr. Raven, had finked out and pressed for his expulsion. In fact, Mr. Raven had made a terrible scene about it. He wasn't groovy. She had judged him inaccurately. Behind the mean, cold eyes actually were mean, cold eyes.

"Are you ready?" Patsy said. "I've a dental appointment at four-thirty and grocery shopping to do. Anyway, thank goodness, I'm able to hire Bobby as a full-time dishwasher. He won't go around penniless when his family cuts off his money."

Sarah checked the greenbookbag to make certain Jenny and Moses' wedding present was safely ensconced. What was Patsy blubbering about, anyway?

]250[

"Are you ready?" Patsy said. "After the dentist I have to see Dr. Newcombe."

"Who?" Sarah said idly. Bobby as a dishwasher? It was silly, incongruous. Not that there was anything intrinsically wrong in being a dishwasher. He had finally convinced her it was a good scene, but he did have talent of another dimension, didn't he? So wasn't he wasting it washing dishes? He had so much to offer the world, so much to give, so much intelligence. No one would ever know as long as he stayed in the back room of The Café in filth up to his elbows. If she hadn't single-handedly screwed everything up, might it have come out differently?

"Should I make coffee?" Patsy said, peering into the coffee cannister. "I'll make instant, that's all you have."

"Yeah," Sarah said.

Patsy poured water into the pot and turned the flame on. "I'll go late to the dentist's," she said.

"Yeah," Sarah said. It wasn't too late to go around to The Café and say a quick good-bye to Bobby.

"My analyst says my chronic lateness is deliberate hostility."

"Yeah," Sarah said.

"I do it intentionally, he said," Patsy said.

"Yeah," Sarah said.

"What do you mean, yeah?" Patsy said irritably. "It's annoying."

Sarah looked at her with curiosity.

"I'm going to see Dr. Newcombe because I don't happen to agree with my analyst."

"What's Dr. Newcombe, a palmist?" Sarah said.

"Another analyst," Patsy said. "I don't think mine's too good. I thought I'd try another."

"Yeah," Sarah said.

Patsy frowned. "Are you being nasty?" she said. "You keep saying yeah. It's very annoying."

Sarah looked down at her shoes. Perhaps she ought to change them. She could unpack her yellow suede boots. Bobby thought they were pretty and he might as well see her the last time in something he admired.

"Just cool it," Sarah said. "Don't take me too seriously. Don't let things get the best of you."

] 251 [

Patsy stirred the water with a fork. "That's what my analyst says," she said.

"Yeah," Sarah said. Why was it that Patsy's cheeks were all puffed up like a squirrel storing nuts? She really ought to lose some weight.

"You probably have separation anxiety," Patsy said.

Sarah walked into the living room and unzipped her suitcase. Somewhere under the clothes were the boots, way down at the bottom. She dug around till she found them and took them out. Would she ever see Bobby again? He might come to New York sometime to visit her. Yet she knew it would be different. They would never be the same again, and furthermore, she would probably be with somebody else by then, a really far-out type, a Village or Lower East Side cat with a beard and a top hat.

She pulled on her boots and laced them up her leg. The lump in her throat was hardening. And wasn't it stupid.

"Don't cry," Patsy said, bringing the coffee into the room, "don't cry. It's unattractive."

Sarah tied the knot on the lace. "I'm not crying," she said, sniffing back the tears. Patsy was right. It was corny to cry. She was turning into some sort of provincial cornball. Someone might think she came from the Midwest, if she wasn't careful. And wasn't it an utter stupidity to cry over a boy? Probably New York was bursting with cats just like Bobby Trees. In her career as an opera singer or a great dancer, she would find an exact replica of Bobby Trees, maybe hundreds of them.

"Drink," Patsy said, pressing the coffee into her hand, "drink and hurry."

Sarah took a sip of the coffee. It scorched her tongue and throat but the hotness was good. She was purging herself of all love thoughts connected with Bobby. What was the point? There was no reason to let yourself feel if those feelings couldn't be realized. She sighed. After today she wouldn't see him again, so why bother to have feelings about him? It was better to think of the possibilities than the non-possibilities, the non-possibilities just tore you into nasty little shreds.

It might be better when she arrived in New York to study pop singing as she had once planned, then barge right into the opera field. Of course, if she stayed with Jenny and Moses she could take her time in deciding. She wouldn't have to spend her money on rent right away. She would have a chance to decide what she wanted to do, what she wanted to be.

"I think I'll put their wedding present in the suitcase," she said, taking the *Kama Sutra* out of the greenbookbag and placing it in the suitcase.

"The *Kama Sutra?*" Patsy said. "Is it good?"

"I think so," Sarah said. "It's kind of a gas."

"Let's go," Patsy said. "I'll help you with the suitcase."

"There's a lump in my throat," Sarah said. "I hate to admit it."

"Yes," Patsy said, "I understand. It's separation anxiety."

They carried the suitcase down the stairway and out onto the porch and down the stairs into the front yard. Next door an old lady was burning leaves.

"Oh, it's lovely," Sarah said, smelling the air. "It reminds me of the Midwest. I mean that's the only thing I liked about the Midwest—when we burned the leaves in the autumn."

They heaved the suitcase into the back of the car and Patsy climbed into the driver's seat.

"All set?" she said, turning on the ignition. Sarah nodded and threw her coat around her shoulders and put on her hat. "Yeah," she said, getting in. The old lady waved as they pulled away from the curb.

"I can't stand it," Sarah said. "It's too sad. I'm leaving, I could cry."

"Control yourself," Patsy said, lighting a cigarette and swerving around a cat that was creeping into the street. "Control yourself. Don't cry." She drove rapidly down Massachusetts Avenue, passing the second-hand store where Sarah had first met Bobby.

"I can't stand it," Sarah said. "I feel very old, like the woman burning leaves in the yard."

"Control your fantasies," Patsy said, licking her bottom lip.

"Yeah," Sarah muttered, trying to ignore the lump in her throat. It was going to fill her entire mouth. She looked at Patsy's pink face. Patsy pig. Patsy pig. Maybe if she could just wrench her mind off her sadness for two seconds, she would feel better.

Patsy pulled up in front of The Café. "I'll wait in the car," she said, "you go ahead and say good-bye. He's in there shooting a segment of the film. There're others around, too."

Reluctantly, Sarah opened the door and got out of the car. The front door of The Café was open. She could hear sounds inside. She looked through the car window at Patsy's round face. The moment had come. Couldn't anyone help her now? Patsy stared back, uncomprehendingly, then rolled down the window.

"What is it?" she said irritably. "I've got to hurry. I'm late to everything today. Hurry up!"

Sarah turned around. Yes, the moment had come. Oh, God, if only she didn't have to say good-bye to Bobby.

The Café was brilliant with lights when she walked in. There was Bobby standing with his back to the door, directing a group of people with a long, flat ruler.

"No," he said to a girl in a red-fox fur coat, "stand over there." He propelled her toward one corner and pushed her against the wall with the ruler. "Good," he said, "good."

"I've got to go soon," the girl snapped; "you've kept me waiting for one hour."

"Well, all right, it's time for a break," Bobby said; "everyone take a break. Be back in ten minutes. Remember the position."

"Yep, Mr. Fellini, sir," she said, leaving.

One by one everyone filed past until there was no one but Sarah and Bobby standing beneath the Klieg lights.

"I came to say good-bye," Sarah said, feeling shy for the first time in her life. It was all so painful. It would have been so much easier to write a note saying farewell.

"I'll miss you," Bobby said, his thin, finely sculptured nose quivering. "I'll miss you."

Sarah pushed one yellow suede boot in front of her to make certain he would see it. "Patsy's in the car," she said, "and in a great, slobbering hurry. But I wanted to tell you how very sorry I am. I wanted to say I'm very sorry about everything, about that night, about your being expelled."

"Yes," Bobby said, "well, it wasn't all your doing, was it? I mean I had something to do with it." He sucked in the corners of his mouth, making his face a hollow. "There were two of us there, you know."

"Well, I'm sorry," Sarah said. "I'm sorry about Mr. Raven, the toad sadist, about the entire happening." She looked at his beautiful, aristocratic hands. Never, never would they touch her again. It was all so irrevocable, so really final, and so utterly, utterly boring.

"I could go with you," Bobby suggested.

"I better go now," Sarah said. "She's in a great rush."

Bobby relaxed his mouth, letting the air escape through his lips.

"I could go with you," he said.

"I hate to say good-bye," Sarah said, "but good-bye."

"I could go with you," he said, picking up his raincoat. "I've got enough money." He patted his wallet. "They may cut off some of the money, but they can't get all of it. It's in trust, you know. We Anglo-Saxons put our moneys in trust." He smiled.

"And," Sarah continued, not listening, "you could come and visit sometime, maybe." She edged toward the door. She could just run out. In thirty minutes she would be on the plane and headed toward New York and this uncivilized, silly, boring business of saying good-bye would be over.

"All I have to do is go to Eliot House and pick up my clothes. Actually," he said, "I don't have any clothes. Carl took everything except my underwear. He left wearing a new suit my mother sent me. I better get some socks. My feet are cold."

Sarah clutched her greenbookbag. "Some things just can't work out. They're doomed," she said. "You were quite right, Bobby."

"Are you crying?" he said, touching her hand. "Are you crying?"

"No," she said. The lump in her throat was so big it felt as if it might just jump out of her mouth.

Bobby began switching off the lights. "I'm going with you, don't you understand?" he said. "Really, I don't need anything but this raincoat and my socks."

"I'm going now," Sarah said tonelessly.

"Did you hear?" he insisted, holding her arm. "I'm going with you to New York." He paused. "Me. You. Us."

Sarah stared into his violet eyes.

"You're going with me?" she said. "But I'm telling you good-bye."

"New York will disappoint you," he said, bending down to

]255[

fasten the lace on her left boot. "New York will disappoint you," he repeated. "It's no mecca. You won't find it a dream."

Sarah cleared her throat.

"Yeah?" she said. "You're going with me. Oh. I think that's boss." She pushed her thick, black hair over one shoulder and laughed uproariously. Even Patsy, fuming in the car, heard. "It's just boss. It's truly, truly boss. Maybe I'll keep the *Kama Sutra* for us."

"Yes," he said, "yes."

"Bobby," she said, taking his hand.

"Speaking of the *Kama Sutra*, let's go dig the Beatles' latest sound."

"Yes," he said.

"We can do it on the way to the airport."

"Yes," he said.

"I wish Patsy would stop honking that ridiculous horn." She could feel the tears springing to her eyes.